Vau[

The Montana Adventures Collection

The Irish Cowboy

Savage

Vaughn's Hill

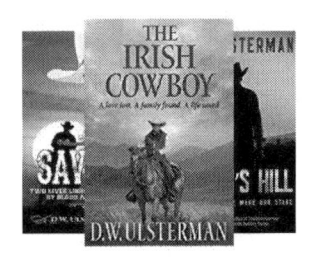

By

D.W. Ulsterman

Copyright: 2022

This is a work of fiction

"Is the best of the free life behind us now?
And are the good times really over for good?
Are we rollin' downhill like a snowball headed for hell
With no kind of chance for the flag or the Liberty Bell."

-Merle Haggard

Prologue

Wet wood and a biting winter wind from the north made for a miserable campfire that gave off far more smoke than heat.

A lone figure sat on a stone in a small clearing next to the sputtering, hissing flames. A thick wool blanket hung over his massive shoulders. He was a huge man with remarkable speed and strength—natural gifts that had once given him a life of wealth and fame.

That was nearly five years ago, though, in a world that no longer existed.

The world now had no electricity, no television, no cellphones, and no supermarkets overflowing with food and goods. The stadiums full of cheering fans were empty concrete carcasses. The million-dollar contracts, multiple homes, fancy vehicles, private jets, or seemingly endless nights filled with beautiful women wanting so badly to please him again and again were nothing more than increasingly faint memories of a time that would never be again.

All of it was gone.

The man picked up a stick and poked at the logs, trying to get the fire to burn hotter. A twig snapped from somewhere beyond the line of trees behind him.

"I mean you no harm, friend." The intruder cleared his throat. He was middle-aged, very thin, with strands of gray hair that stuck out from the bottom of a pointy cap that covered the top of his head. "Might I join you by the fire?"

The big man stood and slowly turned around.

The other man stepped out from the shadows. His sunken eyes widened. "Look at the size of you." He held up his hands as he came closer. "See? No weapons. My name is Carl and like most everyone else in this godforsaken place, I'm cold and hungry." When he grinned, he revealed dark, abscess-oozing gums within a nearly toothless mouth. "I can trade you something." The grin widened. "Wanna have a look?" He snapped his fingers. "Get out here," he barked.

A girl no older than ten or eleven dressed in soiled rags and leather boots that were cracking on the sides emerged from the woods. Her shoulder-length brown hair was tied back in a ponytail. Carl motioned for her to stand next to him. "There's more than one way to stay warm, am I right?" He winked. "Don't let her small size fool you. Even as big as you are I'm certain she'll accommodate the need." He patted the top of the girl's head. "I've taught her well." His eyes narrowed. "Do we have a deal? You get ten minutes with her for some food. Do just about anything you want short of killing her. She can take it." He put his hand around the girl's narrow hips and pulled her close. "She can take it all."

The man by the fire straightened and sighed as the blanket fell away from his shoulders. He reached for something behind him.

"Hey," Carl cried. "I told you I'm unarmed."

The man held a red-stained sledgehammer at his side.

Carl scowled as he scratched at the silver stubble on his winter-burnt face. "I'll be damned. It's really you—the big mute with the hammer. I've heard the stories. Didn't think they were real, yet here you are." Firelight danced within his dark eyes. "You've made some powerful enemies. There's a bounty on you. I suppose you know that already. Not that I'm here to collect. No, I just want a chance to warm myself and hopefully get a bite or two if you can spare it." He pushed the girl forward. "What do you say?

Will she make for a fair trade?" He grabbed the back of the girl's neck and squeezed. "Open your mouth. Earn your keep. Show the man some of what you got."

The girl opened wide. "See?" the man said. "Her teeth are still good. Nice lips—the kind of lips that can help you to forget about your troubles for a while. She might appear dirty on the outside, but I assure you she's good and clean where it counts. You have my word on that."

"It's a trap," the girl murmured.

"Keep quiet," Carl yelled as he slapped the back of her head. He shrugged. "She's an ungrateful brat sometimes, but please don't let that deter you from accepting my offer. She'll deliver and then some. You'll see." He lifted her sweater to expose the flawless alabaster skin of her taught belly underneath. "When's the last time you enjoyed something so smooth? Her body is starting to come in real nice. Not much there yet but just enough to imagine what it'll be like in another year or two."

The big man shook his head while glaring at Carl.

"You really are a mute, huh? Born that way? I remember reading about you in some sports magazine years ago. Said you were something like six-foot nine and nearly four hundred pounds. Seeing you in person now I'd say you're all of that and more. There was mention of a birth defect—born without a tongue or some sad shit like that. You were a big deal. NFL defensive player of the year. Damn near unstoppable if I recall. They called you the bear, or just Bear. Not that any of that matters these days. Nobody is playing or watching football anymore. We're all living in the same hell now."

"Trap," the girl repeated.

Carl's eyes flared. He turned toward her and raised his fist. "I thought I told you—"

Bear strode across the clearing, clamped his free hand around Carl's wrist, and shook his head again.

"She's mine," Carl snarled. "How I discipline her doesn't concern you."

Bear squeezed.

Carl winced. "That hurts."

The girl moved toward Bear.

"She's mine," Carl hissed.

"There are more of them," the girl said. She pointed to the woods. "Hiding. Waiting."

Carl grimaced. "The little bitch is a liar." He tried to yank his hand away, but Bear's grip was iron. "Please," he continued, "I don't want trouble."

The girl shivered as she glanced at Carl. "They hurt me."

Bear returned to his place by the fire, yanking Carl along with him. He put down the sledgehammer and then picked up the blanket with his free hand and offered it to the girl who quickly wrapped it around herself. "Thanks," she whispered.

"You can't have her," Carl shouted. "Not without giving me something in return." His lips drew back from his diseased gums. "I'm warning you."

The girl pointed again. "There."

Two men walked out from behind some trees. They were younger than Carl but just as thin, their bearded faces appearing more wolfish than human—men who had seen plenty of death, most of it delivered by their own hand. The taller one carried a baseball bat. The other held a three-foot piece of pipe.

"She's with us," the taller one said. He licked his lips as he pointed at Bear with the bat. "Say the word, Carl."

Bear let Carl go and picked up the sledgehammer while staring at the other two men. The girl moved behind him.

Carl chuckled as he scurried backwards. "She actually thinks you can save her." He withdrew a knife from the inside of his tattered jacket. "Guess I was wrong about not having a weapon." He smiled. "It's three against one big fella. But I tell you what. Give us everything you have, and we might be willing to let you go."

"I want that hammer," the taller man said.

"Zip it, Hank." Carl's black-gum smile widened. "Apologies. He's impatient."

"You don't tell me what to do," Hank growled. "The hammer is mine."

Carl's cheeks reddened. "For now, we're going to focus on getting the girl back. Then we'll deal with the rest."

"Who put you in charge?" Hank spit to the side. "I sure as hell didn't." He turned to the third man. "Are you going to back me up on this or what?"

That third man hadn't stopped staring at the girl since he walked into the clearing. "I'm with Carl," he replied. "We need to get her back first."

Carl nodded. "That's right. Listen to Jack, Hank. The girl is the most valuable thing here." He looked up at Bear. "And she's ours."

"It was my night," Jack said. "Remember?"

"Yes," Carl replied. "I remember. You'll have your turn. We all will."

Jack started massaging his crotch in slow circular motions. "I better. It's been a few days."

"I thought it was *my* night," Hank said.

"You can go after me," Jack answered. "I'll warm her up for you."

Hank grinned. "Fine by me." He stood next to Carl. "What about the big guy? We're not actually letting him go, are we? I mean look at all that meat on him. I haven't had something that tasty in my belly in a long time."

"He's the bear," Carl whispered.

Jack scowled. "Seriously? This is him?"

Carl nodded. "Pretty sure."

Hank slapped the end of the bat into the palm of his hand. "If that's really him there's a nice price on his head."

"I know," Carl replied. "Vig wants him dead."

"And around here what Vig wants—" Hank started.

"—Vig gets," Carl finished.

"How much?" Jack asked.

Carl shrugged. "I'm sure it's enough to keep us content for a while." He looked at Jack. "You think you and that piece of pipe can take him?"

"By *myself*?" Jack squeaked. "No, we do this together."

Hank stepped forward. "Are you really the one they call the bear?"

Bear reached back and gently pushed the girl further behind him.

"Don't do that," Hank said. "She's ours. Get over here, Reagan. *Now.*"

Reagan shook her head. "No."

Hank's brows lifted. "*No*? You're telling me no?" He spit. "You hear that, boys? Our little Reagan is in serious need of an attitude adjustment."

Jack moved next to Hank. "And I'm just the one to give it to her." He flicked his tongue. "Yes indeed."

"You best step away from the girl," Carl said to Bear from where he stood behind the other two in his group. "Or this is about to get messy."

A log collapsed in the fire, sending a shower of snapping sparks into the night air. Bear tightened his grip on the handle of the sledgehammer.

"How many do they say the bear has killed?" Hank whispered.

"It's just rumors," Jack replied. "Besides, this might not even be him."

"It's him," Carl said. "I'm sure of it. Maybe we should reconsider."

"*Reconsider*?" Jack barked. "You mean give up the girl and slink away from here with nothing? No way. She's the only thing of value we have left."

"Our lives," Carl replied. "We'd still have our lives."

Jack's eyes narrowed. "I'm too hungry and nobody is dying but him. He can't kill all of us."

He was wrong about that.

The sledgehammer slammed into the center of Hank's chest, pushing bone and cartilage inward until slivers of shattered ribs sliced his lungs and punctured his heart. Death was almost immediate.

Jack cried out as he tried to scramble back, but he slipped and fell onto his side. Bear raised the hammer high and then sent it crashing into Jack's skull, cracking it open with a wet crunchy pop. Blood and brain matter oozed from the fracture. Jack gasped twice, eyes bulging, and then lay still.

"Wait," Carl screamed. He dropped the knife. "I meant you no harm. Keep the girl. She's yours. We can all work together. Think about it. You have Vig on your ass. She wants you dead. I can help to get you away from here—you and the girl both. What do you say?"

Reagan walked out from behind Bear. "You hurt me. You touched me. You bit me. You tied me up. You hit me. Over and over and over again."

Carl looked down. "I fed you. I kept you alive." He looked up at Bear. "We could have eaten her, but we didn't. Even when we were starving. The others wanted to, but I stopped them—*me*."

"You're a liar." Reagan's nostrils flared. "You're evil."

"Come now." Carl clicked his tongue. "We've all done things we're not proud of." His eyes begged Bear for understanding. "You've made your point. You've killed my companions. Let me help you or let me go. *Please.*"

Reagan bent down and picked up a rock. "Liar!" she shouted right before throwing it at Carl. His head snapped back as it ricocheted against his forehead, leaving a gash that trickled blood down the side of his face.

"Stop," Carl cried as he wiped the blood away. "I'm leaving, okay? Keep the girl, keep the knife, whatever you want. You'll never see me again."

When Carl turned away, Reagan grabbed another rock and threw it at his back. He flinched, stopped, and then whirled around. "A sweet little piece of ass you might be, but not an hour earlier I'd have slit your throat for that." He glanced down at the knife. "And I might yet."

Bear stepped on the knife with his size-sixteen boot and then shook his head.

Carl grunted. "She's acting all brave now thinking you can protect her, but all I see is a dumb brute with a world of trouble about to be dropped onto his head. Vig is coming for you. You'll both likely be dead in a few days because you were too stupid to accept my offer of help."

"Don't let him go," Reagan warned. "He'll tell them where we are."

"What?" Carl's eyes widened. "No, I wouldn't do that. I'm no friend of Vig's. I avoid her like everyone else. She's death for me the same as she is for you." He stepped back.

Reagan tugged at the sleeve of Bear's coat. "He wants the reward for turning you in."

Carl took a deep breath and then wagged a finger. "I won't do that. You have my word." He cocked his head and pointed to Reagan. "Do you know how much someone like Vig would give for a young thing like her? She'd be a welcome addition to her stable of whores. I'll handle the transaction for you—keep you safe. We could meet up here later and split the profits." He grinned. "Ah, I see the wheels turning now. You'd like that wouldn't you? And who could blame you? We all need what we need, right? Maybe new boots, or a pair of gloves, some canned food, she might just fetch a price that would get you all of those things."

Bear moved his foot back, grabbed the knife, and held it up with the handle facing Carl.

Reagan's mouth fell open and her lower lip trembled. "What are you doing? Don't give me back to him."

"Hush now," Carl cooed as he reached for his knife. "You really should have kept quiet. Putting all of your trust into some stranger in the middle of the woods? I thought you were smarter than that, little girl. Then again, you are just a child. Perhaps the bear will allow me one last time to enjoy your company before you're handed over to Vig." He looked up at Bear. "Or you can go first. I don't mind."

Bear stared into Carl's eyes. That's when Carl realized he wasn't getting his knife back—at least not in the way he thought. He glanced down. The handle was no longer in front of him. He coughed. His legs buckled. He fell to his knees clawing at the blade that was now buried hilt-deep into the side of his throat. "My own knife," he gurgled as he toppled over. "You killed me with my own knife."

Reagan gripped Bear's pinky and squeezed it tight. "You saved me. Thank you."

A wolf howled in the distance.

Bear reached into his jacket and brought out a thin piece of smoke-dried deer meat. "Eah," he grunted.

"You want me to eat?" Reagan replied as she took the meat.

Bear nodded.

"I'll share," Reagan said. "We can sit by the fire and eat it together, okay?"

Bear held up a finger, pointed to the bodies and then pointed at the woods. He grabbed both Carl and Jack by their ankles and dragged them away as if they weighed no more than paper and then returned and did the same to Hank. Then he threw another log on the fire, sat back down on the rock, and motioned for Reagan to join him.

She tore the meat in two and handed the larger piece to Bear. She sniffed hers and then nibbled the tip. "It's good," she said, right before putting the rest in her mouth and chewing hungrily. "It's really good."

It had been a long time since Bear had received a compliment. It felt nice. He happily chewed on the piece of venison while warming his hands over the fire. Reagan rested the side of her head against his hip. Soon she was softly snoring. He reached down to pat her head but then stopped, not wanting to scare her.

"It's okay," Reagan whispered as she pulled Bear's hand down until it touched her hair. "I don't mind." After a pause she opened her eyes and looked up. "You're a good person. I can tell."

"Meh?"

Reagan nodded. "Yeah—you."

Bear tried to say more, but with hardly a tongue there were certain words that were nearly impossible to enunciate. "Ank ooh," was the best he could do.

"You're welcome." Reagan's eyes closed. She fell asleep again with a faint smile on her face.

The fire hissed.

The wolf howled.

As for Bear, he nearly cried, so happy he was to have found someone who treated him like a human being and not the monster this dark existence would have him be. Reagan gave him something he hadn't had in a very long time—a purpose. He stroked her hair and silently promised that as long as he lived no more harm would come to her. If any tried, he would kill them.

He would kill them all.

1.

Six weeks later.

"It seems empty. We should have a look."

Bear put his hand on Reagan's shoulder and held her in place. "Wah."

"We don't need to wait," she said. "There's nobody in there. It'll be dark soon and it's been way too long since I've slept under a roof." She stood and pulled on his hand. "C'mon, let's go."

They crept toward the little shack watching for any sign of trouble. The woods were quiet. Heavy gray clouds hung low in the sky and the air smelled of the snow that would be falling soon.

Bear knocked on the door while Reagan put her hands around her face and peered through the shack's only window. "There's wood stacked next to a stove," she said excitedly. "And a table, some blankets, it's pretty much perfect."

Bear knocked again, waited, and then pushed the door open. He had to duck to step inside. Reagan brushed past him and looked around wide-eyed. "See? Perfect." She pointed to a row of shelves behind the door. "Is that what I think it is?" Three dust-covered cans of pork and beans sat on the top shelf. She grabbed one of them, cleaned it off, and then handed it to Bear. "We're eating good tonight."

Outside the first flakes of snow started to drop onto the surrounding trees. Bear knelt down on a knee and carefully placed a few dry pieces of kindling into the cast iron pot belly stove.

"Check it out," Reagan said as she picked up a box of long matches from the table. "It's almost full." She gave the matches to Bear. "And there's a stack of yellow tablets and some pencils here too. How cool is that?"

Bear tore off a piece of paper from one of the tablets and used it to start the fire. Within minutes the little stove was pushing back the chill and gloom inside of the tiny cabin. He crossed the room, sat at the table, and pulled a tablet toward him.

"Can you write?" Reagan asked.

Bear frowned, scribbled something down, and then held the tablet up.

Of course I can write. I just talk dumb.

"You don't talk dumb," Reagan replied. "You talk different is all."

Bear's writing, despite the great size of his fingers holding the pencil and how fast he did it, was nearly perfect, each letter clear and delicate.

This is how I used to talk—by texting on my phone and letting people read it, but when I was a kid, I used tablets like this to write out what I wanted to say. I could write nearly as fast as people could speak.

Reagan stuck her elbow on the table and then propped her chin against the palm of her hand. "But now there are no more phones." She leaned forward. "Do you miss writing?"

Bear nodded and then wrote some more.

I loved reading and writing. Even when I was playing ball, I always made time for my books.

"What did you read?"

C.S. Lewis, Elmore Leonard, James Baldwin, Charles Bukowski, Decklan Stone, lots of things.

"Never heard of them."

Bear rolled his eyes and then wrote that Reagan was too young to know much about the way the world used to be and that made him sad.

It was so much better then.

"I would hope so because this world totally sucks ass. I learned to read pretty quick, but my writing wasn't so good. I practiced a lot in school. I hated how some of my friends thought I was one of the slow kids. I wasn't slow. Writing was just, I don't know, it was kind of hard. I could do numbers easy. They made sense. Words? Not so much. Numbers say exactly what they mean. Words are like people though—they can lie to you."

Reagan scowled and then continued. "I remember when our school was closed. They said it wasn't safe for us to gather in large groups anymore. We were all told to stay inside and not come out. Soldiers showed up at the homes in the neighborhood to deliver the shots to us. They wore masks, but I could see their eyes and they looked so sad when they were putting the needle into our arms. I felt sorry for them. My dad said things were crazy but that they'd get better. He kept saying that day after day until one day some different soldiers showed up and took him away. They didn't seem nearly as sad as the others, so I didn't feel sorry for them at all. My mom would tell me not to hate people, but I couldn't help hating them. They were bad just like the men you saved me from. I never saw my dad again and not long after that my mom got sick, and she wasn't the only one. Lots of people were getting sick and dying after they got the shots. Mom got weaker and weaker. Right before she died, she gave me over to Carl. He was the neighbor who lived across the street from us. Dad and he used to play golf together all the time. Like me, Carl was one of the few people on our street who didn't get sick after the shots. He promised her that he would keep me safe. What a lie that turned out to be."

I'm so sorry, Bear wrote.

"Me too," Reagan said. "Me too." She tapped the yellow tablet. "Hey, would you mind telling me some of *your* story? We've been traveling together all this time, but I still hardly know anything about you besides you're about the biggest person I've ever seen, and you used to play football. I'd like to read about it. And while you're writing I'll clean up around here so we don't have to eat our dinner surrounded by all of this dirt." When she smiled the whole room seemed to brighten. "What do you say?"

Bear returned the smile, nodded, and then he started to write while Reagan got up and made good on her promise to give the shack a much-needed cleaning. During that cleaning she found a cot folded up against a wall, more blankets, eating utensils, a cast iron pan, several candles, some of which she lit, and a box of hardbound books with a cloth draped over it.

"Huh," Reagan said as she pulled out some of the books. "It's a bunch of cowboy stories written by the same guy." She held one up. "See?" The name on the cover was Remington Wilkes. "It has his picture on the back and it says he lives in a place called Savage, Montana. Where is that?"

Bear held up the yellow tablet.

About twenty miles from here.

"He sure is an old grump. Check it out." Reagan slid the book across the table.

Bear held it up and turned it over. The man on the back cover staring back at him looked like he never learned how to smile. Even his bushy white eyebrows seemed to be frowning.

"All the books have the same picture of him. I like the cowboy hat he's wearing. My dad loved watching those old western movies with the gunfighters. That's what his picture reminds me of—a character from one of those movies." She opened a book. "I wonder if he's still alive."

Not likely, Bear wrote. *The book you gave me was published more than twenty years ago.*

"Twenty years? Gosh, that's nearly twice as long as I've been alive." Reagan dropped the book back into the box. "This must have been his cabin. Maybe that's what the yellow tablets and pencils are for. I bet he came out here to do all his writing."

Bear shrugged.

Reagan pointed at the tablet in front of him. "Have you finished a page yet?"

Bear held up a pencil with one hand and two fingers with the other.

"Two pages—that's good. Keep going while I finish cleaning." Reagan whistled while she worked, her ponytail bouncing against her shoulders, a young girl far older than her years who appeared to have somehow overcome so much earlier trauma.

Bear looked up from his writing for a moment and watched Reagan clean. He knew better than to believe her emotional scars didn't run far deeper than the physical ones. Some people went quiet from pain while others made more noise in an effort to distract themselves from memories they wanted to forget. He wished he could help her to erase the pain of memory, but then he thought that perhaps none of those who now lived should ever forget what happened because to forget might allow it to happen again. He glanced down at the writing on the tablet, each word a reminder of his own suffering and rage following society's collapse.

"The snow is coming down hard now," Reagan said from where she stood looking out the window. "We might be here for a while." She smiled. "I think I'd like that if that's okay with you. This place feels safe and cozy."

Bear nodded.

Reagan nodded back. "Cool. Are you hungry?"

Starving, Bear wrote.

"Me too." Reagan picked up the can of beans she had earlier set on the table. "I didn't come across anything to open this with though." She pretended to bite into the side of the can. "Don't think that'll work."

Bear motioned for her to hand the can to him. He reached into his jacket and took out a knife, placed the can on its side in front of him and cut into the middle of it. Then he grabbed both ends and twisted it open.

"You're crazy strong," Reagan said. "I wish I was that strong. I'd smash anyone and everyone who tried to hurt me." She slid the metal pan under the can and watched as Bear poured the contents into it. The scent of the beans made both their mouths water. Reagan took the pan, set it on top of the stove, and breathed deeply. "Boy, that sure smells good."

Outside, the wind was getting stronger, pushing the snow against the sides of the cabin. Bear added more wood to the fire and then continued writing down his thoughts while Reagan used a spoon to stir the beans. After a few minutes the sauce started to boil. She wrapped a rag around her hand, picked up the hot pan by its handle, and set it on the table.

Bear put down his pencil.

Reagan gave him a spoon. "You better dig in before I eat it all," she said as she scooped up her first bite. She watched Bear do the same. "Well?"

Bear gave her a thumbs up.

Reagan wolfed down her second and third bites. "You know what I *really* miss? Ice cream. Gosh, I'd give almost anything to have a big bowl of it sitting in front of me right now. Not that I'm complaining because these beans sure are great. Still, some chocolate chip mint, I can't even remember the last time I had some." She looked up. "What about you? What food do you miss the most?"

"Beh."

"Huh?" Reagan's face tightened. "Your name?"

Bear shook his head. "Beh," he repeated before taking another bite of beans.

"What's beh?"

"Beh."

"I don't know what you're saying."

Bear picked up his pencil and wrote it out.

Beer!

Reagan giggled. "Beer isn't food."

It is!

"You're silly. Are you saying you would rather have beer than ice cream?"

Bear grinned as he quickly scribbled his reply.

Beer!

He took one more bite from the pan, pushed it in front of Reagan, and then pointed at her.

"You want me to finish the rest?"

"Uh-huh."

"Are you sure?"

Bear reached across the table and spooned out one last bean. "Go aheh."

The fire inside the stove crackled and the candles Reagan had placed around the room burned bright. She finished the beans first and then watched Bear as he continued to write. Eventually, he stopped, looked up, and then put down the pencil.

"All done?"

Bear shrugged.

"What's wrong?"

Bear tore off a single sheet of paper, wrote something down, and then gave it to Reagan.

You won't like the person I was.

"Why do you say that?"

Because I don't like the person I was.

"I told you already that you're a good person. I meant it."

You didn't know me then.

"Then doesn't matter. All that matters is now."

I'm ashamed.

"Like you feel guilty or something?"

Bear nodded.

"Why?"

You're too young to understand.

"Those men you rescued me from—you know what they were doing to me. I'll be ten soon, but I feel a lot older than that. I really don't think there's much you could share that would shock me. But if you don't want me to read what you wrote that's okay. It's none of my business."

My life then seems so stupid now.

"You were famous, right?"

Young, dumb, and spoiled is more like it. There were women—lots of women.

"You mean s-e-x?"

Bear grimaced and then wrote some more.

It feels weird talking about this stuff with you.

"I can just read about it then," Reagan said with a smile. "Or not. Like I said, it's up to you."

I don't want you to think less of me. I hurt people.

"You saved my life, Bear. I owe you big time. Nothing you wrote down on those yellow pieces of paper about who you used to be will change that. Besides, there's always the fire."

Bear frowned. "Fire?"

"You can burn what you wrote. That's what my dad used to say to my mom all the time—burn the past and build the future. I never really knew what he meant by that until after he was gone."

Bear glanced at the stove, looked down at the yellow tablet, and then tapped the pencil eraser against the top of the table. He sighed, set the pencil down, and carefully tore the pages from the tablet and held them in his oversized hands.

"You decide—share it or burn it." Reagan leaned back in her chair with her skinny arms crossed over her chest. "Either way we have food in our bellies and a roof over our heads so it's all good." Her voice lowered. "It really is okay if you don't want me to read it. Believe me, I totally understand."

A blast of wind made the cabin's tin roof rattle. It was going to be a cold and blustery night. Bear looked up, looked down, and then up again. With a long sigh he slid what he had written across the table toward Reagan.

"Are you sure?" she asked.

Bear nodded. "Yeah." He got up, went to the window, and watched the snow falling outside.

Reagan placed the papers in front of her and started to read.

2.
✦✧✦✧

I wasn't always so big. When I had cancer, I was normal sized for my age. They found it on my tongue, which had been sore for weeks. I had just turned six. The doctor told my parents it was an especially rare and aggressive type of tumor. He said radiation might not be enough and that we should consider removing not only the tumor but most of my tongue to be sure all the cancer was taken out.

So, that's what happened.

I went into the hospital able to talk and came out a week later nearly a mute. My mouth and throat were terribly swollen from the operation. I had to sip food through a straw for a while. A month later, I was given my first of three rounds of chemo. Six months after that and I was given the all clear—the cancer was gone.

The kids at school were nice at first, but it wasn't long before some of them would make fun of the way I tried to talk. After a while I stopped trying and just wrote out what I wanted to say. That summer I mostly stayed in my room and read. The following Christmas, my parents got me my first set of weights and I started lifting when I wasn't reading. My mom had been an athlete in high school and college—basketball. She was taller than my dad by a few inches—all her family were tall. It was a mixed marriage. She was black and Dad was white. Despite his smaller size Dad was no punk though. He had boxed in the military and nobody who knew him tried to mess with him because he was quick to set them straight. He told me once that he never went looking to start a fight, but he was damn sure willing to finish one. I liked how that sounded and decided to try to be the same as him—tough.

The summer after I turned twelve, I grew half a foot and came back to school the biggest kid in my class. I had been lifting all that time as well, so I wasn't thin and gangly—I was strong. I started playing football that year. It was football, weights, and reading books 24/7. I wasn't getting teased about not being able to talk so much anymore and girls started to notice me. By the time I was a freshman in high school I was over six foot and about two hundred and forty pounds. I started varsity and at the end of the season colleges were already contacting me about coming to play for them. I had my first serious girlfriend around that time as well. She was older by a few years. That's pretty much how high school went for me—almost all the girls I got serious with were older. I didn't mind. Not one bit.

High school was a blur. It was games, working out, parties, a bit of learning here and there, and then it was off to college. I had nine full-ride scholarship offers to choose from. I picked the University of Miami. Not because they had the best football program or academics opportunities but because when I did my campus visit, they had the best-looking girls. I won't lie. I was girl crazy and the thing of it is, they were crazy for me too. And everything was paid for—housing, tuition, food, tutors, I even had a job monitoring the weight room, which actually meant I was paid to work out, which also gave me all the spending money I needed. It was a great time. We won a national championship my junior year and I was the #1 ranked defensive player in the nation. The NFL wanted me bad. I thought of grabbing the money early and forgoing my senior year, but my parents convinced me to stay and get my degree. They said I had all the time in the world to play football but only one chance to be a college senior so that's what I did.

I blew my knee out the third game of my senior year. Man was I pissed. Pissed at my parents, pissed at my teammates, pissed at the offensive lineman from the other team who had cut my legs out from under me during the play—basically I was pissed at the whole world. First came two surgeries and then months of rehabilitation. The NFL was still interested but not nearly as much as they were the year before. I worked out harder than ever and when I showed up to the NFL Combine the following year, I was nearly four hundred pounds of pure muscle. Nobody was going to stop me from proving to those NFL teams how good I was and how much better I could still be.

"Damn you're big." That was a coach from Dallas who came up to me during the second day of the combine. He was a skinny older guy with these hard, Dirty Harry kind of eyes. "Fast too," he said. "That's what's really interesting about how you play out there, son. I've seen plenty of big strong fellas but not so big and strong as you with that kind of speed. God is funny like that. He took your tongue but seems to have more than made up for it by giving you other things. How's the knee holding up?"

"How does it look like it's holding up?" I texted and then handed the phone to him.

"You'll have to pass a physical. We'll be giving that knee a good looking over."

"No problem," I wrote.

He gave me his card and told me to have my agent contact him directly. Ten days later, I was signing my first NFL contract with my parents standing beside me. It was for three years, fully guaranteed, for seven million dollars and a five-million-dollar signing bonus. I was twenty-two years old and had just signed a guaranteed twelve-million-dollar payday. I earned rookie of the year honors and two years later signed a four-year extension with Dallas for sixty million.

Sixty million for tackling other men on a field. It was crazy. I didn't think it was possible to spend that much money—but I did. I had a house in Dallas, another in Miami, and a condo in Vegas that I used a lot because the strip clubs there were my favorite. I saw my parents less and less. Instead, I bought more cars, more jewelry, chartered private jets, and had a constant parade of women spread out all over the country to spend my nights with. Eventually a few wanted to get serious, asked me to be monogamous. If it meant getting what I wanted from them I'd go along with it and then go out and break that promise the first chance I got. If they complained I cut them loose and replaced them with someone else less demanding.

One woman, an exotic dancer in Atlanta, texted me one day to say she was pregnant and insisted it was mine. She said she wanted money from me whether she kept it or got rid of it and that she had already lawyered up. I offered $50k. She demanded a million. I said no way. She threatened to have the kid and then take me for everything I had. My lawyers asked if I thought I was actually the father. Honestly, I had no idea if I had even slept with her. I knew we hung out, partied, but did we actually do the deed? I couldn't recall. That's how out of control my life had become by then. They suggested $100k to make it all go away. I said fine but with conditions—she was required to do a fetal DNA test so we could confirm paternity. She refused the test. I celebrated this so-called victory by going out and partying for a few nights straight. A couple of months later, I was told by another teammate who knew her that she died of an overdose. Apparently, she had been dead for a week or more before her body was discovered inside of her rat-infested studio apartment. Suddenly my victory didn't feel so much like a victory anymore. I gave a cop some season tickets to let me know if the autopsy indicated if she was actually pregnant or not.

She was.

I felt like such a scumbag.

Welcome to life in the NFL.

After my sixth season I had to have some cartilage cleaned out of the reconstructed knee. That wasn't so bad. I was on crutches for a few weeks. That knee was just one of many physical issues I was battling. My back, neck and shoulders hurt, I had two fingers that had been broken no fewer than six times each and were already turning arthritic, a big toe that was feeling the same, and some constantly sore ribs that sometimes made breathing difficult. I popped anti-inflammatories like candy nearly every hour of every day. The team physician warned how doing that would be hard on my liver. I didn't care. I had a contract to play football that paid me millions and afforded me a life most could only dream of. When the pain got bad, I grabbed for the pills. Wash, rinse, repeat.

Shortly before my 30th birthday I attended a very strange team meeting. There was a representative from the Centers for Disease Control and Prevention there. He told us that as professional athletes with a weekly audience of tens of millions we had an important public relations role to play in an upcoming virus-related health crisis. I was one of the few who actually asked questions, namely how he knew about a health crisis that hadn't happened yet.

Then we learned about the mandatory shots. I said hell no. The coaching staff warned me that I wouldn't be allowed to play if I didn't get the vaccine and that because I would be in violation of my contract I wouldn't be paid either. This was especially tough because my agent was in the middle of negotiating yet another big payday extension. It was nuts though. Why would I get vaccinated for a virus that wasn't there? Nobody seemed to have an answer or if they did, they weren't willing to give me one. I sat out the next game and the one after that. My teammates begged me to just get the jab and be done with it. I started noticing more and more politicians talking about it. Stories of people getting sick were being spread on television and social media. They were actually starting to consider rounding up people who weren't vaccinated for a virus that nobody knew what exactly it was or where it came from or if it was even real.

The team allowed me to come back for an important matchup against Philadelphia that would likely decide the division title. They said the league was still assessing its vaccination policy so until it was finalized, I would be allowed to play. That was the same game where I watched another player collapse and die. We had seen the stories of it happening to soccer players over in Europe, seemingly healthy young men who died suddenly in the middle of a match, but this was the first time I knew of that kind of thing happening in the States. He was a rookie running back named Ellis Banks who we used for third and short situations. Nice kid. Lots of promise. It was his first play of the game. He came onto the field, took the handoff, ran a little sweep over to the left side, and was then brought down after a two-yard gain for a first down.

Ellis never got up from that play. He was face down, not moving—dead. The medical staff worked on him for about twenty minutes, but we all knew he was gone. They hauled the body away on a cart as an entire stadium full of people watched, recording it all with their phones. I overheard one of the doctors say, "He was vaccinated two weeks ago." That's when I saw that same CDC official who had been at the team meeting weeks earlier go up to the coaching staff of both teams and order them to keep playing. I thought there was no way they'd agree to that, but they did. I saw the fear in those coaches' eyes. Whoever that government fella was he scared them bad. Even more disappointing was watching the players walk back out onto the field pretty much like nothing happened. We played on and the fans cheered.

It was so weird, like none of it was real—but it was.

That's when I really started to hate people. A young man had just died, and it took everyone all of about thirty minutes to move on and get back to their clapping and cheering. I'm ashamed to say I wasn't much different. I finished the game. When it was done, though, I cleaned out my locker and left. That was the last game I ever played. I flew home to my parents and not long after that was when the shit really hit the fan.

Mom had agreed weeks earlier to get vaccinated. Then she got sick. Dad was out of his mind with worry and anger. He would appear calm in front of Mom while taking care of her, but when it was just him and me, he would unleash all these conspiracies about how the government was covering up something terrible regarding the shots they were forcing everyone to get. He was convinced the mystery virus that had created all the hysteria was a hoax—that its purpose was to get people to take the shots. I'm still not sure how right or wrong he was about any of that, but what I do know is things had gone from normal to weird very quickly and we were all suddenly living in a world none of us recognized.

Dad said we needed to get out of Michigan—that it was turning into a police state. It was already clear to me that he was right about that. I watched an entire family in the neighborhood that had refused the vaccine be taken away by police. People were losing their jobs. This caused a supply shortage because there weren't enough workers to keep everything moving. The power grid started to go off at different times of the day. And yet, most people kept their heads down and didn't demand answers. Almost all of them did what they were told even when none of it made any sense. Dad mentioned how one of the neighbors had said to him that in parts of Montana things were better. That's where he thought we should go to hide out during all the craziness going on, but by then Mom was suffering from multiple mini strokes that left her barely able to move. Dad urged me to go to Montana by myself, but I refused to leave them alone. They needed the help. The store shelves were empty. Food was getting scarce and winter was coming. With the power going out more and more they couldn't even reliably heat the home.

Eventually the power went off for good and so did everything else. There were no phones, no electricity, no fuel, nothing worked. That's when the looting started in the cities and then quickly spread to the suburbs near where we lived.

The temperature started to consistently drop below freezing. Thank God the house had a fireplace. We were actually burning wood cut from the trees in the yard to stay warm. Dad was meeting regularly with some of the other men in the neighborhood to set up patrol schedules in case the looters showed up. A few of the neighbors had guns, but ammo was in short supply. The rumor was that the government had confiscated nearly all of the ammunition in the country months earlier. A box of shells was now worth more than gold.

Mom passed away in January. We buried her in the backyard. It took me hours to dig that hole because the ground was so hard. Dad changed after she was gone. I watched the light steadily going out in his eyes. He stopped caring. What little food I was able to scrounge up he hardly ate. Every so often, though, he'd remind me to get myself to Montana before it was too late. "Word is people there are doing okay," he'd say. "They are being left alone to fend for themselves."

Left alone. That sounded like the place I wanted to be because in our little corner of the world in Michigan things had gone from bad to worse in no time at all. A house a block from ours burned down one night. Some said it was looters. Others said it was the home's owner who set the fire after his wife and three kids all died within days of each other. "It's the vaccine," he screamed while standing in the middle of the street the night before the fire. "It's the vaccine." The next day his house was a charred pile of nothing.

The looting got worse. Neighbors were stealing from neighbors and it wasn't long before neighbors were killing neighbors for food and water and anything else of value. I would stand on our porch just before dark every night and glare at anyone who gave our house a look, hoping my size would be enough to make them move on. Meanwhile, Dad stayed in his room and slept more and more.

Soldiers woke us up one morning, banging on the door. There were two of them and they were both armed. They said it was a "wellness check" but given the questions they were asking it seemed they were most concerned about whether we had any weapons or not. Dad snapped. He was raging at them to get out, saying it was none of their business what we did or didn't have. Then he cut one of them with a knife. It was little more than a scratch. I tried to intervene, to calm the situation, but was ordered at gunpoint to get back.

The injured soldier was younger than the other one—he couldn't have been more than nineteen or twenty. He looked down at the blood on his arm. Then he raised his rifle and pointed it at my dad.

"Go ahead," Dad said. "See if you got the balls to pull that trigger."

The rifle fired.

I couldn't move. I couldn't breathe. Dad doubled over into a pool of his own blood. He lay on his back and stared at me for what felt like forever even though I know it was only a few seconds. "Montana," he gasped. "Listen to your old man. That's an order."

"What's he talking about?" the soldier who shot him asked.

The other soldier shrugged. "No clue."

"You killed him," I cried in my garbled, tongueless way. My dad told me what needed to be done. He didn't speak the words, but I saw it in his eyes. The only way for me to get out of that house alive was to do it alone—to be the only one left to walk out of there.

I had spent years perfecting the ability to move quickly and powerfully at the snap of the ball. This would be no different. Those soldiers never had a chance. I grabbed the one closest to me, ripped the rifle from his hands, tossed him aside, and then put two rounds into the other one's chest, killing him almost instantly.

"Please don't," the remaining soldier begged as I pointed the rifle at him.

I moved toward the kitchen counter, picked up a pen and paper, and scribbled my reply.

"I have to," I wrote. "You'll report me."

Sweat covered the soldier's face as he read my response. He looked up, his eyes bulging. "There's nobody to report you to. It's all falling apart out there. More and more of us are deserting. We're running out of food, ammo, everything. Nobody knows who's in charge."

"Is that really why you were here?" I wrote. "To find stuff to take from us?"

The soldier looked away. That was his answer. They were no better than the looters.

I put down the pen, aimed and fired, but nothing happened.

"I told you." The soldier glanced down at the other rifle that lay on the floor next to the dead soldier's body. "We're running out of ammo. We came here with just a couple of rounds each."

That meant one round remained in the second rifle and we both knew it. The soldier dove for the gun. I stepped on the barrel, grabbed him by the neck, and slammed his face into the carpet. When he rolled over to grab hold of my leg, I clamped one hand around his neck, picked him up, and threw him across the room. The side of his head struck the corner of the fireplace mantel.

Disoriented, he stumbled toward the front door, but I reached him first, grabbed hold of his face between my hands and then snapped his neck. It wasn't like the movies. A man's neck doesn't break easily. It took almost all of my strength to do it. The sound it made is something I'll never forget but God knows I've tried.

That was the day I became a killer. I felt sick about it, but my dad's voice pushed that sickness aside.

"Son," he whispered. "You did good. You did what was needed to be done."

When I started to speak, he shook his head. "Just listen. The old jeep in the garage is ready. The keys are in it. Both tanks are full and there's more fuel strapped to the back. It won't be enough to get you all the way to Montana, but it's a start. There's also a duffel bag sitting in the passenger seat with a map, dried fruit, bottles of water, a knife, and a first aid kit. I wish I could have left you more, but at least it's something." He closed his eyes and groaned in pain. I rested his head in my lap. "Hurry," he murmured. "Don't bother putting me in the ground. There's isn't time. Just go."

Dad coughed loudly as he grabbed hold of my arm and opened his eyes. "Now."

And then he was gone.

I disobeyed my father.

I didn't leave right away.

I took time to bury him in the yard next to my mother.

With only a few hours of daylight left I opened the garage door, started the jeep, and backed out onto an empty street. Rows of homes sat still and dark. The soldier's rifle with the one round left in it sat propped up against the passenger seat next to the duffel bag. I took out the map. Dad had already drawn a line that linked the location of our home to just inside the border of Eastern Montana.

It was about a thousand miles.

I drove away and didn't look back and have been on my own ever since.

Until now.

Reagan put down the pages Bear had written and looked up at him. It was still snowing outside. "Hey," she said.

He turned around. Shame still colored his eyes.

"Sit down next to me."

The chair groaned under Bear's considerable weight. He avoided looking at Reagan.

"Thanks for sharing all of that with me."

Bear shrugged.

"I'm glad. Now I know you so much better. You don't have anything to be ashamed of."

Bear closed his eyes and clenched his fists.

Reagan got up, stood next to him, and hugged his neck. "We're a team now, right?"

When Bear didn't answer, Reagan squeezed him tighter. "Right?"

Bear nodded. "Righ." He turned in his chair and hugged Reagan back.

"It's okay," she whispered. "What you did—it was all okay."

Bear lowered his face into Reagan's shoulder and for the first time since having his tongue cut out when he was a boy, he allowed himself to cry.

3.
✦✧✦✧

By morning the snow was halfway up to the cabin window.

"I bet there's almost three feet out there," Reagan said.

Bear had earlier already pushed the door open enough to allow him to scoop up some snow in the pot and then melt it on the stove so that they had water to drink. *We're going to need more wood soon,* he wrote.

"Plenty of trees around here for that," Reagan replied.

And food.

"I'm not worried."

Are you hungry?

"Yeah."

Then you should be worried.

"Stop being such a big grump."

Bear grinned as he wrote out his reply. *If the big shoe fits.*

Reagan poked him in the arm. "Grump-grump-grump." She suddenly straightened and her eyes widened. "There's a man on a horse outside."

Bear looked out the window.

"What's he want?" Reagan asked.

Bear picked up the sledgehammer he had left by the door. The horse shook its head and snorted while the man continued to stare at the cabin. He wore a tan cowboy hat, long brown duster jacket, leather gloves, and jeans. His lean face was hidden underneath a full white beard and matching eyebrows that sat above a pair of flinty eyes. A bolt-action rifle was strapped to the side of the saddle. The horse, like the man's hat, was also tan.

"How'd he find this place?" Reagan put her face next to Bear's so she could get a better view through the window. "It's in the middle of nowhere. He looks pretty old. Do you think he's dangerous? I wonder if his gun has bullets."

Bear pressed his finger to his lips and then continued to watch the man outside.

"Sorry," Reagan whispered. "I guess I tend to blabber when I'm nervous."

"Would you mind opening that door so we can talk?" the man shouted in a sandpaper and kerosene voice ripped and torn by decades of tobacco smoke.

Reagan's eyes got even bigger. "It's the same hat." She turned away, grabbed one of the books from the box she had found earlier, and held it up. "See?" She showed the book to Bear. "It's him—Remington Wilkes."

The features of the man on the horse and the author pictured at the back of the book were similar, but it was hard to tell for sure because of the beard.

"Same cowboy hat," Reagan repeated.

Bear pointed to the table and chairs and then wrote for her to wait inside.

"I really don't think he's dangerous," she said.

"Hello?" the man outside yelled. "I know you're in there because of the smoke coming out of the stove pipe. As you can see, I'm armed, but I have no interest in hurting you. I just want a chance to talk. There's something inside that I need to get and then I'll be on my way. You're free to stay if you like—not my concern."

Bear and Reagan remained quiet and watching.

"There's a box of books in there," the man continued. "The photo on the back is me in case you were wondering. This is my place."

"I knew it." Reagan set the book down on the table. "I told you it was him."

Again, Bear pressed his finger to his lips and then repeated the gesture for her to sit.

"Are you going to talk to him?"

Bear nodded.

"Good. Make sure to apologize. It's his cabin after all."

Bear opened the door and stood outside.

The man whistled. "Damn, look at the size of you." He pushed open his jacket to reveal a gun hanging from his hip. "Are we going to have any trouble?"

Bear shook his head.

"What's the big hammer for?"

"Protection," Reagan said. She stood next to Bear despite his having told her to stay inside. "And he knows how to use it."

"Huh," the man grunted. "Wasn't expecting to see a kid step out of there."

Reagan scowled. "I'm not a kid.

The man tipped the brim of his hat. "Apologies, young lady. I imagine you're right about that. If you've managed to survive this long in the nightmare that we're all living in I doubt there's much innocence left in any of us." He gave Bear a hard look. "This man isn't holding you against your will, is he? Because if he is—"

Reagan reached up and squeezed Bear's hand. "He saved me. He's my friend."

"Okay then," the man replied. "My name is Remington Wilkes."

Reagan nodded. "I know. That's what the books say."

The man shifted in the saddle. "That's right."

"I'm Reagan. This is Bear."

Remington's bushy brows lifted. "He's the bear isn't he? I've heard of him. You weren't kidding when you said he's good with that hammer. Do you know about the bounty Vig put on you?"

"Sure, we know," Reagan answered. "Do you work for her?"

Remington flinched. "*Me* working for garbage like Vig? Not likely. My place in Savage is thankfully well beyond her influence—at least for now."

Reagan pointed at the rifle strapped to the saddle. "Do you have bullets?"

"Let's hope neither of you have to find out."

Bear gripped the sledgehammer with both hands and raised it to his chest.

"Easy now," Remington said. "My answer wasn't meant as a threat."

Reagan tugged on Bear's sleeve. "It's okay."

Remington leaned back in the saddle and grimaced. "It's been a long ride and my horse and me could use some rest. You mind if I come inside? It *is* my place after all."

"What's your horse's name?" Reagan asked.

"This here is Peanut." Remington stroked the horse's neck. "Named her after my great uncle Hap's horse. It's originally his property that I call home back in Savage. He's long gone—left the land to his grandkids, but they both live in different parts of the country. At least I hope they're still living. Hard to know for certain these days. I reached out to them some time ago and made a more than fair offer on the place. They were willing to sell to me because it meant the ranch would stay in the family. I've been there ever since. I used this cabin here for hunting elk and to kick around story ideas in my head. Built it myself. I'm no carpenter, but I can fake if I'm motivated to. As you already know by now it's nothing fancy, but it'll do in a pinch."

"Why aren't you hiding out here?"

Remington gripped the saddle horn with both hands. "That's a good question, Reagan. Now pay attention." He pointed to the clearing's perimeter. "All those trees make it difficult to see what's coming. The land is flat, so the cabin is vulnerable to attack from all sides. Back at the ranch there's a hill named after my ancestor who first settled there—Vaughn's Hill. Only one way to the top of it, a narrow little trail that you have to take by horse or walk. I could defend it for days or weeks if I had to. Hap and his grandkids did that very thing once—true story."

Reagan shivered a little from the cold. "You said you were here to get something."

"That's right."

"What is it?"

"I'm not ready to share that with you just yet."

"What about Peanut?"

"There's a nice dry area under those trees by the side where she can get her feet out of this snow."

Reagan looked up at Bear. "Should we let him in?"

Remington cleared his throat. "I'm not really asking. You wouldn't really try to keep a man from his own home, would you?"

"This isn't your home," Reagan replied. "You live on a ranch in Savage, remember?"

"Well, aren't you a little stickler for details."

Reagan shrugged. "Just saying."

Remington grinned. "That you are." He nodded at Bear. "Am I good to come in?"

"I think it's okay," Reagan whispered.

Bear looked down at her, then up at Remington. After a few seconds of hesitation he stepped back and motioned for Remington to come inside.

After leaving Peanut under the branches of a large pine tree Remington walked into the cabin. Reagan sat at the table while Bear stood in front of her still holding the sledgehammer.

"Nice and warm in here," Remington said as he closed the door behind him. "You've burned through most the wood though." He leaned the rifle against the wall by the door.

"We plan to get some more," Reagan replied.

"Gonna be wet."

Bear straightened to his full height as he stared at the rifle.

Remington lifted his head and sniffed. "You found the beans."

"That was our dinner last night." Reagan pointed to the two cans left on the shelf. "There's more."

"I see that." When Remington started to cross the room, Bear took a step toward him. Remington took off his gloves and jammed them into a side pocket of his jacket. "Still don't trust me, huh?"

Bear shook his head.

"Look," Remington continued. "The rifle is way over there and as for this shooter—" he tapped the butt of the revolver that hung off the belt around his narrow waist, "—it's empty. I fired off the last two rounds yesterday on my way here."

"Why?" Reagan asked.

"Road pirates—a couple of real scarecrows. They looked to be near starving. Actually felt sorry for them. Guessing they wanted Peanut for food. They scurried away after I shot at them. Don't worry; I made sure they didn't follow me here."

"How do you know for sure?" Reagan stared at Remington while she waited for an answer.

"You like to ask a lot of questions of people, don't you?"

"I don't like questions nearly as much as I like the answers to them."

Remington chuckled. "How old are you?"

"Going on twelve." Reagan pushed a chair away from the table. "Want to sit down?"

"A chance to rest my feet? You won't have to ask me twice." Remington looked up at Bear. "That is if he'll allow it."

"He'll allow it," Reagan said.

Bear stepped aside.

Remington groaned as he sat.

Reagan leaned forward. "You have a lot of wrinkles on your face."

"Among other places."

"How old are you?"

"The oldest one in this room."

Reagan rolled her eyes. "I know *that*. Are you a hundred?"

"A hundred?" Remington scratched at his beard. "Geez, am I actually looking *that* used up these days?"

Even Bear grinned.

"No," Remington continued. "I'm not a hundred."

Reagan cocked her head. "Then how old?"

"I'm a few years shy of seventy."

"Wow," Reagan whispered. "That *is* old."

Remington winked. "Don't I know it." Then he tapped the floorboards with the worn heel of his boot.

"What are you doing?" Reagan asked.

"It's the reason I'm here." Remington got up. "I need to move this table." He looked at Bear. "You mind giving me a hand?"

Bear grabbed both sides of the table and easily lifted it up.

"Put it over there," Remington said before he knelt down and rapped the floor with a knuckle. "That's it."

Reagan got on her knees across from him. "What?"

"You'll see." Remington took out a pocketknife.

Bear immediately clamped a hand over his shoulder.

"You mind?" Remington said as he winced at the pressure applied by Bear's grip. "I'm just using the knife to open up the floor."

"A secret place!" Reagan exclaimed.

Bear withdrew his hand.

Remington nodded. "Something like that." He stuck the tip of the knife in between two boards until one of them popped out. "There we go." He handed the board to Reagan. "Put that beside you." Two more boards were removed. Remington reached down into the dark hole. "Got it." He held up a canvas duffel bag, set it next to him, and then had Reagan hand him the boards so that he could put them back.

"Good as new," Reagan declared.

Remington pushed himself up. "The floor might be, but as for me," he said as he rubbed his lower back, "not so much."

Reagan stared at the bag. "What's in it?"

"Gum."

"*Really?*"

"Among other things." Remington pulled the table back and then put the bag on top of it. "I'll show you." He glanced at Bear. "I'll show you both."

Bear and Reagan leaned down as Remington unzipped the bag and pulled it open. He reached in and then took out a pack of Black Jack gum. "See?" He handed it to Reagan. "For you."

Reagan gazed at the baby-blue packaging as if she had just been given the keys to the universe. "Seriously? I can have it?"

Remington smiled. "Just save me a piece. I used to chew it all the time back when I smoked cigarettes."

"You smoked?"

"This face didn't get like this all on its own." He patted the front of his jacket. "These days I stick to a bit of pipe tobacco from time to time."

"You're a lot nicer than your picture."

"The author photo you mean?" Remington adjusted his hat. "That was the publisher's idea. He demanded I look the part. Not that I can't be ornery, but unless there's an actual problem then why not be content? I'm a hell of a nice guy—until I'm not. I never did much care for the photo they ended up using—made me look like I was in a state of constant constipation. I suppose I shouldn't complain. At least I sold enough of those books to keep me from having to do honest work." The next items he took from the bag were four boxes of ammo—one for the revolver he wore and the other three for the rifle. "These are why I made the trip all the way out here. A gun without a bullet is like water without the wet—pretty much useless." He returned the ammo into the bag, zipped it closed, and then placed it by the door next to the rifle.

"Are you going to stay for dinner?" Reagan asked.

"Will you be cooking up some more of those beans?"

Reagan's eyes sparkled when she smiled. "Yup."

Bear scowled.

"What's your friend think about the possibility of my staying?" Remington glanced at Bear. "Because from where I'm standing, he doesn't look too thrilled."

"We'll talk about it," Reagan said.

Remington reached for the door. "You do that. I'm going to be outside trying to scrounge up some grass under those trees for Peanut to eat." After he opened the door, he looked up at the clear blue sky. "Sun is out. Snow is melting. Tomorrow should be a decent day for heading back to Savage."

The door closed.

Bear grabbed a pen, wrote something down, and then slid the paper toward Reagan.

Don't be so trusting of strangers.

"You were a stranger to me not too long ago, remember? Why don't you like him?"

I didn't say I didn't like him. We just need to be careful.

"I like him and I want him to stay."

Why?

"Why not?"

We don't know if he can be trusted.

"I trusted you. Was I wrong about that?"

Remington walked in holding a pile of twigs and branches in his arms. "Managed to scrounge up some wood that's reasonably dry. Should burn okay." He set the wood down next to the stove and then looked at Reagan and Bear. "Well?"

"You can stay the night," Reagan said.

Remington brushed his hands off on his jeans. "Does she also speak for you, big fella?"

Bear sighed, looked at Reagan, and then nodded.

"And I'll even sweeten the deal," Remington said as he pointed at the cans of beans. "Dinner is on me."

The rest of the day was spent gathering more wood. Bear also started to read one of Remington's books while Remington sat snoring in a chair by the fire. Right before dark Reagan had Bear open both cans of beans. She emptied them into the pot and put it on the stove.

"You mind if I add a little something to it?" Remington reached into his jacket and then withdrew a few stringy strands of dark dry meat. "Rabbit."

"How'd you get that?" Reagan asked. "They're so hard to catch."

"Maybe some day I'll get to show you." Remington dropped the meat into the pot. "That's sure to kick those beans up a notch."

Bear's nostrils flared as he licked his lips. Reagan stirred the pot for a few minutes and then declared that dinner was ready. The three of them sat around the table sharing the rabbit-flavored beans from the pot.

"Mm," Remington said after swallowing his last spoonful. "You're a fine cook, Reagan. Those are without question the finest beans I have ever had."

Reagan blushed. "Thank you."

Soon after, the last of the wood was put into the stove, the candles were blown out, and a deep sleep visited each of them.

Hours later, Reagan sat up in the dark. "What was that?"

"Horse is spooked." Remington crept toward the door. "Could be wolves." He opened one of the boxes of ammo and carefully loaded the rifle. Then he looked through the window.

"See anything?" Reagan whispered.

"No." Remington continued looking.

Peanut squealed loudly. Something outside was agitating her.

Remington turned and pointed at Bear. "Stay inside and keep her safe."

"What are you doing?" Reagan asked.

"I'm going to find out what's going on out there."

Remington paused before pushing the door open. The glow from the fire allowed Reagan to catch a glimpse of his eyes. She realized then that the photo of him on the back of his books had it right.

Remington Wilkes was a killer.

The door opened and darkness walked outside.

4.
✦✧✦✧

Remington aimed the rifle. "I'll tell you just once—get away from my horse."

The road pirate emerged from the trees and stood in the moonlit gloom. He was tall and lanky with narrow shoulders, a stick of a neck, and a face buried beneath a full blond beard. "Nice place," he said.

"You shouldn't have followed me here."

"Had nothing better to do. Besides, I'm so hungry I could eat—" he paused "—a horse."

"Where's your little buddy?" Remington asked.

"Here," another voice answered.

Remington glanced to his right and saw a second man holding a machete approaching. "Not another step."

The second man stopped. "You're the boss." He was bald, shorter than the other, with a salt-and-pepper beard, but just as emaciated looking. It appeared neither man had eaten in several days. "Are you alone in there?"

"None of your business," Remington replied. "Now go stand next to your partner."

"And if I don't want to?"

"I'll kill you."

The second man grinned. "Not if you're out of bullets."

"Don't try me, kid. Remember, none of us can afford to waste ammo on warning shots these days. When I shoot, it'll be to put a hole in you. I promise you that."

"You don't scare us old man," the taller of the two road pirates said. "We decided we like it here. We'll take the horse, the cabin, and whatever is in it."

"Anything else?" Remington growled.

"That'll do for now," the shorter one said.

"You two have names?"

"Why do you want to know our names?" the taller one asked.

Remington's lips drew back slightly from his teeth. "For the graves it looks like I'll be digging soon."

The tall one chuckled. "You sure like to talk tough, don't you? I like you, old man. You can call me Shane and that's Brad."

"Brad and Shane," Remington repeated. "Short and simple."

Shane's eyes flashed a warning of impending violence. "He might be short, but I'm not simple.

"That's not how I meant it." Remington shrugged. "Actually, I like your take better. He pointed the rifle at Brad. "Short." Then he pointed it at Shane. "And simple."

"I'm tired of hearing him talk," Brad said. "My feet are freezing. Let's finish this. He's just an old man with an empty gun."

"Still thinking this rifle is empty, huh?" Remington aimed it at Brad. "You better be sure about that because you won't get a second chance to be wrong."

Shane took a step toward Remington. "That's a bolt action. You really think you're fast enough to shoot us both before one of us gets to you first?"

Remington's smile matched the cold glare of his eyes. "This is your chance to find out. I'll say this—I'm plenty fast to get at least one of you."

"Why aren't you afraid?" Brad asked. "Most everyone we come across these days is afraid. They'll do just about anything we tell them to."

"Sorry to disappoint you."

"I mean it," Brad continued. "You're acting like this is nothing. We're half your age and have you outnumbered. You should be begging us for your life."

"That's the funny thing about killing," Remington replied. "The more of it you do the easier it gets. Now, can we please hurry this up? I'd like to catch a few more winks before the sun comes up."

"Can't wait to cook strips of that horse over a fire," Brad said as he licked his lips. "I can taste it already."

Remington clicked his tongue. "Big mistake."

Shane took another step. "What is?"

"Talking about my horse like that."

"Why do you care so much about a stupid horse?"

"A man like you wouldn't understand."

"Try me."

"Better yet, you and your friend turn around and get the hell out of here."

Shane's smile lacked several teeth. "You said you were going to kill us."

"Truth be told, I'd rather not."

"Because you can't," Brad scoffed. "It's like we thought—no bullets. All you can do is talk."

"Hold on," Shane said. "I want to hear him explain why he thinks a man *like me* wouldn't understand his feelings about a horse."

"A horse doesn't respect weakness," Remington answered.

"You're calling me weak?"

"Calling it like I see it."

"A man your age probably doesn't see so well."

Brad crept closer. Remington's eyes narrowed. "You sure seem determined to leave me no choice but to shoot you dead."

Shane charged from the opposite side.

Remington fired at Brad and then turned to do the same to Shane but hesitated when he saw his horse standing in the background. A missed shot might hit Peanut. That second of hesitation allowed Shane time to reach him and grab the tip of the rifle and shove it away. Remington tightened his grip as he was pushed backwards by Shane's momentum.

"He shot me," Brad cried. "The sonofabitch really shot me."

"Stop your whining," Remington bellowed. "I warned you."

Shane grabbed hold of the rifle with both his hands and tried to yank it away. "I'm going to scoop your eyes out of your skull and eat them," he hissed.

Remington kicked Shane's shin and then pushed back with a strength that surprised the younger man. Their breath billowed out between them when it struck the cold night air. Shane was tiring already as he struggled to keep his grip on the rifle. "You're dead, old man," he gasped.

"Look behind you," Remington replied.

"Nice try." Shane gritted what remained of his discolored teeth. Then he struck something behind him—something big.

"Told you," Remington said.

"It's him." Brad stumbled forward, his bloody hand covering the bullet hole in his shoulder.

"Who?" Shane asked, seemingly afraid to turn around and find out for himself.

"The bear," Brad whispered, his eyes wide.

Shane let go of the rifle. "We're just trying to survive out here the same as you."

"Same as me?" Remington shook his head. "No, we're definitely *not* the same. I don't go around threatening to kill a man's horse or to take his property from him."

"I'm bleeding bad," Brad whimpered. "Am I going to die?"

Remington turned and fired into the middle of Brad's forehead. The road pirate fell to his knees, eyes wide and his mouth open, dropped the machete, and then collapsed face-first into the snow. "Looks that way," Remington muttered.

Shane started to run, but Bear snatched him by the neck and flung him to the ground. When he rolled over, he was holding a pistol. Bear stopped. Shane got back onto his feet with the gun held out in front of him. "I didn't believe the stories, but you're actually as big as they say." He glanced at Remington. "Why didn't you tell us the bear was inside the cabin?"

"Would that have made a difference?"

"It might have. I mean just look at him—he's huge. Last I heard he had a little girl with him. Is she here too?"

Remington aimed the rifle at Shane's chest. "Why'd you wait until now to show your weapon?"

"Element of surprise I suppose."

"Or it's empty."

"We accused you of being out of bullets too," Shane said. "That didn't turn out so well for Brad, did it? You don't strike me as the kind of man who makes a habit of repeating other people's mistakes."

"So, you're saying you're locked and loaded?"

"I'm saying you won't know for sure until I pull the trigger. Now, do you mind answering my question?"

"What question was that?"

"The girl," Shane said. "Is she in there?"

"Why do you want to know?"

"To confirm the rumors is all."

"Why would a dead man care about rumors?"

"You're not killing me."

Remington arched a brow. *"No?"*

"You shoot me; I shoot the big fella. From where I'm standing it's clear you don't want to see that happen."

"Or I shoot you and you don't do anything but crumple up and die like your dead friend. Then I go back inside and sleep like a baby."

"We just wanted something to eat."

"Actually, you wanted to take by force what wasn't yours. The problem for you is that you finally ran into some people who are willing to fight back. You and I both know you two would have hacked us up into pieces with that machete if we had let you."

"Fine," Shane said. "Brad is dead. I learned my lesson. Now I just want to be on my way."

"I bet you do," Remington said between clenched teeth.

Shane took a step back while keeping his pistol pointed at Bear. "Don't make me shoot him, old man. Be smart and let me go."

Peanut shook her head and pawed at the earth. When Shane glanced in the direction of the noise created by the horse Bear charged, grabbing hold of the gun and ripping it away. Shane fell and then crab walked backwards in the snow while looking up fearfully at the giant man looming over him.

Bear quickly inspected the pistol and then tossed it aside.

"Empty?" Remington asked.

Bear nodded as he raised the sledgehammer over his head.

"Please," Shane sobbed. "Don't kill me."

"Stop."

Bear looked back.

Remington partially lowered his rifle.

Reagan stood in the cabin doorway holding the pot used to cook the beans. "He's hungry. There's a little left. He can have it."

"No," Remington said. "That's not a good idea. You should go back inside. This will all be over soon."

"But he's hungry," Reagan repeated. "We should help people when we can. How will the world get any better if people like us aren't willing to help people like him?" She stared at Remington. "We helped you, didn't we?"

"That man down there isn't me."

Shane got up slowly with his hands held out in front of him. "Listen to the girl." He eyed the pot.

Remington tipped his head toward the cabin. "Go inside, Reagan."

"No." Reagan went to Shane. "I'm sorry there isn't more."

Shane grabbed the pot and buried his face in it, loudly licking the sides and bottom. "Thank you," he mumbled. Within seconds the pot had been licked clean. He was on the verge of tears when he handed it back to Reagan. "You're an angel."

"Now you need to go." Reagan pointed into the darkness. "And don't come back."

"I hope some day to be able to repay your kindness." Shane nodded at Reagan. "I truly mean that." He glared at Remington. "Don't you dare shoot me in the back."

Remington's eyes fired the bullets that his rifle wouldn't. "I won't so long as you keep your word. We don't see you ever again."

Shane picked up his gun and then fled into the night.

"I sure hope that show of mercy doesn't come back to bite us in the ass." Remington lowered the rifle. "But my gut says it will." He sighed. "It won't be safe for you two to stay here. The word about how to find this place will spread. Others will come."

Reagan smiled. "That's why we're going with you to your ranch in Savage."

"You are?" Remington looked at Bear. "*Well?*"

Bear shrugged.

"So, where she goes you go."

Bear gently put his arm around Reagan's shoulder. "Yeah."

Remington nodded. "Fine. We leave at first light. You two can try to catch a few more winks while I keep watch."

"I'm not tired anymore," Reagan said. "I'll keep you company."

"Do I have a choice?"

"Don't you want me to keep you company?"

Remington thought about it and then grunted. "You know what? I wouldn't mind that one bit. Thanks."

Reagan's warm smile was a rare remnant of better times and nearly forgotten days when innocence still had a safe place in the world. "You're welcome." The smile faded and her face turned contemplative. "Will I like your ranch?"

"I don't see why not."

"Is it safe there?"

"Yes, at least for a while longer it should be."

"Mr. Wilkes?"

"Call me Remington."

"Remington, the man you killed outside, did he deserve to die?"

"I think so."

"But you don't know for sure?"

"I think I'm sure."

Reagan frowned. "You can't *think* you're sure. You're either sure or you're not."

"Then I'm sure."

"Did that man want to hurt us?"

"He did."

"And that's why you shot him."

"Yes."

"Okay." Reagan yawned. "Do you mind if I close my eyes for a little bit? You can still talk to me if you want though."

"You can close your eyes. I don't mind."

"Remington?"

"Yeah?"

"Goodnight."

"Goodnight, Reagan."

Bear poked at the coals in the fire and then sat by the stove watching and listening to the exchange between the other two. After Reagan fell asleep Remington looked back at him and nodded. That brief nod was the unspoken acknowledgement of what both men now understood to be their shared purpose—protecting Reagan with their lives.

Remington prayed that he would be up to the task.

5.
✦✧✦✧

The closer they got to Savage the more Remington talked about the place he called home. Reagan sat atop Peanut with him while Bear walked beside them. They had left the cabin at dawn and the sun's place in the sky indicated it was now around noon. It was slow going because they were carefully avoiding any of the main roads that crisscrossed Eastern Montana in the hope of getting all the way to Savage without being seen by anyone else.

"Once we work our way around Glendive," Remington said, "we'll stick to the valley along the Yellowstone River. That'll take us to the Wilkes' ranch and Vaughn's Hill. I think you'll like it up there. On one side you look down at all the property that surrounds the little ranch house that was built by Vaughn Wilkes and on the other side are these endless views of the Yellowstone and beyond."

Reagan kept stroking Peanut's mane. "Sounds nice."

"It is," Remington replied. "I'm really looking forward to getting back."

"How long can we stay?"

"For as long as it's safe."

"For forever?"

With a light flick of the reins Remington had Peanut go on the right side of a cluster of fallen trees. "Maybe." He pointed west. "Over that way is Glendive about ten miles from here. We should make the banks of the Yellowstone before nightfall. You ever camp outside next to a river?"

"No. Can we swim there?"

"I'm afraid it'll be too cold for that. We might try some fishing though."

"*Really?*"

Bear looked up at them with eyes full of the same excitement as Reagan.

"We'll see," Remington said with a chuckle. "I should have some line and hooks saved up somewhere in my saddlebags."

Reagan spread her arms out wide in front of her. "We'll catch a giant one."

"You never know," Remington replied. "For a long time, people have been coming from all over the world to fish the Yellowstone."

"Is it a big river?"

"Nearly seven hundred miles long—from up in the north along the South Dakota border all the way down past Billings and then deep into the western corner of Wyoming. It's a very old river that dates back to when the glaciers first retreated from the continent thousands of years ago. The various Indian tribes who once dominated these lands called it the Elk River and considered it a thing of great power. They travelled, fished and hunted its shores for generations."

"What happened to the Indians?"

"Well, many different tribes came and went over all that time, one tribe pushing out another and so on and so on, but eventually white settlers arrived and they pushed the remaining tribes from the land and onto reservations."

"I learned about reservations in school. They're like prisons, right?"

Remington adjusted his cowboy hat. "I suppose in many ways that term could apply."

"And now it seems like we're being pushed away too just like what happened to the Indians."

"That's a very astute observation, Reagan, with one important difference."

"What's that?"

"The Indians were put onto reservations by force. What's been happening to America and much of the world more recently is what I would call a self-inflicted wound, meaning we did it to ourselves."

"You're saying it was our fault."

"Yes, that's exactly what I'm saying."

Heavy clouds had returned and snow started to fall. Reagan shivered. "Do you think it's snowing in Savage?"

"It might be."

"Will we be able to stay warm?"

"It'll be plenty warm there—I promise."

Bear stopped and then held his hand up for the others to do the same.

"What is it?" Remington asked as his own hand drifted to the revolver on his hip.

Bear pointed at something moving on the horizon.

Reagan leaned forward in the saddle. "It's a man."

"Your eyes are no doubt better than mine." Remington squinted. "It appears you're right. I'd wager he's about a thousand yards from our location."

Bear took out a pad and pencil, wrote something down, and then handed it to Remington.

He could be following us and/or scouting for a larger group.

"My thoughts exactly," Remington replied after reading the message. "We'll track a bit further west for the next couple of miles. If he stays within sight of us or starts to come any closer, we'll have to decide how we want to respond."

"Maybe he's an Indian." Reagan said matter-of-factly.

Remington continued to stare at the lone figure on the horizon. "Not likely." He looked up. "We have at least a few more hours yet until dark. I'm pretty sure we can still make it to the river before then."

The snowfall was increasing though the temperature continued to warm. The flakes would hit the ground and then begin to melt soon after. Far to the north the skies appeared to be clearing, hinting at possible improvement in the weather.

After traveling for another hour Remington pulled back on the reins and turned in the saddle. "Any sign of our mystery man?"

Bear climbed atop a large boulder and then looked out at the miles of prairie grass that stretched out before him. He shook his head.

"That's good," Remington said. "It means we aren't being followed." Bear hopped off the boulder and then handed him another note.

Or he's being more careful not to be seen by us.

Remington gave the big man a wry smile. "Thanks for the optimism." He pointed north. "The grass is thicker and greener here. That means we're getting closer to the river. Just another hour or so to go and then we'll make camp for the night and be to Savage by noon tomorrow."

That hour passed quickly and soon all three of them heard the unmistakable gurgling of water moving over stone. "There!" Reagan said excitedly. "Is that the Yellowstone?"

"That's it," Remington replied.

Sunlight broke through the late afternoon clouds and shimmered off of the slow-moving water's surface. The group found a flat spot fifty yards from the river's bank that was a mix of reddish earth and stones surrounded by prickly green shrubs and clusters of pine trees.

Remington led Peanut to the river so she could have a drink while Bear and Reagan made a firepit out of a circle of rocks and then went off in search of wood for the fire. The clouds were gone and the sun was still out, though the dropping temperature hinted at the evening chill that was soon to come.

"We found lots of wood," Reagan said upon their return as Bear dropped a full armload of twigs and limbs near the firepit. "We even saw a hawk sitting in a tree. Bear said it was watching us to make sure we were going to be good neighbors. That made me laugh. I don't know why. It just did. Probably because the hawk looked so serious and I could imagine that's *exactly* what he was thinking."

Remington pulled out a roll of fishing line from his saddlebag. "Anyone interested in river trout for supper?"

Reagan clapped her hands together. "Yes!"

"First we have to find some bait and we'll need to hurry before it gets too dark."

"Bait?" Reagan looked around. "Where?"

Bear held up a finger and then disappeared into a nearby thicket. He emerged seconds later holding a crumbling pine tree log that had been rotting on the ground for some time.

Remington nodded. "Very good. There's a man who knows what he's doing."

"You're using wood for bait?" Reagan crinkled her nose. "That's weird."

"Not the wood," Remington said. "What's inside the wood." After Bear put the rotting log down and then pulled it apart Remington pointed at the white grubs inside. "There. That's our bait."

Reagan crinkled her nose even more. "What are those?"

Remington picked out a few of the cream-colored grubs and then held them in the palm of his hand. "Bark beetle."

"The fish like those?"

"They sure do." Remington placed a grub onto the hook at the end of his ten-foot-long fishing line, which also had a small rock tied to the middle of it.

"What's the rock for?" Reagan asked.

Remington started walking to the riverbank. "That helps to keep the bait closer to the bottom where the fish are hanging out."

"Fish hang out?"

"They sure do."

"That's silly."

Remington grinned. "No, that's fishing. Now, where do you think a good place is to throw our line in?"

"The water."

"Yes, but *where* in the water? You have to find a spot that's deep enough and the water is moving slow enough so that the fish don't have to try too hard to stay in one place."

Reagan sighed. "Boy, fishing sure is complicated."

Remington looked out at the river. "Any ideas?"

"Over there," Reagan said. "It's moving slow around that clump of grass growing out of the water."

"That looks like a *great* spot. Let's give it a shot." Remington threw the line in, watched the rock and bait sink below the surface, and then he held on tightly to the other end. "Now we wait."

"For how long?"

"That's up to Mr. Fish."

After getting the fire going Bear came and stood next to them as they all watched and waited for a bite. The sun's quickening descent cast long shadows over the water. After ten minutes Remington pulled the line in, added another grub, and then flung it back into the water.

"Seems like Mr. Fish is sleeping or something," Reagan said. "It's almost dark."

"Patience," Remington whispered. "I think I just felt a bite."

Reagan's eyes got big.

"There," Remington said. "That was definitely a bite. Now take it. C'mon fish, you know you want to." He leaned forward. "Ah!" he cried out as he jerked the line tight. "We got it hooked."

The fish broke the water's surface with a loud splash as it struggled to break free from the hook. Bear strode into the water up to his knees and carefully started to pull the line in.

"Careful," Remington said. "Don't lose it."

Bear plunged his hands into the river and then held up a brown trout that was nearly as big as his forearm. He threw it onto the grassy shore where Remington grabbed hold of it and promptly broke its neck.

Reagan winced. "Poor Mr. Fish."

Remington hooked a thumb into the fish's gills and lifted it off the ground. "Well done, Bear. Thanks for the help. Make sure to dry yourself off by the fire. It's going to be a cold one tonight. None of us need to be coming down with pneumonia out here." He looked at Reagan. "And thank you for picking out such a good fishing spot. Tonight, we eat like kings."

"You mean a queen," Reagan said.

"Of course," Remington answered with a tip of his cowboy hat. "A queen." His head snapped up at the sound of Peanut's high-pitched whinny. He dropped the fish and drew his revolver. "Stay here," he told Bear. "Might be something. Might be nothing. I'll let you know."

Peanut remained where Remington had left her tied up to a tree near the campfire. Her head lifted and her ears pricked forward as he approached. His eyes strained to see what was troubling her. "What is it, girl?"

The last gasp of sunlight had fallen behind the hills in the west. The fire crackled, churning out dark tendrils of acrid smoke that made Remington's nose twitch. Perhaps it was the smoke that had made Peanut uncomfortable.

There—movement behind those rocks. Remington pulled the revolver's hammer back. "I'm armed," he said. "Come out slowly with your hands where I can see them."

"I mean you no harm," a voice answered from the darkness. "I'm the one you saw earlier. Your group and I were walking in the same direction."

"What are you doing here?"

"Saw the fire." The voice was older, deep, and confident. "Thought you might not mind the company. If I was wrong about that I'll be on my way."

Remington's head swiveled from side to side as he tried to make certain there weren't others hiding just beyond the fire's light preparing to ambush him. "On your way to where?"

Silence.

"Did you hear me?"

"Savage," the man replied.

Remington cocked his head. "Savage? Why?"

"I'd rather not say."

"I'm not giving you a choice. Tell me what's waiting for you in Savage."

"Do you intend to shoot me if I don't?"

"Shoot you? Not unless you give me cause."

"Ah, then my initial impression was correct."

"What the hell are you talking about?"

"That you are not road pirates."

"We're a long way from any road pirates and I assure you that we intend to keep it that way."

"The big one with you. . ."

"What about him?"

"Is he the bear?"

"Why do you want to know?"

"The stories of him are spreading far and wide. He has become something of a legend—one that certain powerful people would like to see eliminated."

"You mean Vig."

"Yes."

"What do you know of her?"

"Not much and I don't care to."

"Is that why you're going to Savage? To get away from Vig's influence?"

"Perhaps."

Remington kept his gun aimed at the darkness in front of him. "I'm going to need you to come out of there. Do you have any weapons?"

"No."

"You sure?"

"You have my word."

"I don't know you, so your word doesn't mean much."

"My name is Lucian—Lucian Cross. Now you know at least that much about me."

"It's a start," Remington said. "Let's have a look at you, but don't try anything. If you do, I'll kill you where you stand."

"You sound very convincing."

"Good. Now come on out—*slowly*."

Lucian was nearly sixty and of average height and build with a long, deeply lined face that was home to a pair of unusually dark eyes that were kind yet also intimidating, reflecting a world-weary wisdom that can only come from hard-won experience. He walked toward the campfire with a backpack over his shoulder and his hands up, his thin lips pressed tightly together across his hairless face as he looked through the flames and smoke at Remington.

"I'll be damned," Remington whispered. "Reagan was right about you."

Lucian Cross was an Indian.

6.
✦✧✦✧

"Tell us your story, Mr. Cross."

"My story?"

Remington swallowed the last sliver of pan-fried fish. "That's right. We want to hear how you came to be sitting on the banks of the Yellowstone with us eating trout under an open Montana night sky."

"Ah," Lucian said. "Now I understand." He sat up straight and looked at Bear and Reagan. "Do you two wish to hear my story as well?"

They both nodded.

Lucian wiped the corners of his mouth with the back of his hand and then cleared his throat. "Very well." He paused, looked down, wrapped the blanket more tightly around his shoulders, and let out a forlorn sigh. "I will consider this like a lecture, though I fear I'm terribly out of practice. You see, I am, or rather I *was*, a professor of anthropology at a small public university in North Dakota. It was a campus of nearly five thousand students and staff. I complied with the vaccine mandate as did nearly all of my colleagues. The students were required to do so as well as a requirement for enrollment. I recall the university president sending out a memo regarding how pleased she was to be able to report the university was fully vaccinated prior to the beginning of classes for the new semester. We thought we had done the right thing and that we were all safe.

"One noted member of our staff, a professor I knew reasonably well in part because we were both lifelong bachelors without wives or children, did not comply with the mandate. He was a brilliant man who had earned his doctorate from MIT and then subsequently devoted the next thirty years of his life to the study of cellular biomechanics, which had earned him much-deserved recognition throughout the scientific community. Some thought he was wasting his considerable intellectual talents at our little university, but he had once explained to me that it was there where he was allowed to pretty much do what he wanted. He had been quickly granted tenure, allocated a considerable annual research budget and the space to create a program of study to his particular liking.

"That is until he wasn't. He had refused to take the vaccine and to my great shock, his tenure apparently offered him no protection regarding that choice. We crossed paths on his last day as he was cleaning out his office. I shared with him my disappointment over his sudden departure. His response was to say how much he pitied me and all the others who had so willingly given up their sacred right of personal choice. That was the exact term he used—sacred right of personal choice. He asked if I knew what was in the vaccine. I said no. He rolled his eyes at me, cursed, pointed, and cursed some more, calling me an idiot, a puppet, a tool of tyranny. I had never before witnessed him in such an aggressively negative state.

"He was convinced that within the year people would be dying en masse because of what they had allowed to be injected into their bodies. He raged about the dangers of spike proteins, viral overload, severely compromised endocytic pathways, inflammatory toxicity of the internal organs, all terms I knew little about. I asked why our government would inflict such harm on its own people to which he replied it wasn't yet time to try to apply specific determination to the wrongdoing, be it intentional, incompetence, or both, but rather to deal directly with the wrongdoing itself. The rest, he said, would shake out eventually but not until the damage had already been done. That damage, he warned, could be tens or even hundreds of millions of dead or incapacitated and a complete collapse of society as we knew it.

"I watched him leave with a box of his personal items under each arm. When I asked where he would go, he simply stated somewhere remote and safe and strongly suggested I prepare to do the same. I really should have listened to that advice—but I didn't.

"Three weeks into the new semester, I began to notice serious issues unfolding all around me. My classes were nearly empty. There were reports of more and more staff calling in sick. Even supply deliveries to the campus were being mysteriously delayed. Then I began to receive word from extended family living on reservations throughout North Dakota. People were going to hospitals and within weeks or days were dying there in ever-increasing numbers. Reservations have long been places of crime and violence, but the stories I heard then indicated they had quickly devolved into all-out war zones. National Guard soldiers arrived on campus not long after. All classes had been cancelled and students were ordered to either return home or remain secluded in their dorm rooms.

"That week, three staff died suddenly of apparent heart attacks or strokes. All were under the age of sixty. The panic was growing. The students who remained on campus were increasingly agitated, scared, and understandably angry—we all were. More soldiers arrived, heavily armed but clearly just as worried as we were about what was actually going on. You saw it in their eyes, these young men and women without answers, following orders they didn't understand, and in the end, only wanting to return to their own homes and loved ones so they could help to keep them safe.

"The news reports were oddly indifferent to the increasing evidence that the vaccines the government had mandated were the likely cause for the very health crisis those same vaccines were supposed to protect us from. We continued to be told the answer was yet more vaccines. I knew in my gut that something was very wrong, but like so many I simply watched and waited, convinced normalcy would eventually return.

"One day, a handful of students violated the lockdown order and waged a brief protest in front of the campus administration building—emphasis on brief. They were promptly arrested by soldiers and taken away to some unknown location. I expected to witness outrage over this from my colleagues, but none spoke up about it—not a single one. The university president said nothing. Nor did the local media. It was as if the protest and subsequent arrests of those students never happened. By then there were likely fewer than a thousand of us left on campus.

"Then, as quickly as the soldiers had arrived, they were gone. The next day, the power was out for nearly nine hours. The day after that and it went out for good. There was no cell service either, no television, no radio, no running water. I recall thinking at the time how quickly this happened, but in reality I now realize I actually saw it coming for weeks but stupidly chose to ignore all of the warning signs. But for very few exceptions it seems we all did.

"Then the real violence started. I had a little apartment about a mile from campus that had been my home for many years. The entire complex was burned to the ground. It was one of many fires that had been started that week. I made it back to campus, but on the way there I saw bodies in the street. Some had clearly been victims of violence, but others appeared to have simply dropped dead. I returned to my office, bolted the door, closed the blinds, and hid there for the next two years. Sometimes at night I heard screaming in the courtyard outside. The administrative building was burned. Then the gymnasium. I knew it was only a matter of time before the anthropology complex was next. So, I packed what few items I deemed necessary and left for more rural areas in the hope that fewer people also meant less danger.

"I would walk in the early morning hours and then find a place to hide during the rest of the day and night to avoid being seen by others. This went on for weeks until I came upon an encampment near Sheep Creek in the northwest corner of South Dakota. There were ten of them—four men, three women, and three children. One of the couples and their child were Lakota from the Pine Ridge Reservation to the south. As a descendent of the Assiniboine people of North Dakota I hoped our shared Native American heritage would be enough to afford me the opportunity to earn their trust and companionship. You see, I was by then near starving and desperate for help. Winter was fast approaching, and I knew I would likely be unable to survive entirely on my own. Others in the group were from Canada where they said things were just as chaotic. Another couple said they had family in Mexico who urged them not to seek refuge there because the cartels had already taken over most of the country and the daily beheadings numbered in the hundreds.

"The group only allowed me to stay with them for a night and then demanded I go. That was when I first heard the name Vig. They had fled her territory weeks earlier but warned that territory was quickly expanding as more joined her forces. The rumor was that shortly after the power grid collapsed, she had somehow managed to break into the National Guard armory to the south near Rapid City. It was there she stockpiled the weapons and ammunition that allowed her to so quickly become the most feared warlord in the region. And so Vig's power has grown and spread incrementally, day by day, week by week. Few have stood up to her and none have apparently survived long after doing so." Lucian gazed at Bear. "Except for you."

"I took to hiding in large culverts for safety," he continued. "Finding food was an increasingly difficult challenge. Out of desperation I returned to the encampment at Sheep Creek where I was greeted by yet more death. Road pirates, likely working under the authority of Vig, had visited them. Four lay slaughtered on the ground, their faces blown off by a shotgun at close range. The others, including the children, were gone. Part of me thought they might have escaped, but I know that isn't likely. They are no doubt dead by now or surviving as slaves of Vig and her road pirates. Such is the truth of these times we now live in. I left that encampment, fearful the road pirates might return, and resumed my existence going from culvert to culvert, surviving on a diet of roots and bugs.

"Ah, but then came a happy respite in the form of a small cluster of apple trees near a long-abandoned barn. Most of the fruit had already fallen to the ground by then but it remained edible. I gorged myself that first day and became so sick I thought I might die. It passed, though, and then I was more careful, eating only a few apples at a time. My strength returned, I put on some weight, and my mindset greatly improved. Funny how a full belly can completely transform one's outlook for the future.

"The winter there at the barn was terribly difficult. Each night I buried myself under a pile of old hay and straw, sharing the space with a multitude of rodents I heard scurrying about in the dark. I soon grew thankful for their company though. I wouldn't ever describe the flavor of raw mouse as pleasing, but it kept me alive.

"One night, I awoke to the smell of smoke and the sound of flames. The barn had been set ablaze by two men I spied through gaps in the wood plank wall as they stood outside watching. They were both armed, which meant they were likely more of Vig's road pirates. It seemed their numbers had become legion—there was no escaping them. I managed to creep away and hid in the tall field grass that surrounded the barn where I remained until morning. Only after I was certain the men were gone did I dare to raise my head and begin to make my way further west into Montana."

"And now here you are," Remington said.

Lucian nodded. "Here I am, blessed to find some semblance of kindness in this increasingly cruel world for which I am both grateful and in your debt."

Remington grunted. "By kindness you mean us."

"That's right."

"Hmm." Remington scratched at his beard. "We weren't so kind to the road pirates we met some ways back."

"I assure you I don't mistake your kindness for weakness, Mr. Wilkes. You are traveling with the bear after all."

"You never really answered my question regarding why you're heading to Savage."

"I could ask the same of you," Lucian replied.

Remington shrugged. "It's my home. Now it's your turn."

"It's silly but I'm doing so based on a news story I read years ago about a rancher there who had against all odds successfully fought back against the federal government. Being Indian you can likely understand how such a story would appeal to me."

"Go on," Remington said softly, his eyes narrowing.

"This rancher, I don't recall his name, was fighting for his land, his family, his legacy. The final battle was said to have been waged in a place called Vaughn's Hill. I hadn't thought about that story in a very long time, but after the collapse of everything around me I found myself thinking about it almost daily. Savage,

Vaughn's Hill, I don't know why, I can't explain it, but I need to get there."

"Hap Wilkes," Remington said.

Lucian scowled. "Who?"

"The rancher's name from the news story you referenced—his name was Hap Wilkes."

"The same last name as yours."

"That's right. That ranch, Vaughn's Hill, it's my home. Hap Wilkes was an especially strong and determined branch in my family tree. I never actually met him, but I heard plenty of stories."

"How remarkable. It's kismet."

"What's that?" Reagan asked.

"A term very similar to that of destiny," Lucian replied. "Meaning it was meant to be."

Reagan stood and poked at the fire with a stick, causing a shower of sparks to drift up into the blackness above them. "I want to say something."

"Go on," Remington said, his eyes shining beneath the brim of his hat. "Share what's on your mind."

"Why did the grown-ups let this happen? Why didn't anyone stop it? Mr. Cross, you said that you waited for things to get back to normal, but they never did. It seems like everyone was waiting—waiting for someone else to make things better, which means nobody was doing anything. And now what? The world has gone so dark, and people are so mean. I don't like it. I don't like it one bit and I try really hard not to be angry, but sometimes I just can't help it. The adults, the ones in charge, you all really messed up my future."

Bear scribbled something down and then handed the paper to Reagan.

We sure did and now we owe it to all of you to make it right.

Reagan looked up. "But how do you make it right?"

"We do what we should have been doing a long time ago," Remington answered. "We fight back. That doesn't mean we'll win, but we have to at least try." He folded his hands together so tightly the knuckles turned white. "I promise you that Reagan. As long as I draw breath I'll fight for your future, and I know Bear feels the same."

"As do I," Lucian said.

Remington rubbed his face and then looked up at the stars. "We leave at first light. Tomorrow is a new day."

"Savage," Lucian replied. "Tomorrow we see your home, the place that has brought this odd group of misfits together—a writer, a professor, a football player, and a very wise young lady."

Remington lay back, pulled his hat down, and closed his eyes. "All that's missing is a little dog named Toto."

Sleep came quickly to each of them—except for Reagan. She lay on her back, a blanket pulled up to her chin, staring at the winter moon and wondering if the world would only continue to get worse and worse. If God existed, perhaps he or she or it had finally given up any hope and was now willing to stand back and allow the destruction of humankind to play out to its ultimate and final conclusion.

It sure seemed that way.

7.
✦✧✦✧

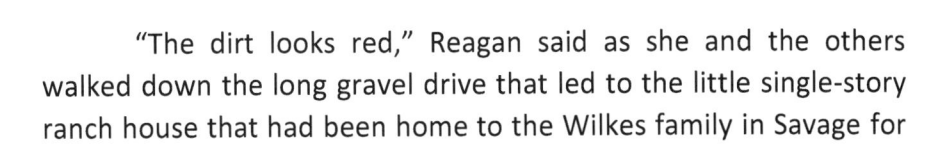

"The dirt looks red," Reagan said as she and the others walked down the long gravel drive that led to the little single-story ranch house that had been home to the Wilkes family in Savage for generations.

"It's the iron-oxide that gives it that tone," Remington replied. "Great for most plants but plays hell on water systems. That iron tends to accumulate deposits inside of well pumps and pipes."

"It's a natural fertilizer," Lucian added. "Iron oxide makes plants tougher, more tolerant of extremes."

Remington nodded. "That's right, Professor, and most who have lived out here for any amount of time would say it's done the same to the people of Savage as well."

Lucian glanced at Remington. "Made them tougher you mean."

"Exactly," Remington replied as he walked alongside Peanut. "Eastern Montana isn't for the weak that's for damn sure."

"It really is beautiful in an unconventional way."

"Unconventional?" Remington chuckled. "Not sure how I should take that."

"I meant it as a compliment. It's a place of timeless contradiction—the reddish-brown earth, the vibrant blue sky, endless stretches of fields, rivers, and streams, and complemented by the sprinkling of hills and mounds; I better understand my own ancestors' reverence toward the region."

"Timeless contradiction." Remington nodded. "That is an apt description indeed. If I am ever allowed the opportunity to write again, I'll be sure to borrow it."

Reagan pointed to the east. "Is that Vaughn's Hill over there?"

"It is," Remington answered. "That's where we're going after I grab a few things from the house."

Lucian put a hand over his eyes as he looked at the hill. "What do you use for shelter up there?"

Remington walked up to the home's little covered porch and reached for the door. "You'll see. I'll just be a second." He returned holding two cans of beans that were identical to the ones Reagan and Bear had earlier found in his hunting cabin. "I was saving these for a special occasion. It's been an awful long time since I had guests at the ranch, so I figured this qualifies."

"Will we get to eat any more fish?" Reagan asked as she hungrily eyed the cans of beans.

"Absolutely," Remington replied. "The river is on the other side of the hill. I have a few more surprises for you as well." He gave Peanut's backside a soft slap. "Lead the way, girl."

Peanut walked slowly down a path that dissected the tall field grass while the others followed close behind. The temperature was the warmest it had been in months. Patches of snow still covered parts of the ground but more and more of it was melting away.

"I like this place," Reagan said.

Remington looked back at her. "Why is that?"

"It feels like it wants us here."

"I know what you mean."

"You do?"

"Sure. Some places just feel right, and this is one of them."

Lucian grabbed a stock of grass and rubbed it between his fingers. "And no road pirates?"

"Not yet," Remington answered. "But I suppose sooner or later some of them will show up. That's why I made the trip to pick up the ammo from the cabin. I wanted to be prepared. My first year hiding out here I foolishly wasted far too many bullets on target practice and hunting. I had no idea ammo was going to become so scarce so quickly."

"No one did," Lucian said, "but at least in more remote places like this people had time to prepare. The cities were already drowning in violence even before the collapse. Speaking of which, do you stay in contact with others in Savage?"

"My closest neighbor is the McGreevy place. The last time I spoke to Morning McGreevy was a few months ago. She stopped by the house to make sure I was okay. I let her know that if she ever needed the safety of Vaughn's Hill, she was welcome to it. She has a beautiful bit of property, but like the other places around here, it's mostly flat, exposed, and vulnerable to attack. She's salt-of-the-earth, the real deal. Lost her husband about, oh, I guess it's been nearly ten years now—tractor accident. Has a grown son who she said is safely hunkered down on one of the San Juan Islands in the Pacific Northwest. She might be out this way again soon. I'd love for you all to meet her."

Peanut reached the narrow trail that meandered its way between earth and stone to the top of Vaughn's Hill. "Here we go," Remington said.

Halfway up Lucian paused to turn and look behind him at the valley below. "Besides you and Morning McGreevy are there any others left in Savage?"

Remington slowly ran his hand down Peanut's powerful neck. "Sure, but as you can see there's a lot more land around here than people. That's Eastern Montana—miles and miles of space. If you wanted to be left alone, I mean *really* left alone, not many places are better than here to do just that. I do still see the Richland County sheriff driving by from time to time though."

Bear scowled and then motioned with his hands like he was steering a car. "How?"

"Apparently, he stocked up on fuel or somehow still has access to it, I'm not sure. The last time Morning was by she mentioned he was still out and about ready to chase off any road pirates that might show up. Sheriff Potts is like me, getting long in the tooth, but like most who call Savage home he's good people. He played a big part in helping my uncle Hap defend this ranch against the feds all those years ago. If he's still getting up every day, putting on the uniform, and working to keep the community safe from the madness all around us now then God bless him."

The group continued up the trail. When they reached the top of the hill, Remington took off Peanut's bridle and the saddlebag so she could wander around nibbling on what little bits of grass she could find. He turned and faced the valley below and spread his arms wide. "Not a bad view, eh?"

"Aesthetically pleasing but more importantly," Lucian said, "tactically superior to staying in the house below."

Remington nodded as he lowered his arms. "Exactly. From up here we can see what's coming from miles around and really only have to worry about defending the trail. The backside of the hill has a way down to the river, but if you didn't live here, you'd never know it was there." He tilted his head. "Over here is the tent. C'mon, I'll show you."

The thick canvas tent was large—forty by forty and twenty feet high in the pitched center, all of it held down by metal stakes stuck deep into the ground. "Took me all of four days to get this thing up by myself," Remington remarked as he pulled open the entrance flap. "Check it out."

The floor was bare earth, compacted by the bottom of Remington's boots repeatedly walking over it. A firepit had been placed in the middle of the tent. There was a small opening in the center of the roof to allow the smoke to escape, similar to an Indian tepee. Near the firepit was a well-worn, wood-framed leather chair.

Reagan ran to the chair and then looked back. "Can I sit in it?"

Remington smiled. "Sure. That chair originally came all the way over from Ireland. It was one of the few items in the house I made sure to pack up here. It's been in the family for generations."

One of the walls had a stack of dry wood planks that went up nearly to the ceiling. Remington explained the wood was the remains of the old barn that used to be on the property. He spent weeks the previous summer dragging pieces of it up the hill to be used as firewood during the cold winter months. "It stays reasonably warm in here with the fire going," he said. "I won't pretend it's five-star accommodations, but it works."

"Impressive," Lucian replied. "You've done well."

"Where does Peanut stay?" Reagan asked.

"In here with me," Remington answered. "She's a housebroken horse. Right before dark she'll poke her head into the tent and wait for me to tell her she can come in. Does all her business in a corner of the hill outside. Never had an accident in here, which, now that I think of it, is a better track record than I have. Speaking of which, if you need to use the bathroom, I put in an outhouse behind the tent with a view that looks down at the Yellowstone. It's actually quite a nice spot to do some sitting and thinking." He went over to another wall where several large boxes were. "There are plenty of blankets, pots, pans, bowls, and jugs for water. I pack it up from the river and then boil it over the fire to be safe. No need to survive the apocalypse only to die from dysentery."

Bear handed a note to Remington.

We don't want to be an imposition.

"Imposition?" Remington took off his hat and ran his hands through his thinning white hair. "Your being here is no imposition. I welcome the help and the company."

"What do you do for food?" Lucian asked.

"Fish from the river, rabbits in the valley when I can catch them, and vegetables."

Lucian's brows arched. "Vegetables?"

"I told you I had some surprises. Follow me." Remington went outside and then walked to the back of the tent. "I actually put this up before the tent."

It was an igloo-shaped greenhouse made of plastic framing that was covered in transparent PVC. "Ordered it online some years back and then never got around to putting it up. Found the box when I was preparing to move things up to the hill and figured it was time to make use of it. The tomatoes are coming in real nice. Should be ready in a week or two and I've been living off potatoes for some time now—one a day for the last few months. Also have a nice batch of carrots and onions that are almost ready as well."

"Can I help you grow the vegetables?" Reagan asked.

Remington's eyes twinkled. "You sure can. And I'll boil us up some potatoes to go with our beans tonight for dinner. How's that sound?"

Reagan licked her lips. "Delicious."

Bear pointed at something in the valley below. Lucian turned around to see what it was. "A vehicle," he said.

"That's the sheriff I was telling you about," Remington replied. "And that's the main road that takes you into Savage. Weird seeing a moving car, isn't it?"

"A rare sight indeed," Lucian said. "Vig's road pirates would no doubt like to get their hands on the sheriff's source of fuel."

"He'd likely blast them to hell if they tried."

Reagan walked to the other side of the greenhouse where a tree grew. "What are these stones?"

"Those are the Wilkes family graves," Remington answered. "The most recent one at the end is my uncle Hap's. He lived a long hard life and died alone in the bedroom in the house down at the bottom of this hill. In fact, it was Sheriff Potts who found the body. He told me once how Hap had this look on his face like he was enjoying a pleasant dream when death took him, which was out of character because apparently Hap wasn't the grinning kind. The sheriff figured that whatever it was that Hap had found in the beyond must have pleased him. What that might have been will forever remain a mystery, but what I do know is that he risked everything including his very life to protect this land. Maybe winning that war with the feds was what gave him some much-deserved peace in the end."

Lucian stared down at the grave marker. "The day which we fear as our last is but the birthday of eternity."

"Emily Dickinson?" Remington said.

"Seneca," Lucian replied.

"Ah, a fan of the classics."

Lucian shrugged. "Standing on this hill beside the grave of the man who once so bravely defended it, well, it just felt . . . appropriate."

"I appreciate the sentiment."

"Not nearly as much as we appreciate your hospitality."

Remington grunted. "That's enough of the gratitude parade. We have some work to do before supper. There's water to be hauled up from the river, a fire to be started, and potatoes to be cleaned and prepared for cooking."

Bear volunteered to haul the water while Lucian said he would take care of getting the fire going. That left Reagan and Remington to dig up the potatoes for dinner.

"They're in there," Remington said as he crouched down by the rectangular growing box he had constructed out of repurposed wood from the old barn. The wood box was full of soft soil with a thick layer of old hay covering it. "See the three rows? The one nearest to us is ready for picking. The second row will be ready in a few weeks and the third one in a few weeks after that, and by then, the first row will almost be ready again. We just continue to rotate the row we're picking from. Each row should have about twenty to thirty potatoes in it. It's my version of the Ruth Stout method."

"Who is that?"

"Ruth Stout was something of a renaissance woman from Kansas in the late eighteen hundreds who then moved to New York shortly before the new century. While in New York she was a bookkeeper, a nurse, and even spent time in Russia helping out with famine relief. In the nineteen thirties she moved to a fifty-five-acre farm in Redding, Connecticut with her husband. Ruth was forty-six by then, what many considered middle-aged or even old at the time, but it was also the same year that she discovered her true calling—gardening. She spent years following the more conventional methods of planting and harvesting, namely the work-intensive annual tilling of the earth, but with inconsistent results. She grew frustrated with having to depend on someone to help her with the hard work of tilling and so, one year, she decided to skip the tilling and simply plant the seeds and cover them with a mulch. The result was remarkable—her best harvest yet. And so, the Ruth Stout method was born. She became famous for it, was a frequent contributor to the leading gardening periodicals, and was among the most influential gardeners of the twentieth century. She enjoyed her success for quite a long time, dying at the age of ninety-six in the midst of a final late summer harvest."

"Geez," Reagan whispered, her eyes wide with wonder. "Ninety-six." She looked down at the dark green leaves of the potato plants. "How many do we pick for dinner?"

"Depends on the size of the potato." Remington pointed to one of the taller green stalks. "I bet that's a big one. Dig your hands into the straw and find out."

Reagan smiled excitedly as her fingers plunged beneath the surface.

"Well?" Remington said.

"I think I feel something."

"Okay, pull it out and have a look."

Reagan held up a fist-sized potato. "One more?"

Remington nodded. "One more should be perfect."

They left the greenhouse with Reagan holding tightly to both potatoes just as Bear was returning with the buckets of water. The three of them went into the tent where Lucian was placing another piece of wood onto a roaring fire.

"Already feeling warmer in here," Remington said. He looked at Bear. "I see you found your way down to the river okay and you made it back here in half the time it takes me."

Reagan ran to Lucian and showed him the potatoes. He told her well done and that he would help her to clean them.

Bear set the buckets down near the fire and then hugged Reagan and thanked her for getting the potatoes. "Have you ever heard of Ruth Stout?" she asked him. When Bear shook his head, she explained how Ruth was an old farmer who lived for almost a hundred years because she found out farming was a lot easier than people thought and she spent the last fifty years of her life proving it to them.

The tent was soon filled with the aroma of boiled potatoes and canned beans seasoned with salt and pepper. Light was provided by a battery-powered lantern that Remington recharged each day with a solar panel that hung from the side of the tent outside. Each of them sat on the ground around the fire and nibbled on their meal, wanting to savor it and make it last for as long as possible. Lucian declared the potatoes to be the best he had ever eaten.

"Tomorrow we'll check the rabbit snares," Remington said. "And then after that perhaps we can try some fishing."

"And more potatoes?" Reagan asked.

Remington plopped the last of his potato into his mouth. "Of course."

Lucian got up, clasped his hands in front of him, and looked down at the others. "I am so grateful to have met you three." His brow furrowed as he fought back tears. "These last few years, well, you know as well as any how horrible they have been. And yet here we are now, sharing dinner for a second time, talking, laughing, and already planning for an even better tomorrow. I could not ask for a more capable and caring group as you. Thank you, Remington, for inviting us here and sharing your home. Thank you, Bear. Thank you, Reagan. Thank you all."

"My pleasure," Remington said.

Bear stood, walked over to Lucian, clasped his shoulders, and then hugged him so tightly Lucian groaned.

Reagan pursed her lips and shook her head. "That's my Bear—always so emotional."

Bear reached down, scooped her up over his shoulder, and then tickled her sides until she begged him to stop. He carefully set her down and then lightly put his giant paw of a hand on the top of her head. She looked up at him and smiled. He looked down and did the same.

It was a good night but secretly each of them wondered in their own way how many more nights like this they would be allowed to have. Surely the world beyond Savage would find and punish them eventually.

It was only a matter of time.

8.
✦✧✦✧

They awoke to the rumbling roar of angry thunder.

Peanut's eyes rolled back white as she nervously shifted where she stood just inside the tent entrance. Remington turned on the lantern and then got up to comfort her as a hard rain pelted the canvas roof. "Wind is picking up," he said. "We should stay put in here until the storm passes. If anyone is cold, I can get another fire stared."

Lucian sat up and stretched. "I believe we're fine, Remington, but thank you."

"Is it still dark out?" Reagan asked as she rubbed the sleep from her eyes.

Bear looked up at the small opening in the ceiling and then nodded.

"There now," Remington whispered to Peanut while petting her shoulder. "It's okay." Peanut turned her head and nudged his chest. "Sorry, I don't have any carrots. You're going to have to wait."

"Can we work in the greenhouse today?" Reagan asked.

Remington looked back at her. "You bet."

"I wouldn't mind taking a crack at some fishing," Lucian said as he stood and then folded his blanket. "Perhaps Bear might wish to join me?"

Bear gave him a thumbs up.

Lightning cracked across the valley followed by yet more thunder. Remington poked his head outside and then withdrew and closed the flap. He had to nearly yell so that he could be heard over the din of the storm. "This keeps up there could be some flooding in the valleys."

"I was meaning to ask you," Lucian said.

Remington walked up to him. "Yeah?"

"Is there anywhere to clean up around here?"

"You mean like a bath?"

"Exactly."

"I've been using a bar of soap and the river from time to time. Fair warning, though, it's a damn cold endeavor."

"I can imagine."

"But if the stink gets too heavy on you then you got to do what you got to do."

Lucian lifted his arm, turned his head, and sniffed. "I fear I've about reached that point."

"The soap is kept in a little satchel tied to a tree branch down at the river just up from the fishing hole. You'll see the grass is all trampled down there. It's easy enough to find. If the weather clears and you decide to do some fishing, feel free to wade on in upstream and clean yourself up. I doubt the fish will mind too much."

"Thank you—I might just do that." Lucian looked down at Reagan. "Is something wrong?"

Reagan blushed as she started to do a little tippy-toe dance with her blanket wrapped around her. "I have to go potty."

Bear went to her, leaned down, and then let Reagan hop on his back and wrap her arms around his muscular neck. She giggled. "Your beard is so scratchy."

"You're going to get wet," Remington warned. "Here, this might help a little." He placed a blanket over Reagan's head and Bear's shoulders. "At least it's not quite as dark out there now. You should be able to find your way to the outhouse easily enough."

Lucian stood next to Remington as they both watched Bear stride into the stormy gloom with Reagan on his back while holding the sledgehammer in his hand—a mountain of a man atop a hill, leaning into the wind, seemingly as immovable as the hill itself. "I would not want to be the one who gets between that man and his determination to protect that child," Lucian said.

"That's an understatement," Remington replied. "Never seen a man so big move so well."

"I've heard some of the stories."

"As have I."

"Do you think they're true?"

Remington shrugged. "If he managed to kill some road pirates here and there, I have no problem with that."

"How many?"

"Dead road pirates?"

"Yeah."

"No idea but it was enough to get Vig's attention and put a price on his head."

Lucian's mouth tightened.

"What?" Remington asked.

"I wonder if his continued presence here might end up being a danger to us all."

"Not open for discussion, Professor."

"I don't understand."

Remington faced Lucian. "Yes, you do. This is *my* hill, *my* tent, *my* hospitality. That man out there can stay for as long as he chooses to."

"I wasn't suggesting he couldn't."

"No? Because it kind of sounded like you were."

"I assure you I wasn't."

"I don't know how things were done where you come from, the academic world and all that, but in Savage people live up to the promises they make. Their word is their bond. I know a lot of other places might dismiss that kind of sentiment as antiquated or clichéd, but around here it's still our way of life and we sure as hell don't turn our backs on friends because it might become *inconvenient*."

"I said his presence could be dangerous not inconvenient."

"And I'm saying it doesn't matter the particular word you used because Bear will be the one who decides if he stays or leaves. Have I made myself clear?"

Lucian nodded. "Crystal."

Remington clamped his hand over Lucian's shoulder. "Good."

A gust of wind buffeted the tent fabric, causing the framing to shift and creak. Lucian glanced up. "Will this thing hold?"

"This isn't the first storm I've had to ride out up here. We'll be fine. In fact, I bet by noon the sun will be making an appearance."

Bear pushed the flap open, stepped inside, and lowered Reagan down.

"Everything go okay out there?"

Reagan scrunched her face together. "Kind of icky."

Remington dipped his head. "The outhouse or Bear?"

"The outhouse," Reagan answered with a smile. She waved her hand in front of her nose. "Phew."

"Well, it *is* an outhouse," Remington said, "not a bed of roses. Did you see the stack of old newspapers and magazines I left in there?"

"I didn't have time for all that reading."

"Those weren't for reading. They were for—"

Reagan closed her eyes, shook her head, and sighed. "Mr. Wilkes, I *know* what they were for and, yes, I found them."

"Very good."

"I'm so embarrassed."

Remington chuckled. "Nothing to be embarrassed about."

"That's easy for you to say."

"Why is that?"

"You're old."

"I'm not following."

Reagan smirked. "Everyone already expects you to be gross."

"Oh, I see." Remington pointed at Bear. "Have you been teaching her to be so darn feisty?"

Bear held up his hands and laughed.

Reagan pretended to glare at Remington. "Mr. Wilkes, I was born feisty."

"I believe it." Remington cocked his head. "You hear that?"

"What?" Lucian said.

"Exactly—it stopped raining."

"It appears your prediction for better weather is already proving true."

Remington pulled his hat down tighter, opened the flap, and took Peanut outside. "It usually does. I've found that weather can be rather predictable if you pay attention to what it's trying to tell you and any place that has as many farms as Eastern Montana learns to listen right quick because if they don't their crops are sure to suffer the consequences of their ignorance." He cocked his head again. "Now I *know* you hear that."

Lucian opened the flap. "It sounds like a dog."

Reagan gasped and ran outside. "It *is* a dog. Look!"

The medium-sized mutt with short bristly gray and white hair was sniffing the ground where Peanut stood about fifty yards from the tent. Peanut lowered her head and snorted at it. The dog paused and then crept forward carefully until their noses briefly touched.

"Can it stay with us?" Reagan asked.

"We're not even sure it wants to," Remington answered.

Reagan clapped her hands together. The dog looked up and then barked, which in turn appeared to annoy Peanut who shook her head and trotted away.

"Come here, boy," Reagan yelled as she began to run toward the dog. Bear strode ahead of her and told her to wait. Reagan pouted. "Why? It's just a dog." She leaned to the side to get another look. "Great, you scared him away."

The dog took off running toward the trail that led down the hill.

"Probably best," Remington said. "Although. . ."

Lucian looked at him. "Although what?"

Remington dug the heel of his boot into the dirt. "Just something I recall hearing about a long time ago."

Reagan turned around. "Not fair—no secrets."

"There was a dog that belonged to my uncle Hap," Remington continued. "That was actually its name—Dog. It was killed up here on this hill—shot by some government agents. That's how the story went anyways."

"They killed your uncle's dog?" Reagan bit her lower lip. "Why would someone want to hurt a poor little dog?"

Remington looked out at the field that stretched across the top of the hill. "They flew in on a helicopter right over there, near where Peanut is standing now. That's what Hap's grandkids told me. They were here with him at the time and saw it all happen. Those damn feds got out of the chopper and the dog took off after them. All he was doing was trying to protect Hap. The one in charge, some piece of human garbage named Tuttle, ordered his men to fire. They blew the poor thing's head off."

"So bad things happened back then too."

"Yes, they did, Reagan. It seems bad things have always been part of the human condition."

"What happened to that Tuttle guy?"

Remington straightened and then looked to the east. "He was trampled to death by a herd of wild horses on the other side of this hill."

Reagan's eyes widened. "Trampled?"

"That's how it was told to me."

"People shouldn't hurt other people or their animals," Reagan said.

Bear's head dropped and his shoulders slumped.

"Unless they have to," Reagan quickly added as she reached out and squeezed Bear's fingers.

The clouds were pushed farther west as the sun covered the hill in its warm embrace. Lucian tilted his face up toward that warmth and grinned. "We have been blessed with another fine day."

From somewhere in the valley below came the sound of barking. Remington's hand went to the gun on his hip. "Someone's coming." He and the others walked to the edge of the hill and then looked down.

A rider on a horse galloped toward the ranch house.

Lucian pointed at something further away. "Two men are following," he said.

"Road pirates," Remington growled as he removed the revolver from its holster.

The rider suddenly stopped, jumped off the horse, and then turned to face the men while aiming a shotgun at them.

"That's a woman," Lucian said.

Remington's eyes narrowed. "Yes, it is, and those men are about to wish they never crossed her."

The woman walked calmly down the middle of the drive with the gun out in front of her. She wore a cowboy hat, jeans, and boots with spurs that clinked with each step she took.

The men slowed and then stopped, likely realizing the easy victim they thought they had found wasn't so easy after all.

"Who is she?" Lucian asked.

The woman continued walking.

"That," Remington said, "is my neighbor, Morning McGreevy."

The men raised their hands and then backed away.

Morning kept coming.

"Twelve gauge?" Lucian asked.

"Good eye," Remington replied. "And those two idiots down there don't have the sense to move away from each other. If they keep standing so close together like that, she'll be able to hit the both of them with a single shot."

As if somehow hearing Remington's remark one of the men turned and ran while the other continued to stand in place and beg for his life. Morning fired at the man still in front of her. He clutched at his chest, stumbled forward, and then collapsed onto his side.

"If the other one gets away he'll soon be bringing more here," Lucian said.

Morning looked back, put two fingers to her mouth, and whistled. Her horse immediately took off running toward her. She grabbed hold of the saddle horn with one hand, the rifle with the other, and then lifted herself smoothly back into the saddle.

Remington holstered his gun. "Trust me—he isn't getting away."

The man was fast but not nearly fast enough. With her horse running at a full gallop, it only took Morning a few seconds for her to catch up to the second man. From her position high atop her horse, she lowered her head, aimed, and then blasted him in the back of his head. After he dropped Morning pulled on the reins, turned, and headed back toward the house without looking down at the two bodies.

"She probably wants to say hello and apologize for the noise," Remington said. He started walking. "C'mon, it'll give you a chance to introduce yourselves." When he realized the others weren't following, he stopped and turned around. "Don't worry. Morning is actually quite friendly in her own way."

It took Bear a few tries but he finally managed to say the words. "Aren't we all?"

"Exactly." Remington continued walking. "The sun is shining down on two dead road pirates. That's a good day in my book. Let's not keep her waiting because that wouldn't be very neighborly of me."

Reagan pulled on Bear's hand. "Let's go meet her."

Lucian hung back for a moment, looking down at the bodies strewn across the gravel driveway below. *Two dead road pirates*, he thought. *How many more are already on their way to replace them?*

In the distance the last of that day's thunder seemed to answer Lucian as it made the ground beneath his feet tremble.

Where one storm leaves another is soon to follow.

9.
◆✧◆✧

"I'm really sorry about the mess on your driveway, Remington. I'll clean it up."

"No need to apologize, Morning. We watched the whole thing from up on the hill. You made short work of those road pirates. Well done."

Morning McGreevy was in her late forties, with straight, shoulder-length brown hair that was dissected by a one-inch-wide silver streak that started near her widow's peak and ran the length of her head. She was of average height but thin and wiry, with hawklike eyes that hinted at a sometimes volatile temper that was quick to show itself when provoked. The natural beauty of her youth was still visible but now appeared to be at war with the more recent years of loss and struggle she had endured. She stood next to her horse holding its reins and pointed at the group behind Remington.

"I didn't know you had company."

"These are my new friends," Remington said. "This is Lucian, this is Reagan, and this is Bear."

Morning stared at Bear. "Are you *the* bear? The one Vig is so determined to get her hands on?"

Bear nodded.

"You're certainly a big one, I'll give you that."

Reagan stepped forward. "And he's smart too. Just because he can't talk so good doesn't mean he's not smart."

Morning's tone softened considerably when she looked down at Reagan. She stuck out her calloused hand. "Hello there, Reagan. It's a pleasure to meet you."

"Your name is Morning—Morning McGreevy," Reagan said as she shook hands.

"That's right."

"It's a pretty name."

"Thank you. I like your name too."

Reagan shrugged. "It's okay."

"How did you come to know old Remington here?"

"We met at my hunting cabin," Remington replied. "I was there to get some supplies."

"Ammunition?"

"That's right."

"Just fired off my last two rounds of shotgun shells," Morning said. "You don't happen to have any you could spare, do you?"

"Sorry, I just have ammo for my rifle and revolver."

"You killed the bad men," Reagan said.

Morning looked out at the bodies of the dead road pirates. "Sorry you had to see that."

"I didn't mind."

"No?"

Reagan shook her head. "I know all about bad men. They probably wanted to hurt you like they hurt me."

The natural hardness in Morning's eyes was replaced by motherly instinct. "Men hurt you?" she asked softly.

Reagan sighed. "I don't like to talk about it. Bear saved me though." She smiled. "He's a good one."

Morning looked up at Bear again. "You've been keeping her safe?"

"Yeah," Bear answered.

"If you don't mind my asking, why is it tough for you to talk?"

"No tongue," Reagan said. "He had cancer when he was a boy."

Morning's gaze lingered on Bear long enough that he looked away. "We've all been kicked around hard in one way or another by life it seems."

Lucian cleared his throat. "Were those road pirates you killed the first you've seen around here?"

"They're the first I woke up to find sniffing around my property. I warned them I was armed, but apparently all they saw was a woman without a man around. I suppose that was enough to motivate them to try to take what wasn't theirs—including me."

"That didn't end well for them," Remington said.

Morning's jaw clenched. "No, it didn't."

"And now what?" Lucian asked.

"What do you mean *what*?" Morning's eyes flashed annoyance. "I'll take care of it. They'll be buried and gone by the afternoon if that's what you're asking."

"Not exactly."

"Then explain what you mean or shut up about it."

"Are you certain they were alone?"

"Certain? No. I didn't really have time to interview them before they decided to attack me at my home. What I do know is this. If I had let that second one go then there would definitely be more coming this way. Look, the sheriff has been doing his best to run these road pirates off, but we all know that eventually there's going to be a group of them who will try to pillage Savage the same as they've been doing everywhere else."

Lucian persisted. "Those two men won't be reporting back to wherever it is they came from."

"Duh. That was pretty much the whole point of my killing them—so they couldn't do that very thing."

"You're not understanding *my* point, Ms. McGreevy."

"It's not Ms., it's Mrs. I may have lost a husband but not my name and I don't care what *your* point is. I did what I did, and it's done—end of story."

"I wasn't questioning what you did; I was merely trying to ascertain potential future complications after the fact."

"The only potential future complication you should be worried about right now is my boot up your ass." Morning looked at Remington. "Where in the hell did you get this guy?"

Remington was about to respond when he was cut off by the sound of an approaching vehicle. It was the sheriff's patrol car slowly swerving around the bodies on the gravel drive. "This is the busiest my ranch has been in ages," he said.

Dillon Potts had been the Richland County Sheriff for more than thirty years. These days it seemed every one of those years was etched across his once handsome face like a roadmap of tragedy and despair. Since losing his entire family to the vaccine the burden of that pain continued to cut deeper and deeper within him. His body ached nearly as much as his soul. The hair he kept mostly hidden under his cowboy hat had long ago thinned and gone white; the arthritis in his knees made getting into and out of his patrol car a wince-inducing routine; he'd lost too much weight, and his vision seemed to worsen a little more each day. And yet as tired as Dillon was of all the death and destruction around him, he continued to put on the uniform and do his sworn duty to serve and protect the citizens of Richland County to the best of his abilities. Without the job he likely would have put a gun to his head and ended it soon after his wife had gasped her last breath while he held her hand and cursed God for taking her from him. The job gave him purpose and that purpose gave him the strength to keep on living.

"Sheriff Potts." Remington tipped the brim of his hat. "Good to see you."

Dillon grimaced. "Couldn't help but notice the new speed bumps on your driveway."

Remington grunted. "Damn road pirates."

"That was my doing," Morning said. "They were on my property earlier."

"How'd they end up here?" Dillon asked.

"They chased me and then I chased them."

"Clearly you did more than just chase."

"I did."

"Give them any warning first?"

"I tried. They wouldn't listen."

"So, it was justified."

"Self-defense."

"One of those men was shot in the back, Morning."

"I couldn't let him get away. He would have brought more of them here. None of us want that mess—you included."

Dillon looked like he might smile. "You almost sound like you want me to thank you."

"Nah. I just want to be left alone to dig the holes to bury them in."

"Fair enough." Dillon took off his hat and ran his hand through what little hair remained. "Now, who are all of you?"

Remington first introduced Lucian, Reagan, and then Bear.

Dillon pulled his hat down as he looked up at Bear. "You know what I'm going to ask you."

"I'm him," Bear replied.

"I watched you play football. You were something."

"He's more than just a football player," Reagan said. "He's my friend."

This time Dillon did smile. "I can see that." He gave Lucian a long looking over. "Are you from the reservation up north?"

"Because I'm Indian?"

"I thought the acceptable term was Native American."

"Sheriff, that's one of the few benefits I've seen since the collapse of modern society—nobody cares about political correctness anymore. Whatever we choose to call each other no longer matters because there are far more important things to worry about such as life and death. As to where I'm from, no, I am not from the Fort Peck reservation, but I am familiar with it as many who are descended from my tribe have long called it home."

"The reason I mentioned it is because I used to be able to contact the tribal police chief up there on my shortwave at the station, but I haven't been able to for going on a year now. I know the reservations were hit especially hard by violence and bloodshed following the collapse. I thought you might know something regarding how he's doing."

"I'm sorry, Sheriff, I have no information on the current conditions at Fort Peck."

"You said you have descendants up there. Are you Assiniboine?"

"I am—and proudly so. Before the madness took our world, I was a professor in North Dakota."

"How'd you end up with these four?"

Lucian's mouth tightened. "This is starting to feel like an interrogation."

"Don't take it personal, Professor. It's my job to ask questions." Dillon glanced at Morning. "You'll vouch for him?"

"I just met him and the others the same as you," Morning said. "Ask Remington."

Dillon locked eyes with Remington. "Well?"

"He seems to be honest enough," Remington replied. "Now, if you don't mind, I'd like to ask *you* something, Sheriff."

"Yeah?"

"Besides the tribal police chief up at Fort Peck, have you been in regular contact with others on your shortwave?"

"Sure."

"So, you have an idea of what's going on in other parts of the country?"

"I suppose I do."

"And?"

Dillon sighed. "And you probably don't want to know."

"That bad?"

Dillon nodded. "That bad."

Bear wrote something down and passed it to Dillon.

Tell us.

Dillon stared at the two words for some time before looking up. "Let me put it to you like this. I started out a few years back getting regular updates from twenty-nine other law enforcement officers from across the country. That number is now down to five. The rest have gone silent. I figure most if not all are dead or on the run. The bigger cities went first, but like an aggressive cancer the chaos is spreading with people like Vig and her road pirates getting more and more dangerous in our own backyard. We've had it good here in Savage, but our time is coming. Three months ago, I was communicating with the sheriff out in Harding County, South Dakota. That's just a little over two hundred miles from here. There were about forty of them holed up inside of a church in a little place called Riva. Vig's road pirates were constantly attacking and they were running low on ammo and food. He was begging for help— help I was in no position to provide. I haven't heard from that sheriff since."

"Two hundred miles isn't nearly enough space between what happened there and here," Remington said.

"Exactly." Dillon's eyes betrayed the weariness that lay so heavily on his shoulders. "Like I said, our time is coming."

"Do you think those road pirates today were Vig's?" Morning asked.

"Were they armed with guns?"

Morning shook her head. "No."

"Then it's hard to know for sure. Everything I've heard says that Vig's primary forces are well armed. Those two back there might have just been a pair of stragglers hoping to join up with her and trying to prove their worth. That doesn't mean they didn't deserve to get what you gave to them. No doubt they were still the kind of scumbags we want to keep away from here."

Remington looked down at Dillon's sidearm. "How are you doing on ammo and fuel?"

"Enough to put up a short fight but not nearly enough to hold out for more than a few days. As for fuel, the tanks at the station are less than a third full now and the generator I use to power the pumps has been getting harder and harder to start. I've already cut back on my patrols up to Sidney."

"And how many of us do you think are left around here?"

"No more than a few hundred spread out over about fifty square miles."

"That's it? *A few hundred*?" Remington closed his eyes and pinched the space between them. "The rest are just . . . gone?"

"Yeah." Dillon exhaled. "The vaccine took out at least half. As for the rest—who knows." He looked up at Vaughn's Hill. "Before this is over those few of us left might all end up on that hill of yours. It seems like just yesterday I was up there fighting alongside Hap against the Bureau of Land Management and that son of a bitch Tuttle."

"You should come for dinner, Sheriff," Reagan blurted out. "You and Morning. We're going to catch fish and pick some vegetables and maybe even have some rabbit too."

"Rabbit? Those critters are tough to find this time of year. They don't like to come out when it's this cold."

"I put out quite a few snares," Remington said. "Caught a nice one last week."

"Well?" Reagan continued. "Will you two come for dinner?"

"Maybe next time," Dillon replied.

Reagan looked at Morning. "What about you?"

"Fresh fish," Remington added.

"I'll come if the sheriff does," Morning said.

Dillon frowned. "That's not fair."

"C'mon, Sheriff," Morning continued. "It'll do us both some good to get out."

"You go."

"We *both* go."

Dillon scratched at the stubble on his cheek. "You can make good on that promise of some cooked rabbit?"

"I'll do my best," Remington answered.

"Fine, though my knees and back aren't looking forward to walking that trail to the top of the hill."

"A little exercise won't hurt," Morning said.

"I do have a couple cans of beef stew I could bring. At least then I'd feel like I was contributing something to the meal."

"Some of that stew would be great." Remington stuck his hands into the back pockets of his jeans. "So, we'll see you back here right before dark?"

"Sure," Dillon answered. "I'll be here."

Reagan smiled and clapped. "It'll be a party."

Morning's eyes twinkled, which made Dillon's eyes narrow. "*What?*" he growled.

"There's one more thing."

"The answer is no."

"I haven't even asked you yet."

"I already know what it is."

"Bring your guitar."

Remington beamed. "What a fantastic idea."

"I said no," Dillon repeated.

"Please," Reagan begged. "If we had some music then it really *would* be a party. We could sing and dance and everything."

Dillon turned and walked to his car. "Fine. I'll think about it."

After he drove away Morning looked down at Reagan and winked. "He's going to bring his guitar." She slapped her thigh. "Now, it's time I get to work burying those bodies."

Bear stepped forward and passed Morning a note.

I'll help you.

Morning shrugged. "Okay. I'll be back in a few with the shovel." She lifted herself up into the saddle and then looked around. "Huh."

"Something wrong?" Remington asked.

"Not sure. I just had a strong feeling of being watched."

Everyone turned and looked as well.

"I don't see anything," Lucian said.

"I didn't see anything either," Morning replied. "I felt it."

Reagan squinted into the sun. "Is it more bad men coming to get me?"

"That won't happen," Morning said as she gripped the reins tightly. "Bear won't let it. None of us will."

Reagan grinned. "I know."

Morning took off down the road on her horse.

"I like her," Reagan said. She looked up at Bear who stood watching as Morning galloped away. "Do you like her too?"

Bear pretended not to hear the question.

Reagan didn't ask it again.

His silence was her answer.

10.
✦✧✦✧

"I haven't been fishing since I was a kid, and I haven't been a kid in quite some time. How about you?"

Bear sat on a rock staring at the line that disappeared under the waters of the Yellowstone River. Lucian and he had been watching and waiting for nearly an hour without a single bite to show for their efforts. Bear held up his tablet so Lucian could see the words.

Never caught one.

Lucian handed the line to Bear. "Then it's long past time we change that."

Bear wrapped the line around his finger.

"Maybe you'll have better luck than me. You certainly couldn't do any worse." Lucian picked up a thin black rock that was next to his feet and held it up. "Obsidian. Somewhat rare in these parts. Likely carried here from the north via the confluence of the Missouri and Yellowstone rivers. Do you know why obsidian was so highly prized among the continent's original tribes?"

Bear shrugged.

"Weapons and tools," Lucian said. "The foundation of humankind's modern era. Obsidian is natural glass forged over millennia out of volcanic fire—a beautiful remnant of ancient geological distress." He turned the stone over in his hand. "It was belched from the earth's innards and then cooled quickly, a process which gives it its uniquely dark sheen. For thousands of years the people of these lands prized obsidian above all other materials." He dropped the stone. "Now it sits here among all of the other rocks, ignored and worthless." He sighed. "Another victim of society's so-called progress."

Bear pulled in the line and held up the end with the hook attached to it. The bait had fallen off.

"Here." Lucian handed him another bug. "Try that."

With fresh bait in the water Bear tied the line to a rock, wrote another note, and handed it to Lucian.

How do you think all of this ends?

"Do you mean how it ends for us here or the world out there?"

Bear nodded.

Lucian chuckled. "I'll take that to mean you want me to speak to both scenarios."

Bear scribbled another note.

Us, the world, everything. Where does it all go from here?

"I don't know, Bear. I'm like everyone else—keeping my head down and trying to survive."

Give me your best educated guess.

"Just so you know, I wouldn't place my intelligence as being superior to yours or anyone else's. I might have been a professor, but the fact is some of the most idiotic people I've known were academics. Perhaps you could help me out by asking about something more specific so I'm not firing blanks into the proverbial intellectual abyss."

Will the chaos ever end?

"The simple answer is also the hardest—no. Society was full of chaos before the collapse but the institutions running most everything were able to distract us from it with things like thousands of streaming channels, millions of online videos, phones that chirped and chimed and vibrated to us both night and day, as well as twenty-four-seven news that rarely ever reported actual news that wasn't in some way meant to be mass manipulation. Right now, there are figures like Vig who, because they have the most guns, have become, for lack of a better term, warlords. Eventually those warlords will, if they haven't already, start fighting each other as they try to expand their territories. This isn't new. Humankind has been doing that since the beginning. We simply have been living so comfortably for so long that we forgot our own history and just how appallingly nasty we can be to one another."

Why did the vaccine kill some but not others?

"The answer is likely similar to why a disease kills some and not others. Perhaps it's due to genetics, environmental factors, or just dumb luck."

Are you saying the vaccine is a disease?

"In this case I would agree the two terms are one and the same because the end result has been millions upon millions of dead. I recall a lecture I attended years ago where the speaker was a billionaire who had made his fortune in technology. He declared his intent to us that day that he would soon be redirecting his focus toward better managing what he considered to be the ever-worsening crisis of overpopulation. I have thought of that lecture often since the collapse because if I had that man's vast resources and influence and wanted to greatly reduce the planet's population in one fell swoop, a virus created as a vehicle for mass vaccination that would then kill more than half the population would be an ingenious way to go about it, don't you think?"

Murder is what it is.

Lucian nodded. "Certainly, but anyone who spends even a little time going through history can find example after example of murdering institutions that considered human life to be nothing more than an inconvenience to their hunger for more riches, power, and domination of others. The Native American tribes of this continent practiced brutal forms of war and subsequent slavery for thousands of years—long before the first white people ever set foot here. Those deadly imperfections of the human condition were later modernized so that instead of thousands of dead over months or years those deaths could accumulate in a matter of days or even hours. Germany's Hitler is estimated to have killed some thirty million. Stalin's Soviet Union nearly forty million. China's Mao likely killed as many as Stalin and Hitler combined and the one thing all of these monstrous governments had in common was their desire to divide and conquer and then to control nearly every aspect of people's lives and to wipe out any and all opposition. There was a time when American education studied those examples with disbelief that such governments could exist. Ah, but over time this nation began to replicate those very same authoritarian tendencies that not so long ago horrified us until we became the willing architects of our own tragic demise."

A hawk circled overhead, likely watching what they were doing by the river.

Lucian folded his hands over a bony knee. "Would you mind answering some of my questions?"

Bear tugged on the fishing line a little and then shrugged.

"I'm fascinated by the legend that surrounds you," Lucian continued. "So many now whisper of the bear. Some do so fearfully while others speak of you with great reverence. You have become a beacon of hope to them—a power that chooses not only to fight back against the madness but fight back and win. I do apologize for the forwardness of this question and understand if you choose not to answer, but I am so curious to know how many of Vig's road pirates have you killed since the collapse?"

Bear stared straight ahead for a moment, looked down at the fishing line, and then over at Lucian.

"Take your time," Lucian said.

Bear gave Lucian the fishing line and then wrote his response.

Too many.

"How many is too many?"

I don't know.

"I think you do, Bear. Don't carry that burden around alone. Free yourself from such secrets by telling me."

I'm not proud of it.

"Of course not."

Why do you care to know?

"I've never met someone like you."

You mean a killer?

"That's right."

I'm not a killer. I'm just a man the same as you.

Lucian shook his head. "We are *not* the same, Bear. I cannot do what you have done. I lack the strength and the courage. Saying it out loud I now realize how much I envy you. Tell me what it's like."

Bear scowled.

"To kill," Lucian whispered as he leaned forward. "What's it like to take a life not just once but repeatedly?"

Every life I've taken has in turn taken just as much from me.

Lucian mouthed the words as he read them. "That's quite profound but it also begs the question—what then is left of you now?"

Bear's scowl remained as he wrote his reply.

As much or as little as is required.

"You're not a monster."

I know.

"What you have been forced to do isn't your fault. We've all been made victims of this madness."

Nobody forced me. I chose to kill those men.

Lucian's eyes widened. "Why?"

Why not? Their only purpose was to harm others. My purpose was to stop them. Unlike others, I refuse to be made a victim.

"How many? Ten? Twenty? *More?*"

If you keep asking me that question, I'll be adding you to the total.

The hawk circled once more and then dropped from the sky. A rabbit squeaked as the hawk's talons and beak tore into its flesh. Seconds later, a lone coyote bounded across the field toward the commotion. The hawk spread its wings and screeched at the intrusion.

The coyote charged. The hawk, weighed down by the rabbit corpse it refused to let go of, barely escaped as the coyote's jaws snapped shut inches from its tailfeathers. The coyote sniffed the ground, licked rabbit blood from some blades of grass, and then sat and stared at Bear and Lucian who watched it from across the river.

"Neither the hawk nor the coyote kills without purpose," Lucian said as he turned his head toward Bear. "I believe the same can be said for you." He paused. "I have a confession. Yesterday, I voiced concern that your presence here might be more trouble than benefit."

"Why?" Bear asked.

"You're Vig's most wanted right now. From what I've heard she's not one to forgive and forget."

Bear wrote some more.

You shared this concern with Remington?

"Yes."

What did he say?

"He basically told me to shut up and not to mention it again and let me tell you—that is a man who says what he means."

Bear smiled. "Yeah?"

Lucian nodded. "He made it clear I'd be the one to go long before you would. It seems you've made quite the impression on him. Actually, you've made quite the impression on me as well."

The fishing line went tight in Lucian's hand. He flinched. "Oh, that was a bite."

Bear stood, watching the water and waiting.

"There," Lucian said. "Another one." He handed the line to Bear. "Your turn."

Bear gave the line a jerk and then started to pull it in.

"Fish on!" Lucian exclaimed. He pointed across the river at the coyote that was still watching them. "He sure looks interested in finding out what you've caught."

With a loud splash the fish darted and dived as Bear continued to pull the end of the line toward the shore. The coyote looked up at something in the sky and then took off running.

Lucian turned around. "Wonder what spooked him."

They both heard it before they saw it—a low whirring rumble accompanied by a dark speck against the backdrop of blue sky.

Bear stopped pulling the line.

Lucian crouched down behind a shrub and suggested to Bear that he do the same.

The whirring rumble grew louder.

"It's been a long time since I've seen one of those."

Bear still had a hold of the fishing line.

The helicopter was moving fast and getting closer.

"That's a National Guard chopper from South Dakota," Lucian said. "I recognize the logo. I wonder who is flying it?"

Bear watched the chopper drop lower as it neared the river side of Vaughn's Hill. Whoever was flying it had to have been able to spot Remington's tent by now. Bear couldn't see those inside the chopper, but he knew. It took some effort, but he managed to say the name.

"Vig."

And then the gunfire started.

11.
✦✧✦✧

At the same time that Bear and Lucian were dropping a fishing line into the river Remington and Reagan were pulling carrots from inside the greenhouse. Reagan held hers up and asked if it was a good one.

"That's a prize winner for sure," Remington said. "And mine is almost as good. We can add these to the canned stew that the sheriff is bringing by later."

"And some potatoes."

"Absolutely."

"And rabbit."

Remington winked. "If we're lucky."

Reagan continued to fire off questions and comments ranging from why dirt smells the way it does, how is it possible for birds to fly, why fish can breathe underwater, to how far away the sun is. Remington listened patiently, answered as best he could, and listened some more, amused by Reagan's youthful enthusiasm.

"I tell you what," he said. "I'm going to do just a little more work in here while you go back into the tent and set the vegetables by the fire pit." He held up a pinky-sized carrot. "And I'll have you give this one to Peanut later."

"Okay," Reagan happily replied as she scooped up the carrots and potatoes and then walked out of the greenhouse.

Remington added water to some of the pots, used his fingers to stir the dirt in others to help oxygenate the soil, and then he stood wincing while pressing his hands against his lower back that had been paining him for some time. *Getting old sucks,* he thought, *but I suppose it's better than the alternative.*

When Remington stepped outside, he tilted his head toward the tent. Reagan was talking to someone. He walked in quietly and watched as she stood nodding in front of the old Wilkes family chair. No one else was there.

"Uh-huh." Reagan looked directly at the chair. "Okay. I'll tell him."

"Who are you talking to?" Remington asked.

"You don't see him?"

"No."

Reagan pointed. "He's sitting right here. Now he's looking at you—he's looking at you and smiling. He had mean eyes at first, but now they're nice eyes like yours. The hat is the same too. He doesn't have a beard though."

Remington stepped toward Reagan and the empty chair. "Does he have a name?"

"Of course he has a name. I told him mine and he told me his. He also has a nickname and says that you would know it."

Remington, thinking Reagan's imagination had gotten the better of her, played along so that he wouldn't hurt her feelings. "How would I know his nickname?"

Reagan shrugged. "He's the one who said it."

"Who?"

"The Irish Cowboy. That's his nickname."

The hairs on the back of Remington's neck stood up.

Reagan looked up and smiled. "He's your great-uncle Hap."

"Oh. What does he want?"

"To tell you something. He was going to have me do it, but now he says he'll tell you himself."

"I'm sorry, Reagan, but I don't see anyone else here but the two of us."

"Don't be silly. He's walking right next to you."

"I guess your eyes are a lot better than mine because—"

The words were a whisper of a whisper and yet Remington heard them clearly, spoken in a low rasp that was so much like his own—the voice of an old man. It wasn't his imagination or some trick of the mind. No, he heard those words but more importantly he felt them too, like a heavy stillness pressing up against him.

"Be ready, boy—they're coming."

Remington turned toward the voice. He reached out to touch something that was there but wasn't. His hand closed on empty space. "Hap?" There were no more words, nothing to see, no indication anyone or anything had been there at all.

"He's gone," Reagan said.

Remington clenched his fists to stop his hands from shaking. "Where?"

"Someone else named Shirley was waiting for him. She calls him Happy, and he said this is his happy place. Isn't that funny?"

"I need to sit down."

Reagan patted the old chair. "Here you go. Hap said it was his chair, but I don't think he'd mind. You're family after all."

Remington shuffled over to the chair, settled into it, dropped his head, and buried his face in his hands.

"Hey, are you okay?"

"I'm fine." Remington rubbed his eyes and looked up. "Did that really just happen?"

"What?"

"I think Hap spoke to me."

Reagan shrugged. "So?"

"That's not possible."

"Why not?"

"Because he's dead." Remington regretted putting it so bluntly to Reagan, but she didn't seem to mind.

"Dead doesn't mean gone," she replied. "He likes it here. I do too. Isn't that why you're here? Because you like it?"

"Sure."

"Then why such a sad face?"

Remington scratched at his beard. "I can't really explain it and I don't think I should even try."

Reagan shrugged again. "Okay. Are we going to go outside to look for rabbits?"

"Just a minute." Remington locked eyes with her. "Did you hear what Hap told me?"

Reagan nodded. "He said to get ready because they were coming."

We both heard it, Remington thought. *I don't know how or why, but it happened. There's no denying it.* He cleared his throat. "Do you know who *they* are?"

"The ones who are coming here?"

"Yes."

Reagan's face tightened as her brows drew together. "The bad people."

"The bad people?"

"Uh-huh."

"Did Hap say anything else to you?"

"He said there are times when the only choice is for the good to take a stand against the bad and that this is going to be one of those times but that I shouldn't worry because we aren't alone. This hill has power—a *lot* of power—and Hap isn't the only one watching out for us."

Remington's fingers dug into the arms of the chair. "Who else is watching us, Reagan?"

"Morning knows him."

"Morning McGreevy?"

"He's her great grandfather. His name is Cy. He had to fight the bad ones once just like Hap did. He says that's what true cowboys do—they fight the fights that no one else will."

Remington knew the name. The McGreevy family's Savage history went as far back as the Wilkes'. "Has Cy McGreevy ever talked to you as well?"

Reagan shook her head. "Nope—just Hap, but I'm pretty sure he wouldn't lie about it."

"How do you know that?"

"I just do. Remember how I said he had nice eyes like yours?"

"Yes."

"Those kinds of eyes don't lie." Reagan looked up at the opening in the tent's ceiling where the sun was shining through. "Do we still have time to look for rabbits?"

Remington got up. "I gave you my word, so we better get going."

"See?" Reagan said. "You and your eyes don't lie."

"I appreciate the confidence." Remington tipped the brim of his hat. "And I'll do my best to keep proving you right." *Ghosts and rabbits,* he thought. *What a day this has turned out to be.*

When they stepped outside, they both heard a dog barking from somewhere in the valley below. Reagan ran to the edge and looked down. The dog, the same one they had seen earlier at the top of the hill, was trotting through the field by the house sniffing the ground as he went until he suddenly stopped, turned, and started barking loudly at something neither Remington nor Reagan could see.

Then Remington heard a windy roar coming from above. Reagan pointed at the dark metallic flash in the sky. "What's that?"

"Get inside," Remington said. "Now." They went into the tent together. Remington grabbed the rifle. "Stay here." He put a hand on Reagan's shoulder. "I mean it. Stay here and don't move, okay?"

"Okay," Reagan answered.

Remington returned outside and looked up. The chopper was closer, no more than five hundred yards to the east. He walked to the other side of the tent where the Wilkes family graves were located and took a position under a nearby tree, watching, waiting, and hoping the chopper would pass over them and then move on. *Whoever it is they had to have already seen the tent,* he thought.

The chopper kept coming. Remington could feel the air around him throbbing to the mechanical beat of its blades. He raised the rifle, aimed, but didn't fire. "Keep going," he said through gritted teeth. "Don't start trouble where none need be."

Down in the valley the dog continued to bark. The chopper turned slightly, dropped lower, and faced the hillside. *Bear and Lucian are still down at the river.* Remington regripped the rifle and cursed under his breath. The chopper continued to hover in place. *What the hell do you want?*

Whoosh-whoosh-whoosh went the blades as the chopper started to edge closer to the hill as Hap's words echoed in Remington's ears: *"Be ready, boy—they're coming."*

Remington's finger tightened against the trigger. *Friend or foe?* he thought. *They're checking out the tent, the top of the hill, the house below—all things road pirate scum would love to get their hands on.*

The sound of gunfire was partly muffled by the din of the chopper, but Remington still heard it and knew that the bullet was either meant for him or for Bear and Lucian down at the river. So, he did the only thing he could.

He returned fire—twice.

The chopper immediately veered and started to climb. Remington aimed again and pulled the trigger for a third time. White smoke belched from the tail section. He prepared to fire again but decided it was already too far away. Every bullet was precious, and he couldn't afford to waste a single one. The chopper was retreating and as far as he knew everyone else was safe.

That would have to be enough.

For now.

12.
✦✧✦✧

"Tell me that's what I think it is."

Dillon glanced up at Remington while carrying a box of something over one shoulder and a guitar that hung off of the other. "I figured we all could use something to wash the stew down with."

Bear took the box, set it down near the firepit and then opened it. He looked up grinning like a kid on Christmas morning. "Beer!"

"It seems Bear likes beer," Remington said with a chuckle.

"May I?" Bear held up a can that looked comically small in his oversized hand.

"That's what I brought it for," Dillon replied. He also took out two cans of stew from his coat pocket and gave them to Remington. "As promised."

"A case of beer, some vegetables, rabbit meat, and two big cans of stew." Remington shook his head. "I suddenly feel like the richest man in the world."

Morning grabbed a couple of beers and handed one to Lucian. "Who knows," she said. "The way things are going out there you just might be." She pulled back the tab and held up her can. "Slainte."

Remington tapped his beer against Morning's. "Good on you for helping to keep it Irish up on this hill. Hap would definitely approve—slainte."

"Can I try some?" Reagan asked. Bear let her have a sip. Her lips drew back against her teeth as she shook her head. "That's disgusting."

The others laughed and then it quickly became uncomfortably quiet.

Remington shifted on his feet. "I'll get the fire going."

"Not to be a buzzkill," Dillon said, "but we need to talk more about what happened today with that chopper visit."

"I know." Remington dropped some wood into the firepit. "We will. Let me start this fire and then we can sit around enjoying some pre-dinner beers and hash it out."

Reagan poked Bear's thigh and looked up at him. "Are the chopper people coming back?"

Bear shrugged.

"We'll be ready if they do," Morning said right before tipping her head back and taking another drink.

Remington stepped away from the firepit and watched the smoke billow up toward the opening in the tent ceiling. "Once we have some hot coals going, we'll get that stew cooked up." He took a long drink of beer, closed his eyes, and sighed. "So good. Thank you, Sheriff. I really needed this."

"It's been a while, hasn't it?" Dillon tapped the top of his can. "Who would have thought we'd be living in a time when such a simple pleasure like a beer would turn into something so rare and remarkable."

"That's because the world went batshit crazy on us," Morning said. "I still don't understand how it happened. I watched it happen, I lived it, but for the life of me I still don't get *how* it happened."

Remington reached down and grabbed a second beer. "Never underestimate humankind's potential for stupidity."

"Or it's willingness to orchestrate its own extinction," Lucian added.

"All I know is this," Dillon said. "For six months before the vaccine we had three deaths in the entire county that were directly attributed to the virus. In the six months *after* the vaccine was made available, we had eighteen deaths that our county health officials were putting down as virus related. You would think a six-hundred-percent increase in deaths would have been more than enough for them to tap the breaks on the vaccine mandates but instead they kept pushing for people to get the jab. I was asking questions back then, wondering what the hell was going on. Nobody, and I mean *nobody*, wanted to give me answers. The year after that, well, you all know what happened then. The number of people dying from the vaccines was—"

"Biblical." Lucian took a drink. "So many lives lost. It hurts to think about it."

Morning gave him a hard look. "Then don't. We need to focus on the here and now not the then and gone."

"Those that fail to learn from history are doomed to repeat it," Lucian countered.

Remington poured the canned stew into a pot, added the vegetables and strips of salted rabbit, stirred it all together and then placed the pot over the fire. "Won't be long now."

"Until then," Dillon said, "let's discuss the chopper."

"Sure." Remington sat in the chair and leaned back while sipping his beer. "What do you want to know?"

"Did you get a look at who was piloting it?"

"No, but if I had to put money down on it, I'd say they were Vig's people."

"Road pirates."

"Yeah."

"Road pirates with the ability to attack from above." Dillon pursed his lips. "That's not good."

"No, it isn't," Remington replied. "Pretty sure I damaged that chopper though. Saw smoke coming from the tail section after I shot at it."

"Maybe it crashed on its way back to wherever it came from," Morning said.

Remington emptied his beer and reached for another one. "Would be nice to know for sure. I'd hate to wake up to the sound of it dropping down on this place again."

Bear held up his tablet.

We could look for the crash. The sheriff has a car and fuel.

Dillon wagged his finger. "Hold on there. That's a big ask—and a damn dangerous one."

"Doesn't mean he's wrong to suggest it." Morning nodded at Bear. "I'm in."

"I'm not going to waste what little gas I have left driving around looking for a crash site that most likely doesn't exist."

"LoLo's," Remington said as he slowly stirred the stew. "How far is it?"

"Absolutely not," Dillon answered.

"Eighty miles to the west of here?" Remington continued. "That sound about right?"

Dillon wiped his nose with the back of his hand. "I said no."

"Eighty miles, a hundred at the most," Morning added. She looked at Lucian. "Do you know of it?"

Lucian nodded. "Yes, but I don't personally know the owner if that's what you're really asking."

"If I was really asking you that then I would," Morning said. "But you've *heard* of the owner, haven't you?"

"Because he's an Indian like me?"

"Have you heard of him or not?"

"I have."

Morning rolled her eyes. "Was that so hard to admit?"

Bear wrote on his tablet again.

What is LoLo's?

"It's a bar deep in the woods halfway between the Fort Peck and Fort Belknap reservations that never shut down even after the collapse," Morning answered. "At least that's the rumor. LoLo's has always attracted a criminal element."

"Criminal element." Dillon grunted. "That's putting it mildly. Word is it's as bad now as it has ever been—murdering smugglers and cutthroats the lot of them."

"But I bet someone there knows something about that helicopter," Remington said. "Especially if it's Vig's."

Dillon hooked his thumbs into his belt. "You can't be serious about us driving all the way out there hoping to find someone who would give us that kind of information. We're just as likely to have our throats slit. In case you haven't noticed I'm an old man and so are you."

"Wasn't your daddy an old man when he stood shoulder to shoulder with Hap and pushed the feds off this very hill?"

"This isn't that, Remington."

"Lost your will to fight, eh?"

"No, I'm just not looking to die by being stupid."

"That's coward talk."

Dillon's eyes were steely slits. "Watch it."

Remington got up from the chair. "There it is. *That's* the sheriff I know. Now, you take that toughness, drive it on out to LoLo's, talk to some of those snakes who have a knack for knowing things the rest of us don't, and find out who the hell got their hands on a chopper. We can't just stick our heads in the sand and hope it never comes back. You know I'm right so do the right thing."

"We'll be okay, Sheriff," Morning said. "You and Remington are both armed, and we have the bear. Nobody will mess with us."

"What about Reagan?" Dillon replied. "She shouldn't be anywhere near that place. You know how valuable a girl like her would be to people like them."

"I'll stay here with her." Remington put a hand on Reagan's shoulder. "Morning can take my rifle. That still leaves me with a revolver. You'll be fine. We'll be fine. It's a good plan. We need to find out about that chopper, and this is the best way we know to do it."

"So much for saving what little fuel I have left. I'll likely use up an entire tank of gas with all of that driving."

Morning shrugged. "Why bother with putting gas in the tank if you're not going to use it for a good cause? Besides, you can be out there and back in a day."

"*If* we get back," Dillon said.

"We will." Morning looked at the others. "Are we in agreement then? We head out for LoLo's first thing in the morning."

Bear and Lucian nodded. Dillon took off his hat and slapped it against his thigh. "Dammit, Morning."

"Is that a yes?" Morning's brows lifted.

Dillon pushed his hat back onto his head. "Okay—I'll do it."

"Excellent timing, Sheriff," Remington said.

"Why's that?" Dillon growled.

"The stew is ready."

They ate and drank in silence while sitting around the fire. Even Reagan seemed apprehensive over the trip the others would be taking the next day. After some more beers, though, the mood lightened. A few smiles followed, some chuckles, and then Morning finally pushed away the heaviness altogether by demanding Dillon play them a song.

"I'm out of practice," he warned.

"You sure grabbed for that guitar quick." Remington opened another beer. "Admit it, Sheriff—you're dying to play something. You secretly always wanted to be a singing cowboy."

Dillon groaned as he lowered himself onto the ground. He sat cross-legged and strummed the strings. "These old knees of mine—I may never get back up."

"Then you better make it a good one," Morning said.

"Any requests?"

Reagan folded her arms over her bent knees and then rested her chin on them. "Play something for all the ones who are gone."

Dillon wasn't prepared for her words to hit him so hard. His head dropped. He had lost so much—they all had. He looked up, eyes wet, and gave Reagan a smiling sigh. "I'll try, but I fear it might be a sad or angry one."

"That's okay," Reagan whispered. "Sometimes it's good to feel sad and angry because it means you're remembering all the people you wish were still a part of your life and as long as you still remember them, they never really die."

"You mentioned my father earlier, Remington," Dillon said. "I've been thinking about him a lot lately. He was one tough SOB, a damn fine sheriff, and a good friend to your uncle Hap to the very end. I grew up listening to Merle Haggard because both my parents played him so much, I didn't have a choice and I suppose I sort of resented it at the time. It's funny how you try to put all that space between what your parents liked and what you as a younger person *think* you should like and then the years pass and you eventually come to realize your mom and dad knew a hell of a lot more about the world and how it really works than your ignorant and arrogant self gave them credit for. How's that saying go—youth is wasted on the young while wisdom is wasted on the old? Man do I understand that now. I just wish it hadn't taken me this long. So much time wasted."

Dillon looked at Reagan and then took a deep breath. "The song is called 'Are the Good Times Really Over for Good' which seems appropriate given the mess we're in. I first played it at my father's funeral a long time ago. It always reminded me of my parents' generation and how they weren't the least bit shy about telling people to stop doing wrong and start doing right. Men were men, women were women, and America was still something the rest of the world wished it could be." He picked at the strings, tapped his foot, and started to sing.

Remington knew the words and by the second chorus he was joining in. When the song was over, he asked Dillon to play it again. This time everyone, including Bear after being encouraged to by Morning, sang along, their voices a rebellious refrain that swirled and soared with the fire's smoke, rising up and up and then out into the darkness beyond Vaughn's Hill.

They sang.

They drank.

And they remembered the world as it used to be and mourned its passing.

13.

✦✧✦✧

"It's amazing how quickly the landscape changes out here," Morning said. "After just an hour of driving we've gone from miles and miles of open fields and rolling hills to more and more trees."

"Just wait," Dillon replied from behind the wheel of his cruiser. "By the time we get to LoLo's those trees are pretty much all you're going to see."

Because of his size Bear's knees pressed against the dash even though he had moved the passenger seat as far back as possible. Morning sat with Lucian in the back of the car. They hadn't seen another vehicle since leaving Savage.

"When is the last time you've been out to LoLo's?" Morning asked.

The inside of the cruiser was getting stuffy, so Dillon turned off the heat. "I was part of a multi-agency team responding to a parole violation nine years ago. The guy was a convicted murderer with a long history of armed violence—a real bad dude. There were three other counties as well as the state police involved."

"Did you get him?"

"No. He wasn't there. At least that's what LoLo told us—not that we trusted a word that came out of his mouth."

Morning leaned forward. "So LoLo is an actual person?"

"Yes, he is, though he's also known as Chief on account of his Native American heritage. That's the name I was told he prefers—Chief."

"He's no chief," Lucian said. "I'm not even sure he's actually Native American."

Dillon glanced in the rearview mirror. "Is that right?"

"In the end it doesn't matter," Lucian continued. "LoLo is an embarrassment to all the tribes in the area. None wish to claim him as one of their own."

"Whatever he is, he's been a pain in the ass to local law enforcement for nearly as long as I've been a sheriff. I sure hope we're not making this trip out here for nothing."

Trees now bookended both sides of the road and the way forward was getting darker and darker. Dillon slowed their speed. When Morning asked him why, he pointed at a truck parked sideways in the middle of the road about a quarter mile ahead. He unlatched his gun holster and then told the others to prepare for possible trouble.

"I'll stop about fifty yards from the roadblock so that we have enough room to turn around and get out of here if we need to. Morning, you be ready with the rifle. If things go sideways just pop open the back door, use it as cover, and then shoot to kill."

Morning nodded. Bear gripped the handle of the sledgehammer tightly while Lucian closed his eyes and took a deep breath.

After they were stopped Dillon opened the driver door and stepped out. Two men stood in front of the truck. Neither appeared to be armed. "What's the deal with the roadblock?" Dillon shouted at them.

"Where you headed?" the shorter and older of the two men shouted back.

"On our way to LoLo's."

"You invited?"

"No."

"A regular?"

"No."

"Did you steal those wheels or were you actually a cop?"

"Does it make a difference?"

The taller man smiled. Despite looking at least ten years younger his voice was deeper, and he talked slower than the other one. "We don't like cops."

"I'm not here as the sheriff."

"Sheriff?" the shorter man said. "You must be the one who's been patrolling Richland County like he's still on the job."

"That would be me."

The man smiled and then spit. "That's funny."

"How so?"

"The world has turned to shit and yet you're still getting up and pulling a shift."

"We're going to need to get by you. Can you please move the truck?"

The taller man shook his head. "I don't think so."

"Why not?"

"Don't feel like it."

"I wasn't actually asking. We need to speak to LoLo."

"That's not going to happen without an invitation."

Dillon's patience was wearing thin. "Then invite us."

The shorter man spit again. "I don't think so."

"You best reconsider."

"This is *our* road, Sheriff. We decide who uses it and who doesn't."

"You sound a lot like one of Vig's road pirates."

"Watch your mouth," the taller man said. "We have nothing to do with that crazy bitch."

Dillon nodded. "Glad to hear it. Vig is actually why we're here to see LoLo."

"Go on," the shorter man replied.

"We're hoping he might know something about something."

"And what would that something be?" the taller man asked.

"I'd rather wait to ask him in person."

The shorter man's head lowered as he stared at the cruiser. "How many are with you?"

"Three."

"Armed?"

Dillon placed his hand on the butt of his sidearm. "We are but we don't want any trouble."

"You found trouble," the taller man said. "Rolling up here in a vehicle with fuel and weapons. Were you really expecting us to let a prize like that go?"

"I'm not expecting a damn thing from either of you. Get that truck out of the road and we'll be on our way."

The shorter man laughed. "Old man, you're in the wrong place at the wrong time to be thinking you can order us to do anything. Like I said, you're funny." He paused, spit again, and then continued. "Tell me something."

Dillon's mouth twitched. "Yeah?"

"You actually have any bullets in that shooter?"

"Keep pissing me off and you're bound to find out."

"Car, fuel, weapons, ammo, we haven't had a haul like that in a long time."

"Sorry to disappoint, but you won't be getting any of it."

"Is that right?" The shorter man looked up at the taller one. "Isn't that just like a cop—always trying to tell us what we can and can't do."

Dillon drew his gun. "I mean it."

The taller man stepped out of the shadows and further into the road. His long, greasy hair clung to his forehead and nearly concealed his eyes. His dark beard was sparse and splotchy, like someone had taken weed killer to it. "You're a long way from home, Sheriff, so I'll cut you some slack regarding you not knowing how things work out here. Pulling your gun like that is a surefire way to get yourself killed."

"Just shut up and move the truck."

"No need for rudeness," the taller one cooed. "Pay the toll."

"What toll?"

"That's up to you."

"My toll is the information I have for LoLo regarding Vig."

"Go on."

"What I have to say is for LoLo's ears not yours."

"C'mon Sheriff, you tell us and then we decide if it's worth troubling LoLo with. That's how we do this."

Dillon pointed his gun at the men. "Move the damn truck."

Morning got out from the back of the car, stood behind the passenger door, and aimed the rifle. "We're not asking again."

The shorter man stroked his full beard. "What do we have here? She's not bad looking for an older gal—not bad at all. And a nice rifle to go along with it."

"I know how to use it," Morning said. "Try me—I dare you."

"I believe it," the shorter man replied. He nodded at something in the woods. Four more men emerged, two on each side of the road. They were all holding foot-long fillet knives.

The taller man smiled. "Your move, Sheriff. Put down your guns or we take this to the next level. If you actually have some ammo, then you'll no doubt get some of us, but you won't be able to get all of us. Blood will be spilled—most of it yours."

Dillon aimed directly at the taller man. "Then I'll be sure to take your sorry ass out first."

The front passenger door opened. The six men looked down and then up as they watched Bear slowly stand to his full height. He faced them while holding the sledgehammer in both his hands.

"Oh my," the shorter man said after spitting. Then he packed his lower lip with more chewing tobacco. "Is that who I think it is?"

Bear lowered the sledgehammer and pointed at the truck. "Move."

"And tell your men to get back," Dillon added.

The taller man arched a brow as he looked Bear up and down. "This changes everything."

"Tell me about it," the shorter one replied. "Vig wants so badly to get her hands on him. We need LoLo to know who just showed up at our front door." He took out a walkie talkie and spoke into it briefly, put it to his ear, and then dropped it into his jacket pocket. "Move the truck."

"Yeah?" the taller one said.

The shorter one nodded. "That comes directly from LoLo—he wants us to escort them to the bar pronto."

The taller one looked at Dillon. "You're in luck, Sheriff. LoLo wants to see you. You're going to follow us there."

The other four men had already retreated back into the woods by the time the truck was pulling away. "Well," Dillon said, "looks like we're about to get what we wanted, but I have to say it sure feels a lot like going from the frying pan to the fire."

"We'll be fine." Morning slid back into the rear seat of the car. "And we shouldn't keep them waiting."

Bear still stood next to the car watching the truck drive off. Dillon asked him what he thought about the visit to LoLo's. Bear shrugged.

"They're awful interested in you," Dillon said. "Be ready. They might be wondering how much Vig is willing to pay to have them hand you over to her."

Bear used his finger to write his reply on the car's dirty hood.

They can try.

"C'mon," Morning shouted. "We have to go."

Dillon got in, slammed the door shut, and started the engine. "Yes ma'am."

"Sorry, I just don't want to give them any more time to prepare in case they're planning something."

"Understood," Dillon said as he spun the tires. "Anyone else notice how they didn't seem too worried about taking our weapons from us?"

"Because no doubt the bar will be very well armed," Lucian said. "So much so that they feel safe from challenge."

Bear wrote on his tablet and then held it up so the others could see.

They fear Vig.

"How do you know that?" Morning asked.

Saw it in their eyes.

"If that's true does them fearing Vig help or hurt us?"

No idea but either way we're about to find out.

The truck was waiting for them at the start of a gravel drive that turned off of the main road. Dillon followed them deeper into the woods. The car's suspension lurched and groaned as they drove over and around a series of increasingly large potholes. Dillon had to switch on the headlights because so little sun was able to get through the thick growth of trees. The condition of the road worsened. Dillon slowed to just five miles an hour as he complained he could walk faster than they were driving.

"It's smart," Lucian said. "There's no way to drive fast and anything that tries will make so much noise anyone within a mile will hear them coming."

"Like a natural alarm system," Dillon added.

Lucian nodded. "Exactly."

Morning winced as they drove over an especially deep pothole. "Or they're just too lazy to maintain it. How much further?"

"If I'm remembering right, I'd say we're getting real close," Dillon answered. He glanced at Bear. "Be ready for anything. Who knows what we'll be walking into."

Minutes later, they came to a widening in the road where the truck was parked in front of a long, singly-story stone building that had only one small window by the entrance door. A large blue tarp was stretched over one side of the roof. Two Harley Davidson motorcycles were next to the truck. Dillon pulled up alongside the motorcycles and shoved the console shifter into park. "Here we go," he said right before turning off the car.

"Is this how you remember it?" Morning asked.

Dillon scanned the overgrown clearing and the wall of trees that surrounded the building. "A bit more rundown perhaps but it's almost exactly how I remember it. The tarp is a new touch."

They got out of the car. Dillon made sure to lock it. Morning carried the rifle and Bear had his sledgehammer. Lucian went to the door and prepared to pull it open. "Last chance to change our minds."

"We haven't had a chance to turn back since we were on the main road," Morning replied. "The only way we're getting back now is if they allow it or we shoot our way out."

Lucian grimaced. "I would very much prefer the former versus the latter."

"We all would," Dillon said. "When you open the door, the bar runs almost the entire length of the room on the left side. There should be a few tables on the right. LoLo's office is in the very back next to a storage room. When I was here all those years ago, the place was powered by a generator, but I don't hear anything running so my guess is what little light inside will be coming from candles or battery-powered lamps." He looked at Lucian. "Okay let's see what's waiting for us."

Lucian grabbed hold of the handle. Dillon put his hand over his gun. Bear tightened his grip on the sledgehammer. Morning held the rifle against her chest with the barrel pointed up. All of them in some form or other said a silent prayer that whatever waited inside wouldn't end up getting them killed.

The door was opened.

14.
✦✧✦✧

"There he is—the bear himself. Sir, it is truly an honor to have such a magnificent thorn in the side of Vig as a guest in my humble little establishment. Please, take a seat at the bar and enjoy my hospitality. This round is on the house."

The place smelled like an old cellar—damp and dirty.

LoLo was in his early seventies, six-foot, thin, with broad shoulders and very narrow hips. His silver hair was pulled back from a prominent forehead. Despite his age, the only significant lines on his otherwise smooth face were those that extended from the corners of his deep-set gray eyes. The cheekbones were prominent, the dusky skin unblemished, and the wide mouth turned slightly upwards, hinting at either a playful sense of humor, an inclination for cruelty, or both. His wrists, hands, and fingers were thin, almost delicate, and adorned with multiple gold and silver rings and bracelets. He wore a black-and-red checkered flannel shirt tucked into jeans. An ivory hilt dagger hung from the side of his belt.

The glasses were lined up and then partly filled with whiskey. "The good stuff," LoLo proudly stated from behind the polished wood bar that ran nearly the entire length of the room just like Dillon had described earlier. "Down from Canada. People travel great distances for a chance to drink this and here you are now getting to do the same for free." He locked eyes with Dillon. "You look familiar. Have we met before?"

"I was part of a team that was attempting to locate a dangerous criminal here some years back."

LoLo flashed a crooked smile. "Oh my, a dangerous criminal. Did you catch him?"

"They did eventually, but not here."

"Was I cooperative?"

"You were—not that you had a choice not to be."

LoLo smiled again but his eyes were hard. "We *always* have a choice, Sheriff. It's just that so many choose not to exercise it. I could kill all of you right now . . . but I choose not to. See how that works?"

"I could say the same." Dillon glanced at the mirror behind the bar. Lighting came primarily from the candle chandelier that hung from the low ceiling in the middle of the room. The two men they had followed there were seated at a table behind them. Two more men were at the far end of the bar near the doors to the storage room and LoLo's office. They were both armed with semi-automatic rifles.

"How's that?" LoLo asked.

"We could kill all of you, but we choose not to."

LoLo's smile widened. "You could try."

Dillon grunted. "Funny, Bear said something very similar right before we came here."

LoLo held up his glass. "I guess it's true then—great minds really do think alike." He took a sip, set the glass down, and then nodded at Morning. "And who might you be?"

"Morning—Morning McGreevy."

"Lovely name that fits an equally lovely face." LoLo shifted toward Lucian. "And you?"

"Lucian Cross."

"What tribe?"

"Assiniboine."

"From the reservation up north?"

"No. I am, I *was*, an anthropology professor in North Dakota."

"I figured your story was something along those lines on account of how you talk."

"And how is that?"

"Educated," LoLo said as he poured more whiskey. "I actually have a bit of Assiniboine in me as well on my mother's side." He looked at Dillon. "My men told me you're the Richland County sheriff."

Dillon nodded. "That's right."

"That would make you Dillon Potts."

"How'd you know my name?"

"You're a cop. You do what you do, and I do what I do. I didn't manage to keep this place running for all of these years without knowing the names of those who might want to shut me down."

"Those days are long gone. We're just here for information."

"So I've been told."

Dillon told an abbreviated version of the encounter with the helicopter in Savage. When he finished, he folded his hands together atop the bar. "Well?"

"Well, what?" LoLo replied.

"Is that chopper being used by Vig?"

"Was it turbine or piston powered?"

Dillon shrugged. "How would I know?"

"By the sound. Was there a high-pitched whine?"

"I don't think so."

"Then it was most likely a piston-powered craft that runs off of aviation-grade fuel."

"Thanks for the lesson, but what I really want to know is if that chopper is Vig's or not."

LoLo started wiping the bar down with a towel. "If I were to tell you what I know regarding the chopper what do I get in return?"

"You want payment?"

"Unlike you Sheriff I didn't spend my life sucking off the public teat."

"Is that your way of trying to make stealing from others sound more noble?"

"Just tell us what you know," Morning said.

"He knows about the chopper," Lucian added. "That's why he was asking if it was turbine or piston powered. He wanted you to tell him what *kind* of chopper it is."

Morning glanced at Dillon. "Which means you've already given him something and he's given you nothing in return while still asking for more."

LoLo leaned back and scratched his nose. "If you keep disrespecting me with that tone in front of my men, I might be so inclined to make an example out of you."

"You could try," Morning said as she reached down to touch the rifle that rested against her leg.

LoLo picked up his glass. "I know you've all noticed the two men sitting in the back. Those guns would cut you down in seconds."

"No need for threats," Dillon replied. "A shootout between us would leave both sides damaged and I know you don't want that because sooner or later Vig is going to find her way here to take what you have and you're going to need every last one of you at full strength to fight back."

"That's true," LoLo said, "which is why I'm willing to offer a proposal that would benefit us both."

Dillon shook his head. "Not interested."

"None of us here are stupid, Sheriff."

"What's your point?"

"My point is quite simple—don't act stupid and listen to my proposal with an open mind."

"Go ahead," Morning said. "Say what you want to say."

LoLo poured a fresh splash of whiskey into Morning's glass. "Thank you." He stood back and crossed his arms over his chest. "I propose an alliance. Everyone these days is desperate for supplies and I'm the one, perhaps the *only* one, with the network in place to meet that demand. Ammo, weapons, dry goods, batteries, blankets, even fuel from time to time, I can help you to acquire all of those things."

Dillon pushed his glass toward LoLo. "And in return?"

"I want him"—LoLo pointed at Bear with one hand while pouring more whiskey into Dillon's glass with the other— "working for me."

"Absolutely not," Dillon replied.

"Oh?" LoLo tilted his head. "I wasn't aware you owned the rights to the bear."

"I don't."

"Then how do you know he doesn't want to work for me?"

"I assumed."

LoLo clicked his tongue. "Shouldn't *he* be the one to decide?"

"Maybe the both of you should stop talking about him like he's not actually sitting right here in front of you," Morning said.

Lucian chuckled.

Bear acted like he was writing something on the palm of his hand.

When LoLo went to reach under the bar Dillon drew his revolver. "Slow."

LoLo held up a pencil and a pad of paper. "Sheriff, if I wanted you dead it already would have happened. Now, please put your gun away before my men lose their patience with you. We're not fighting—we're negotiating. I would think you would know the difference."

Bear wrote while the others waited.

I'm not leaving Reagan.

"Who is Reagan?" LoLo asked.

"A girl he saved from some of Vig's road pirates," Morning answered.

LoLo's eyes widened. "Ah, I heard about that—stories of the bear wandering the countryside with a girl in tow. She's a young thing, yes?" When no one replied, he continued. "Bring her with you. I have no doubt we could put her to use here."

Bear roared as he grabbed LoLo by the throat and dragged him over the bar. The four other men raised their weapons and shouted for Bear to let him go. LoLo waved them away, gasping that he was okay.

"Don't," Dillon said as he gripped Bear's shoulder. "If you want to get back to Reagan this isn't the way to do it."

"Listen to your friend," LoLo croaked, his eyes bulging.

Bear let him go.

LoLo coughed as he rubbed his throat. He stood and then leaned against the bar. "You're every bit as strong as you look." When his men started to move toward him, he again waved them away. "I'm fine. Just a little misunderstanding." He glanced up at Bear. "I meant no harm regarding what I said about the girl. Look around. There are no whores here and certainly no children being turned out for the pleasure of others. We're not road pirate scum. I'm a businessman. I was offering her protection not enslavement."

Bear wrote some more.

My apologies.

"Accepted," LoLo said while still rubbing his neck. "I know well the atrocities taking place out there and if it's true you saved her from Vig's road pirates then I know exactly what it is you saved her from."

Was that Vig's chopper that we saw?

LoLo read the question and then nodded to the others as he returned to his place behind the bar. "I believe so. That's why I asked about the sound it made and the fuel it was likely using.

Some of my associates were monitoring a small private airport outside of Broadus a few months back."

"The one off of highway two-twelve," Dillon said.

"That's right. You know of it?"

"Been there a time or two."

"And you also likely know how valuable fuel has become. Aviation fuel even more so because you can drive an older vehicle with aviation fuel, but you can't power an aircraft with regular fuel—aircraft require much more octane or you risk stalling the engine and falling out of the sky."

"You intended to steal the aviation fuel and resell it."

"I prefer the term *secure* versus *steal*, but yes, Sheriff, that was our plan. Unfortunately, Vig's road pirates beat us to it. They descended on that little airport like locusts and took it for themselves and now we know why. We had no choice then but to move on to simpler and safer opportunities."

"The chopper we saw had a South Dakota National Guard emblem on it."

"Makes sense given Vig's strong presence there. She found the chopper but needed the fuel to fly it. Now that we've confirmed the chopper is most likely hers, we have ourselves a serious problem, thus my attempt to form an alliance with you."

"We didn't come here for an alliance. We came for information which you just gave us and for that I'm grateful."

"Vig is coming for you, Sheriff. And likely not long after that she'll be knocking on my door as well. She's insane you know—a bloodthirsty madwoman who won't stop until she controls everything by killing anyone who tries to stop her. We can help each other to weather that storm so that we might continue to survive."

"And how do you propose we do that?"

"Do you need ammunition?"

"You would just give away ammo? For someone who advises others not to be dumb that seems downright stupid."

"I'm not *giving* it away. Rather, consider it a downpayment."

Bear pulled the pad toward him and then wrote some more.

The stronger we are the more damage we do to Vig and the greater his chance of successfully defending himself against her.

"Huh," LoLo grunted. "He has it exactly right."

"We put up a stronger fight in Savage so that you'll have more time to prepare for Vig here," Dillon said.

"Do you have shotgun shells?" Morning asked.

"I do," LoLo answered.

"How many?"

"Enough."

"Enough for what?"

"To kill as many of Vig's road pirates as possible. Are you willing to do that?"

"I'll do it for me and my friends," Morning said, "but not for you."

"You never know—we might someday be friends."

"I doubt that."

"Do you want the shells or not?"

Morning nodded. "Sure, I'll take them."

LoLo tipped his head back and emptied his glass. "That's what I thought."

"Let me get this straight." Dillon scowled as he concentrated. "We're going to leave here today with a trunk full of ammo given to us on a promise to do damage to Vig on the off chance she makes her way to Savage. Do I have that about right?"

LoLo held up a finger. "Pretty much, but there is one condition."

"Here it is." Lucian sighed. "The true cost of making a deal with the devil."

"I may be a devil," LoLo said, "but you and I both know you're no angel. None who have managed to stay alive this long are."

"What's the condition?" Morning asked.

LoLo pointed at Bear. "Him. Now before I get dragged over the bar again let me explain. I'm not asking for the bear to join my little band of merry men permanently. I just need his help this one time. If he does that, and if we are successful, I split the take with you fifty-fifty."

"The take being the ammo you promised us." Lucian shook his head. "Unbelievable. If Bear doesn't help you then we get nothing."

"That's right," Lolo replied. "It's a shipment coming up from Fort Collins, Colorado being delivered to Vig's road pirates. I intend to intercept it long before it reaches her."

"That would be a declaration of war between you and Vig," Dillon said. "Why would you risk that?"

"That's why he wants Bear." Lucian waited until everyone was looking at him before he continued. "Bear is both a powerful weapon that can help ensure success but also an equally powerful distraction. He's not associated with LoLo. Vig has already put a price on Bear's head. She'll be focused on tracking him down and won't think to put both LoLo and Bear as working together."

Dillon glared at LoLo. "If that's true then you can take your offer of giving us some ammo and shove it up your—"

Bear tapped the top of the bar. "Yeah."

"You agree?" LoLo said.

Bear wrote out his answer.

One job. One time. We keep half of the ammo and weapons and you keep your word.

LoLo's smile did nothing to make him appear any more trustworthy. "I promise and as a gesture of goodwill I'll let you leave today with this." He reached under the bar and then brought out a box of shotgun shells. "There are four left." He pushed the box toward Morning. "Enjoy."

"When do you plan on intercepting Vig's delivery?" Dillon asked.

"My people will be in touch, Sheriff. You won't be waiting long."

Morning reached over the bar and grabbed hold of LoLo's wrist. "Don't you dare try to burn us. If anything happens to Bear, I'll be pumping these shotgun shells into your chest. Is that understood?"

"Feisty." LoLo's smile remained. "I like that. Perhaps it's *your* services I should be negotiating for."

"You couldn't afford me." Morning grabbed the box of shells. "Are we done here?"

Dillon stood. "I believe we are."

"Don't forget, Sheriff." LoLo poured himself another drink. "We'll be in touch." He raised his glass at Bear. "Soon."

Dillon made sure the others had already exited the room safely before he turned away from LoLo while half expecting to be shot in the back as he reached for the door. No shots were fired, but that didn't stop him from breathing a sigh of relief when the door closed behind him.

He couldn't wait to get back to Savage and as far away from LoLo's as possible.

15.
✦✧✦✧

Bear bent down, opened his arms wide, and scooped up a beaming Reagan after she sprinted across the field toward him. By the time the group had driven back to Savage the sun hung low in the sky and night was no more than an hour away. Dillon dropped the others off at Remington's ranch and then drove home, promising to check in with them the next day. Lucian had already gone down to the river to bathe, saying he was eager to get the stench of LoLo's off of him.

"I missed you," Reagan said before nuzzling her face into Bear's neck and hugging him tight. Bear lifted her up high and gave her entire body a playful shake before carefully setting her down. "It was fun hanging out with Mr. Wilkes though. We worked in the greenhouse, got some firewood, and walked to the river and checked the rabbit snares and when we were down there doing that, the dog came up to us and walked with us for a while. We call him Dog because Mr. Wilkes says that name still means something around here. His uncle Hap had a dog named Dog and Mr. Wilkes thinks maybe this new Dog is somehow related to the old Dog."

On and on Reagan talked, her sentences crashing into one another. Bear smiled and nodded, listening to every word while Morning walked beside them, quietly admiring how such a physically imposing mountain of a man was also so patient and considerate of those who were the most vulnerable.

"When I was worried about you not coming back," Reagan continued, "Mr. Wilkes said that worrying never did anyone a lick of good and that you would move heaven and earth to get back here to make sure I was okay, and I guess he was right because here you are. He seems pretty smart, and his horse sure likes him. Mr. Wilkes whistled and then Peanut ran all the way across the hill to him. It was really something." She looked up. "Did you have to move heaven and earth while you were on your trip?"

Bear shook his head.

"That's good. At least I think it's good. I don't know how anyone can actually move heaven and earth. I figured that's just something old people like to say."

"He did drag a man across a bar," Morning said. "It was pretty impressive."

"Really?" Reagan kept looking at Bear. "Why did you do that?"

Morning answered for Bear. "The man said something he shouldn't have, and Bear let him know."

By then Remington had walked out from the tent to greet their return. "Everyone back safe and sound?"

"We are," Morning answered. "There's a lot to tell you though."

"I figured. A trip to LoLo's is bound to be interesting at its best and deadly at its worst. Glad to see you all were able to experience the interesting version."

Reagan tapped Remington's leg. "Bear dragged a man across the bar because he said something he shouldn't have."

"Who was that?" Remington asked.

"LoLo," Morning replied. "Grabbed him by the throat and rag-dolled him."

"No kidding." Remington chuckled. "You actually did that to LoLo in his own place and somehow managed to walk out of there alive?"

"He wanted something from us. More specifically, he wanted something from Bear." Morning described LoLo's plan to intercept the ammunition delivery that would soon be on its way to Vig.

Remington scowled. "I don't like the sound of that."

"I'm not too crazy about the idea myself."

"How was he?" Remington asked. "LoLo I mean."

"Greasy."

"Not someone you'd want to do too much hanging out with?"

"Hell no." Morning handed Remington his rifle. "Thanks for letting me borrow it." She showed him the box of shells. "My shotgun is back in business. Speaking of which how did it go here?"

"Fine," Remington replied. "Real quiet, the way I like it." He tousled Reagan's hair. "And this is one great young lady. We worked hard but had fun doing it and she was a big help. I'll be starting supper soon. You two hungry?"

Bear slapped his stomach and nodded.

"Starving," Morning said. "What's on the menu?"

"Boiled potatoes with a touch of salt and pepper and fried rabbit. How's that sound?"

"Perfect."

"I'll get the fire going."

"I'll help," Reagan shouted right before running into the tent.

Remington chuckled. "All that energy. Hard to believe I was ever that young."

Bear stopped, handed Remington a note, and then stuck out his hand.

Thank you for taking such good care of her while I was gone.

The two men shook. "It was my pleasure," Remington said. "I mean that. She's a peach. Knowing what I know about what she went through I'm amazed at how well adjusted she is. It seems she's even managing to recapture some semblance of the innocence that was taken from her." He put his other hand over Bear's. "God bless you for what you've done for that child."

Morning nodded. "I'll second that. We're very fortunate to have the both of you with us."

Bear struggled to get out the word thank you several times. It didn't matter that he couldn't say it clearly. Morning and Remington understood regardless. He was one of them now—a citizen of Savage.

The fire was started, and the meal was prepared. Lucian entered the tent just as darkness covered Vaughn's Hill. He sat next to Remington, gratefully accepted his plate of food, and proceeded to pick at it while staring at the fire.

"You okay?" Remington asked.

Lucian flinched, shaken out of whatever was preoccupying him, and then he sighed. "Lost in my own thoughts I suppose." He took a bite of food. "The rabbit is especially good tonight."

Morning stared at Lucian until he finally noticed. "What is it?"

"Nothing. I'm fine."

"Go on," Morning continued. "Spit it out."

Lucian put down his plate. "I said I'm—"

"I heard what you said." Morning's eyes continued to bore into Lucian's. "I just don't believe you. Was it the trip to LoLo's?"

"Actually, yes."

"What happened?"

"A realization."

"Now you have *me* wondering," Remington said. "You can't put this horse back in the barn now. We all want to know what's on your mind."

Lucian wrapped his arms around his knees. "I'm thinking of leaving here."

Remington swallowed the last of his meal. "Why? Did we do something wrong?"

"No, nothing like that. It was actually something LoLo said."

Bear held up his notepad.

You want to go to Fort Peck.

Lucian's mouth dropped open. "How did you know?"

LoLo mentioned your tribe—the Assiniboine. That's where they're located.

"I have a confession to make. I lied when I said I wasn't from Fort Peck. I was born there. My family's history at that reservation is a long one. As a teenager I only wanted to get away. It was all I could think of. I had no love for my people—only shame and embarrassment. I thought them weak, simple-minded, and incapable of imagining a world beyond the borders of that reservation. It was a place corrupted by those like LoLo—degenerates who used their American Indian heritage as an excuse for their deplorably dangerous and destructive behaviors." Lucian's head fell toward his chest. "Or so I thought."

"Why didn't you like your people?" Reagan asked.

Lucian gave her a thin, pained smile. "Arrogance, resentment, the belief I was intended for bigger and better things. The answer to that question is a very long list indeed and something I now look back on with such regret. For what are we doing here today but living as simply and efficiently as my family did those many years ago? There is no shame in poverty. My people are survivors of a generational genocide and yet in my youth I saw only what I wanted to see and not what I needed to see or what they deserved me to see."

"I doubt there are many who get to our age who don't understand exactly what you mean," Remington said. "Regret? I have enough to fill an entire valley with."

Morning poked at the fire with a stick. "You think there might still be survivors at Fort Peck?"

"I do," Lucian replied. "LoLo all but confirmed it."

Morning put the stick down. "What will you do there?"

"Help others as best I can and hopefully reacquaint myself with the past and possibly find the person I could have been before it's too late. The world is now being reborn. The old world is gone. The new one begins. Why shouldn't I attempt to do the same?"

"It'll be a long walk to get there," Remington said.

"I'll manage. I made it this far."

Remington nodded. "That you did. When do you plan on going?"

"First thing in the morning."

"That soon?"

"Yes, but please know how grateful I am for your hospitality. You have all been so kind."

"Wasn't nothing. You seem like good people, and I was raised to lend a hand to those who could use it. That has always been the Savage way. And who knows? Maybe you'll return to us someday."

"I hope so," Lucian said.

Reagan got up, walked around the fire, and then hugged Lucian around his shoulders. "I'll miss you."

Lucian's smiling eyes threatened tears. "I'll miss you too," he whispered.

Not long after, as the fire's flames flickered, nearly all of them were already asleep except for Lucian. He lay on his back with his hands folded on his chest, looking up at the darkness and wondering if his decision to leave was really the right one. He had fled the reservation as a young man because he yearned to reinvent himself. Now he was an old man returning to that same reservation hoping to reinvent himself yet again.

By the time the first glimpses of daylight filtered into the tent Lucian was already up and ready to go. Remington gave him both water and food for his journey. They all walked outside together and looked down at the shimmering crooked finger that was the river's path out of the valley. Lucian intended to follow that path north until he reached the borders of the Fort Peck Reservation. He shook hands with Bear, Remington, and Morning and then happily welcomed another warm hug from Reagan.

"I do wish we could spare a weapon for you to take with you," Remington said. "I'd feel better knowing you could properly protect yourself out there."

Lucian adjusted his backpack. "The land will provide all I need—including my safety. It shouldn't take more than a week to get to Fort Peck." He straightened and then hooked his thumbs under the straps of his backpack. "And again, thank you."

Remington, Bear, Morning and Reagan stood at the edge of the hillside and watched as Lucian made his way down to the river. "Do you think we'll see him again?" Reagan asked.

"For some reason I think we will," Morning answered.

"Why is that?" Remington wondered.

"Just a hunch."

Remington shrugged. "Maybe you're right." He turned toward her. "What are your plans for today?"

"Going to head home for a bit to make sure everything is okay there. I should be back by the afternoon."

Reagan stood between Bear and Morning. She reached up and held both of their hands. "Can we come see your home?"

"Sure, if Bear wants to."

"He does," Reagan said. "I can tell."

If Bear's skin wasn't dark, they would have surely seen him blush. He gave Reagan a quick nod to let her know he was okay with going to Morning's place.

Reagan smiled up at Morning. "I bet you have a nice home."

"I like to think so."

"I'm excited to see it."

Morning glanced at Bear. He pretended not to notice.

"There he is," Remington said.

Lucian had reached the river. He stopped, looked back at them, and then waved. Remington and the others waved back.

"You said you're sure about seeing him again," Remington continued. "Are you just as sure about him being truthful regarding why he's really making the trip to Fort Peck?"

"No," Morning admitted. "I'm not."

"Don't trust him?"

"Not sure. Do you?"

"You know, I haven't been able to decide that just yet."

Morning knew exactly what Remington meant by that.

She felt the same.

16.
◆✧◆✧

Three days later.

"Who's that down there?" Reagan pointed at two men walking through the field between Remington's house and Vaughn's Hill.

Remington turned toward the tent and whistled. Bear, somehow already sensing trouble, stepped out carrying his sledgehammer, looking more than a little like a dark-skinned version of the Norse God of Thunder.

"We have visitors," Remington said.

Bear stood next to him and then looked down. He held up his thumb and forefinger in the shape of an L.

"That's LoLo?"

Bear nodded.

Reagan pointed again. "The sheriff." Dillon's cruiser was driving slowly toward the house.

"Bet he's already noticed LoLo and the other man walking through the field," Remington said. "This could get interesting. How about I go grab the rifle and then keep watch from up here while you go meet them in the field? I'd prefer we keep them away from the hill if we can. The less they know about what we have the better. The sheriff will no doubt have your back should you need it." Remington looked Bear up and down. "Not that you'd have any trouble taking care of yourself."

Bear nodded and started to make his way down the path to the field while Remington and Reagan went back into the tent to get the rifle. As soon as Bear started crossing the field LoLo and the other man stopped.

"I'm not armed," LoLo shouted. "And neither is he."

"Sit tight," Dillon replied as he walked toward them from the other side with his hand on his gun.

"Look at the size of him," the man with LoLo said. He was in his thirties, short and powerfully built, with a full beard and stringy dirty blond hair that hung down to his wide shoulders. "He's huge."

"Told you," LoLo whispered. "Not too many have gotten to see the bear this close and then lived to tell the tale."

Bear strode through the grass holding the sledgehammer in front of him while looking as if the slightest provocation would have him swinging it at the men's heads.

"This is Jacob," LoLo said. "He's the one who has been keeping an eye on that shipment I was telling you about."

Jacob stepped back as Bear came closer. "You mind lowering that brain basher? I've heard the stories."

Bear stopped.

"What are you doing here?" Dillon asked.

LoLo turned around. "Hello again, Sheriff Potts."

Dillon kept his hand on his gun. "Drop the phony pleasantries and answer the question."

"Just keeping up my end of the bargain."

"You mean the shipment?"

"That's right. It's ready to be taken."

"Where?"

"I'll show you," Jacob answered. "Tomorrow night."

Dillon frowned. "That soon? We haven't had any time to prepare."

"You have until tomorrow. How much more time do you need?"

"You're sure about the location?"

Jacob appeared offended by the question. "I guarantee it. We block the road, come in strong, and take it."

"How far?"

"About an hour's drive south of here."

Dillon glanced behind him. "You two come alone?"

LoLo's sly grin indicated they hadn't. "I can't tell you *all* my secrets, Sheriff."

"I know you didn't walk all this way."

"No, we didn't."

"So, what got you here?"

"Motorcycles."

"Where are they?"

"Hidden."

"Why?"

"In case you decided you wanted them for yourself."

Dillon grunted. "You worried that *I* would be the one stealing from *you*? I'm pretty sure it should be the other way around."

LoLo looked up at Vaughn's Hill. "I've heard the stories about this ranch—the fight that took place here with the feds. You were part of that weren't you, Sheriff?"

"Sure."

"How many guns do you have pointing down at me from that hill right now?"

Dillon shrugged. "Can't tell you *all* my secrets, LoLo."

"I do have a favor to ask."

"Go on."

"We'll need to fuel up the motorcycles for the trip tomorrow."

"You want to use my gas? For free?"

"Come now, Sheriff," LoLo said. "Your half of the shipment will make it more than worth it."

"I'll bring you a can."

"No need to go to the trouble. I'm happy to drive out to where you pump the gas."

Dillon's eyes narrowed. "I bet you are. You want to see exactly where it is and how I get the pumps to work. I don't think so. Like I said, I'll bring a can. Either that works for you, or it doesn't."

"The can it is then."

"I have another question I'd like you to answer for me."

LoLo cocked his head. "Yes?"

"The people moving the shipment—Vig's people. What happens to them?"

"They die."

"There's no other way?"

"Not unless you want them going back to Vig and telling her what happened."

"I'm not in the business of killing people."

LoLo's sly smile returned. "I'm afraid you are now. Take comfort that it's for a good reason."

"What reason would that be?"

"Survival, Sheriff—your survival and the survival of those you care about. You know as well as any that weapons and ammunition are the difference between life and death in these troubled times we now live in. If it isn't Vig who shows up here to take Savage it'll be someone else. Your share of the shipment will go a long way toward protecting you and your friends." LoLo looked up at the hill again. "Where are the others—Lucian and Morning?"

"Lucian left."

LoLo scowled. "Why?"

"He had somewhere he wanted to be. And don't ask me where because it's none of your business."

"You don't know that, Sheriff. What if he's running off to inform Vig about our plans to take her shipment?"

"His leaving had nothing to do with that."

"How can you be so sure?"

"Guess you'll just have to trust me."

"And Morning? Where is she?"

"Again—none of your business."

"Pity, I was looking forward to seeing her again. Will she be joining us tomorrow night?"

"That'll be up to her."

Jacob elbowed LoLo and then dipped his head toward something behind them. LoLo looked and then smiled. "Ah, such impeccable timing. Her ears must be burning."

Morning was on her horse coming toward the others with her shotgun strapped to the saddle. "Everything okay?" she asked.

"So good to see you again," LoLo replied.

Morning ignored him as she focused on Dillon and Bear.

"We're fine," Dillon said.

"Is this about the shipment?" Morning asked.

If LoLo's eyes could eat they would have already devoured Morning in a few ravenous bites. "Yes, we're here about the shipment. Our plan is to take it tomorrow night. Will you be joining us?"

"Haven't decided."

"I welcome your help. You strike me as a very capable woman."

Morning straightened in the saddle, placed both hands on the saddle horn, and then glared down at LoLo. "Here's the thing. I don't like you. We're not friends and we never will be. The less you talk to me, the less you look at me, the better for the both of us. And that goes for your pet there too. Is that understood?"

Jacob started to move toward Morning, but LoLo put a hand on his chest. He smiled and nodded. "Understood."

"You're just going to let her talk to us like that?" Jacob snarled.

"We're guests," LoLo answered. He tilted his head up and inhaled. "I like it here. The tall grass, the hill and the river behind it, it's so serene—truly a place worth fighting for."

Dillon's hand remained on his gun. "Are we done?"

"Until tomorrow night, Sheriff. I assume you'll be driving your cruiser?"

"Makes sense."

"You can follow us."

"You'll be on your motorcycles?"

"Correct. We'll all meet here first. Oh, and please remember to bring the gas you promised."

"I hope you're right about the shipment. We'll be very disappointed if you're not." Dillon tipped his head toward Bear. "Including him."

"Ah yes, the infamous Bear."

"You seem to know more than most about Vig," Morning said. "How much is she offering for Bear these days?"

LoLo looked up at her and then over at Bear. "Apparently not enough because here he stands as free and fearsome as ever."

"How much?" Morning repeated.

"The way I understand it," Jacob said, "is that she's willing to consider a name-your-price option, meaning she'll pay whatever is required to get her hands on him."

Morning leaned forward in the saddle. "Which is more than enough for someone like you to try to earn that reward."

"Me?" Jacob shook his head. "Nah, I want to see Vig cut down not made stronger. I have no quarrel with the bear. Far from it. Give me an army of a hundred more just like him and I'd eliminate Vig once and for all. I've heard the stories. That she-devil needs to be—"

LoLo cleared his throat. "We'll be going now. It's not right that we take up any more of your precious time in this beautiful place."

"Need an escort back to your motorcycles?" Dillon asked.

"That won't be necessary. Besides, I wouldn't want you to know where we hid them."

"That was actually the point of my offer."

LoLo nodded. "I know. This suspicious dance between us is rather fun don't you think?"

"Not really."

"I trust you'll be able to put your suspicions aside so that we can successfully take Vig's shipment from her."

"Don't worry." Dillon paused and then continued. "We'll do what needs to be done."

"I'm counting on it. You do know this will be good for the both of us."

"So you keep saying."

"Because I'm not convinced that you actually believe it."

"What I believe or don't believe isn't your concern."

LoLo's eyes widened. "Oh, but it *is*, Sheriff."

"I'm going to give you some advice," Morning said. "When we're done with this shipment business, you don't ever come back here. Return to that shack in the woods and leave us the hell alone."

"I'll take that advice under consideration." LoLo started to walk away. "See you all tomorrow. Let's go, Jacob."

The two walked down the long drive until eventually they were out of sight. Morning let out the reins so her horse could nibble on the grass. "I want to say something, and I hope the both of you listen."

Dillon and Bear exchanged glances. "Let's hear it," Dillon said.

"I don't like this." Morning shook her head. "I don't like it one bit."

"I feel the same." Dillon looked at Bear. "What about you?"

Bear started writing.

I gave LoLo my word, but if you don't want to go with me, I totally understand.

"I can't let you take that kind of risk by yourself." Morning tilted her head at Dillon. "And I'm betting the sheriff feels the same."

I can handle LoLo. I'll do what needs to be done and return here with the weapons and ammo.

"*If* there are weapons and ammo." Morning ran her fingers through her horse's mane. "We can't trust a single word that comes out of that man's mouth."

Then he'll pay a price for lying to us.

"Is that right?" Dillon sighed. "You think it's wise to be starting a war with LoLo's crew while we have the threat of Vig literally hovering over our heads?"

There won't be a war. It'll be over too soon for that.

"You can't kill the world, Bear, because sooner or later it's going to bite back. You're likely on borrowed time as it is. The difference now, though, is that you now have something besides yourself to live for. There's a girl up on that hill who would be devasted if something happened to you."

We need those weapons and ammo so we can prepare for what's coming.

"Sure, but like Morning says, we don't even know if this alleged shipment LoLo has us running after actually exists."

"It could be a setup," Morning added. "LoLo hands you over to Vig, collects the reward, and slithers back to the hole he came from."

I know the risk and I'm willing to take it.

"Okay, if your mind is made up then that means we're willing to take it with you." Dillon kicked at the dirt with the toe of his boot. "We do this together."

I'll get us back here safe. I promise.

"I believe you believe that."

I don't just believe it—I know it.

A dog barked in the distance. All three turned toward the sound. It was the same dog as before, winding its way through the tall grass. Dillon's melancholy smile matched the faraway look in his eyes. "Funny how the past comes back to visit with you," he muttered just loud enough for the others to hear. "I swear I wouldn't be the least bit surprised if I looked up to see old Hap following that dog through the field." His face tightened. "God, I miss how the world used to be and all those I once shared it with."

"Amen to that," Morning said. "There's not a day goes by, well, you know. . ."

Dillon's shoulders slumped as his head dropped and he closed his eyes. "I sure do."

17.
✦✧✦✧

Morning McGreevy looked up at the five cream-colored cooing doves that had long made her barn their home. The number of doves matched the number of graves behind the barn, the most recent one being for her beloved husband, Waylon.

"You've lived here a long time?" Reagan asked.

"I have." Reagan's forced smile was an attempt to hide the still raw wound left by Waylon's passing a decade earlier. "I first came to Savage when I was a college student and then met a handsome young cowboy at a party. We fell in love, got married, made a family, and this was our home for many wonderful years. Unlike Remington's place, which was primarily an animal ranch when his uncle Hap lived there, Waylon and I turned this property into a successful produce farm. Year after year, no matter the challenges brought on by weather or the economy, he somehow managed to produce some of the most beautiful crops in the area."

"It's nice."

"Yes, it is."

"Then why do you sound so sad?"

The doves continued to coo. Morning wiped away tears and shrugged. "I don't even know anymore. Some days it feels like all the happy has been drained out of me. On the *really* bad days I can't even remember what happy feels like."

Bear, who had been standing quietly beside her, put his arm around Morning's shoulders. She stiffened at first but then relaxed, enjoying the sensation of his warm power around her.

"Why did you come to Savage?" Reagan asked.

This time Morning's smile was genuine. "I found my great-grandfather Cy's journal. Reading it allowed me to experience the world through his eyes. Savage was his home, and his words and experiences became my compass. I was drawn here. The land, the dirt, it spoke to me, and I liked what it had to say. For the first time in my life, I felt like I knew who I was and what I wanted to be."

"I wonder if I'll ever find out who or what I want to be."

"You will. It just takes some time."

Reagan bent down, picked up a long blade of grass, and squeezed it between her fingers. "What if I run out of time before that happens?"

"Why would you think that? Your life has barely gotten started." Reagan remained quiet. "Hey," Morning said, "it doesn't matter what happened to you before. The only thing that matters now is what the future holds."

"I guess so." Reagan dropped the blade of grass. "Can I see where your family is buried?"

"Sure. Follow me." Morning stood between Bear and Reagan and took their hands into hers. "It's in a little clearing behind the barn." The path to the burial site had recently been cut back. Morning said it was a constant battle in the spring and summer to keep the weeds at bay. "The oldest of the graves are Temple and Branna McGreevy. They came to Savage from Ireland around eighteen-eighty and carved out a home here with their bare hands. The next grave is Cy McGreevy, their son and my great-grandfather. Next to him is his daughter, my grandmother, Candace." Morning stiffened as she looked down at the fifth grave marker. "And that's my husband's grave."

"I'm sorry about Waylon," Reagan whispered.

Agitated by the arrival of yet more tears, Morning wiped them away with the back of her hand. "Thank you. He was a wonderful man—strong but patient. A good husband and a good father to our son Cy, who is, I hope, safe at his home in the San Juan Islands in Washington State. I plan to visit him there someday when things settle down."

"You named your son after your great-grandfather?"

"We did. As I mentioned before it was Cy's journal that brought me here, which in turn made everything that followed possible. I was blessed to have many wonderful years with Waylon. Too many people go their whole lives not knowing the kind of happiness we got to experience turning this old farm into a home and thriving business."

Morning turned and pointed to a large stone in the field some fifty yards from the graves. "Waylon was going to use the tractor to move that boulder over to here. He said it would make the perfect sitting rock for me. He knew how I loved to come out here with my coffee in the early morning to think about things as the sun started to come up. He wanted to give me a place to sit, but he also wanted it to be something natural from the property. He was always doing things like that—being so thoughtful and wanting to make me happy. If Waylon wasn't working the fields, he was working on something else. That man didn't know the meaning of the word relax. He always had to be doing something and he loved all his projects both great and small. He was happiest when he was doing something for others. Then the accident happened and there that rock remains, a reminder that Waylon is gone and so many things he had planned on doing around here were left undone. I was almost forty when he died and now I'm nearly fifty and I still miss our life together so much that sometimes it hurts to breathe let alone get out of bed."

Bear strode through the grass toward the stone.

Morning called out after him. "What are doing?"

"He's going to move it for you," Reagan said, smiling.

"I don't think so. That thing has to weigh almost four hundred pounds." Morning jogged to catch up to Bear. "Seriously, you don't need to bother. I don't want you to hurt yourself."

Bear reached the rock, pushed the grass away from it, and then ran his hands over its rough surface.

"Stop," Morning said. "It's too big. You'll break your back."

Reagan shook her head. "No, he won't. One time, I watched him push a tree over a creek so we could walk across it and the tree was bigger than that rock."

"Bear." Morning nudged his massive chest. "I appreciate the gesture, I really do, but this isn't necessary."

"C'mon," Reagan said. "Let him try. He wants to do something nice for you."

"It's too heavy," Morning repeated.

Bear gently moved Morning away, took a deep breath, crouched low, and then wrapped his arms as far as he could around the stone. The veins in his neck and forehead looked like they might rip through his skin as he grunted and grimaced.

"Fine, see for yourself. You might be the biggest man I've ever met, but that rock isn't going anywhere."

The layers of thick muscle in Bear's upper body flexed and rippled from the strain. He shut his eyes, tilted his head back, and growled. The rock moved. Despite the cool temperature sweat covered his face and soaked his dark beard. He lifted the rock higher until he was able to partially lay it against his chest and stomach.

"Told you," Reagan proudly said.

"Lifting it is one thing. Now he has to try to actually move it."

Bear gritted his teeth, grunted some more, and then took a step.

"You're going to kill yourself," Morning declared, but her eyes said something very different. She was in awe of Bear's incredible display of strength. "Careful," she added as he took another step.

"Where?" Bear gasped.

"This way." Morning and Reagan moved in front of him. It took nearly ten minutes for Bear to walk those fifty yards. Morning pointed to an area directly in front of the grave markers. "There," she said.

Bear made certain Reagan was safely standing far enough away and then he dropped the stone with a heavy thud that shook the ground beneath their feet. He put his hands on the rock and leaned over it, gulping air while drops of sweat rolled down his face.

"You're bleeding." Reagan tapped the top of Bear's hand. "See?"

Bear straightened and then turned his hands over. The palms had been rubbed raw. The right hand had a gash. He bent down, wiped his hand on the grass, looked over at Morning and then tried his best to say the word sorry for getting blood on her sitting stone.

"Don't you dare think you need to apologize to me," Morning replied. "Watching you move that thing was nothing short of amazing. I have a first aid kit in the house. We don't want that hand of yours getting infected. Sit tight. I'll be right back."

Reagan watched Morning leave and then she looked up at Bear. "She didn't think you could do it, but I *knew* you could. You're probably the strongest man in the whole world." Her face turned serious. "Does your hand hurt?"

Bear shook his head.

"Morning seems like such a nice lady," Reagan continued. "And pretty too." She paused. "Do you think she's pretty?" Bear sat on the rock and pretended not to hear the question. Reagan laid her head on his shoulder and yawned. "This place makes me tired. Funny how some places do that."

"Okay," Morning said upon her return. "Let's have a look." She took Bear's hand, silently amazed by the size of it. "I'm going to clean it with an alcohol swab so it's going to sting." If it did, Bear didn't show it. He sat watching as Morning carefully cleaned the shallow wound and then taped some gauze over it. "That should do. I'm guessing you're one of those people who heals quick." She put the first aid kit down. "You mind if I sit with you?"

Bear scooted over.

"This is nice." Morning stretched her legs out in front of her. "It's exactly what Waylon wanted to do for me—a place to sit and think in the presence of those who made my life possible."

Reagan looked down at Waylon's grave marker. "Why is it that both you and Mr. Wilkes have family graves on your properties?"

Morning took off her cowboy hat, ran her fingers through her hair, and then pulled the hat back down over her eyes. "It's an Irish thing."

"What's that mean?"

"The Irish know the pain of subjugation. It's in our DNA."

"I don't understand."

Bear arched his brows. He wanted Morning to continue.

"You know about the terrible slavery that took place long ago in America, right?"

Reagan nodded. "The black people from Africa."

"Correct. That version of slavery existed long before we were the United States and lasted for about two hundred and fifty years."

"What's that have to do with the Irish?"

Morning enjoyed seeing someone as young as Reagan being so inquisitive and willing to ask questions. "I'm getting there. Did you know that Ireland was occupied by Great Britain for more than six hundred years?"

"That's a long time."

"A *very* long time and the Irish people suffered terribly for it. Tens of thousands were forced onto ships and sent away to work in places as far away as the Caribbean. Families were broken up. Those who spoke out against the British were jailed, tortured, or even put to death. Their property was seized and their businesses shut down. They could be beaten for doing nothing more than speaking in their native tongue."

"That's horrible."

"Yes, it was, but then it got even worse. In eighteen forty-five a deadly famine swept across Ireland that lasted for seven long years. It was so bad people took to eating dirt to survive. One out of every five Irish starved to death, more than a million in total, many of them children. During this time English soldiers forced thousands of families off of their lands at gunpoint. They took their homes and their food from them and then did nothing to help as they died in the streets. So, you see, the Irish have an instinctive inclination to fight for their land. This is something that has been developed in them over generations. As a people the Irish don't complain about the past so much as learn from it and when they came to America, they did so with an understanding, born from hundreds of years of oppression, of just how important freedom is to all of us."

"Why are there so many Irish in Savage?"

"For a time, the land out here was free and the opportunity to make your own way considerable. That's all the Irish ever wanted—opportunity. So, they moved across America and settled in places like this. The Irish loved what this country used to be because they helped to build it and then defend it when needed—people like Temple and Branna McGreevy, my great-grandfather Cy McGreevy, and Remington's great-uncle, Hap Wilkes."

Reagan frowned as she looked down at the grave markers. "I wish people didn't have to die. I would have liked to have met your family."

Morning put her hands over her knees as she leaned forward. "You're right about all of us dying some day, but you want to know what's a lot sadder than that?" Her voice lowered. "The ones who never learn to be alive while they're here. They get trapped in routine and conformity and never have the courage to break away and be their own person."

"What's conformity?"

"Doing something just because everyone else is doing it."

"Like when everyone was getting the shots that made them sick?"

Morning nodded. "*Exactly*. We need to learn from that if we are to survive. When people allow themselves to fear without reason, they make themselves vulnerable to being made to do just about anything."

"I don't want to be one of those people."

"You're strong, Reagan—a lot stronger than you realize."

"Strong like you?"

"Stronger."

"I don't think so."

Bear held up his notepad.

Those who would give up essential liberty to purchase a little temporary safety deserve neither liberty nor safety. -Ben Franklin

"Wise man," Morning said.

Reagan mouthed the words as she read them. "Why didn't more people fight back like you and Bear and Mr. Wilkes do?"

Morning shrugged. "I wish I knew. I guess at some point we forgot who we were and where we came from. The schools stopped teaching about it. Parents stopped living by example. Our history was erased and then replaced with propaganda that was meant to control minds rather than helping to shape them. Everything became a lie and a manipulation, but most didn't seem to care. They had their phones, their video games, their mindless entertainment, and nothing else mattered."

"It's like the Ben Franklin quote," Reagan said. "They had what they thought was temporary safety and didn't care about losing their essential liberty."

"That's right. We let your generation down, Reagan. Those people right there." Morning pointed at the graves. "They never would have allowed this to happen. I don't care what anyone else says. I know that to be true."

Reagan squeezed Morning's hand. "It's an Irish thing."

Morning laughed. It felt good and she was grateful to Reagan for it. She put her other arm around Bear's waist. "I'd say we three make a pretty darn good team."

They sat on the rock for a while, enjoying the sounds and smells of a crisp, beautiful Eastern Montana day. Eventually Morning said they should be getting back to Vaughn's Hill. Bear scooped Reagan up and put her on his shoulders as they walked the path back to the other side of the barn.

"Hi," Reagan said as she waved at something.

"Who are you waving at?" Morning asked.

"Him." Reagan pointed toward the house that was at the end of the short drive that separated it and the barn.

Morning looked over at the covered front porch. "A man?"

Reagan nodded. "Don't you see him?"

"There's no one there." Morning's eyes narrowed. "Are you playing a joke on me?"

"No." Reagan's brow furrowed as she pointed again. "It's a man in a cowboy hat. He's leaning against the railing smoking a pipe and he's looking right at you."

Bear stopped, glanced at Morning, looked at the house, and then shook his head.

"You can't see him either?" Reagan asked.

Morning wanted so badly to see what Reagan was seeing. "Cy smoked a pipe," she murmured.

"Bye-bye." Reagan waved. "He went back in the house."

"What did he look like?"

"Proud."

Morning frowned. *"Proud?"*

"Of you."

"I don't understand."

Reagan shrugged. "Maybe it's an Irish thing."

Morning continued walking. "Yeah, maybe." She looked back one more time. The porch remained empty, the house still and dark, and yet she wondered if Reagan had somehow seen a version of her great-grandfather Cy. She understood better than most how such a thing might be possible, having experienced something very similar when she was reading through Cy's journal all those years ago.

There were only four doves sitting together at the top of the barn cooing softly as they watched Morning, Bear, and Reagan leave. The fifth dove was suddenly absent. Clouds moved slowly across the sky, temporarily blocking out the sun and casting the property in shadow while the branches of the surrounding trees creaked in the wind. From inside Morning's home, on the other side of the kitchen window that overlooked the barnyard, could be seen the faint orange-red glow of a tobacco pipe burning on and off like the slow, purposeful blinking of an eye.

Reagan was right.

Cy was very proud of his great-granddaughter Morning's fighting spirit.

It was an Irish thing.

18.

✦✧✦✧

"Keep your eyes open for any signs of trouble."

"From LoLo?" Morning asked.

Dillon nodded as he made sure the pair of motorcycle taillights remained visible in front of him. It wasn't yet dark, but it would be soon. "I have a hard time believing he'd come all the way out here with just himself and Jacob. Not when he's attempting to snatch something so valuable from Vig herself."

"It does seem bold."

"I'd say stupid, but LoLo isn't that. At least not in the conventional sense of the word."

"You think he'd actually try to double-cross us?"

"I'd wager it has crossed his mind."

Bear sat in the backseat of the cruiser listening to the conversation. They had been driving for nearly an hour, following LoLo and Jacob to the place LoLo promised would be the perfect spot to take the shipment of weapons and ammunition from Vig.

Dillon pointed to a sign on the side of the road. "The town of Wibaux. I was down this way last year. There used to be five or six hundred people living around here."

"And now?"

"Dead, gone—it's the same old story."

"The damn vaccine."

Dillon's expression was grim. "The damn vaccine."

The motorcycles slowed. Dillon did the same, making sure to keep at least fifty yards between the cruiser and them.

Morning held tightly to the shotgun pointed at the floorboard that rested between her legs. "Is this it?"

"We're about to find out. Like I said earlier, be prepared for anything and everything." Dillon glanced in the rearview mirror to see if they were being followed. Then he looked at Bear. "You ready back there?"

Bear gave a thumbs up. His eyes indicated no emotion, his face unreadable, like he might either kill someone, take a nap, or be content to do both.

"Come on," LoLo said while standing on the side of the road next to his motorcycle. "We need to go over some details." Both he and Jacob were holding pistols.

Dillon turned off the cruiser, checked the trunk latch, and then got out with his hand resting on the butt of his revolver. Morning got out as well while holding the shotgun in front of her.

LoLo cocked his head. "What about the big fella?"

"He's chicken." Jacob smirked. "All muscle but no hustle."

Dillon looked back. Bear remained in the car.

"Well?" LoLo said. "What's he doing?"

"I figure a man as big as he is does whatever the hell he wants," Dillon replied.

"For our plan to work he needs to be seen."

"And what plan is that?"

Jacob rolled his eyes. "I told you they'd be trouble."

LoLo gave Dillon an icy smile. "You aren't trouble are you, Sheriff?"

"Not unless I need to be."

"The shipment will be coming this way soon."

"Uh-huh."

"I need to explain the role you and the others are to play for this to work."

"I'm not much for playing *roles*, LoLo, and we're not your dancing monkeys. You tell me where you want us to be and what you want us to do. If we agree, fine. If not, we'll have to figure it out and then go from there."

LoLo half turned to look behind him. "Note how flat this stretch of road is. It's all open spaces. We'll see the headlights from miles away. You'll park your cruiser in the middle of the road with the hood up and the lights on."

"Like it broke down?" Dillon asked.

"Exactly."

"Seems a bit obvious don't you think? What if they just drive around and leave us standing here like idiots?"

"They won't."

"How do you know that?"

"I've been doing this kind of thing for a very long time, Sheriff."

"Being a criminal, you mean."

"Watch your mouth," Jacob snarled.

"It's fine," LoLo cooed. "The sheriff is nervous is all."

"Nervous?" Dillon shook his head. "More like suspicious."

LoLo shrugged. "I can't control how you choose to think of me. Far more important to the task at hand is if the bear will be joining us or not. Why is he still in the backseat of your car? Time is wasting."

Morning had been quietly watching the exchange between LoLo, Jacob, and Dillon. She couldn't yet put her finger on it, but something felt off. "There are three of us and only two of you," she said. "For someone who just said how long they've been doing this sort of thing, well, that strikes me as a little odd."

"We live in odd times." LoLo looked up. "It's almost dark. We need to go over the plan."

Morning raised the shotgun. "Look at you two practically standing shoulder to shoulder like that. I could spray you with one shot. Might not kill you right off, but it would sure hurt like hell. Now answer my question. Why is it just the two of you? We followed you close and there was no sign of anyone else around. Maybe you had them come out here earlier. And maybe they're watching us right now, waiting for your signal."

Jacob pointed his pistol at Morning. "Don't threaten me."

"This isn't a threat. If I wanted to shoot you, I would have. All I'm doing now is asking questions."

Bear got out of the car with the sledgehammer slung over his shoulder.

LoLo's eyes widened. "Ah, the bear finally makes an appearance. Shall we get to it then?"

"Go on," Dillon replied as Morning lowered her shotgun.

"Move the car into the middle of the road as I said," LoLo continued. "Have the woman stand—"

"My name is Morning."

"Have *Morning* stand near the front of the car with the hood up. Don't let them see your weapon. As for the sheriff and the bear, they will be crouched down on the other side of the cruiser waiting for me to make the first move."

"Where will you be?" Dillon asked.

"Right over there." LoLo pointed to a cluster of shrubs and boulders thirty yards beyond the side of the road. "While they are focused on Morning, Jacob and I will come up from behind and then you and the bear will rise up in front of them. They throw down their weapons; we take the shipment, kill them, and then drive back together to Savage to divide it up among ourselves."

"We're not killing anyone unless we have to," Morning said.

"Fair enough," LoLo replied. "We'll do it your way so long as we leave here with the shipment." He looked at Dillon. "Now please move the car into the middle of the road, put the hood up, and then wait. It won't be long now." He started to move his motorcycle off the road.

Bear pointed at the headlights coming toward them.

"Hurry," LoLo shouted.

The cruiser was moved. Morning stood next to the open hood as Bear and Dillon crouched down behind the car.

"Are you okay?" Dillon whispered.

"Fine," Morning whispered back. She lay the shotgun over the engine, making sure she could easily reach it if needed. "Are you keeping your eyes on LoLo and Jacob?"

"Like a hawk. We'll be ready. Don't you worry."

The headlights were closer. Morning took a deep breath, trying to calm herself.

"Hey," Dillon said. "Can you pull off helpless?"

"You mean if little old me can play the part of a vulnerable woman who doesn't know what to do out here all alone on an abandoned road?"

"Exactly."

"I think I can manage."

"Good. The more helpless they think you are the more they'll relax and the easier it'll be to take the shipment from them without anyone getting hurt."

"From your mouth to God's ears, Sheriff." Morning watched and waited. She tried to spot where LoLo and Jacob were hiding, but it was too dark by then to see much of anything but the approaching headlights. The vehicle slowed and then stopped. It was an older truck with a tarp tied down over the bed. A door opened followed by the sound of boots against pavement.

"Broke down?"

The voice was male, young, with the kind of fake pleasant tone that Morning knew warned of potential trouble. "I'm hoping I just ran out of gas," she replied.

A tall figure stepped into the light. His beard and hair were both long and dark. He wore a denim jacket and jeans. "You alone?"

"Yeah. You're not one of those road pirates, are you?"

"Where'd you get the gas that brought you this far?" the man asked.

"Came with the car."

"Does that say Richland County Sheriff on the side?"

"I guess."

"How'd you come to be the one behind the wheel?"

"The keys were in it."

The man smiled. His face wasn't unpleasant. In a different time and place Morning might have found it handsome. "You took it."

"Looks that way."

"Where you headed?"

Morning shrugged. "Somewhere. Anywhere."

"But not here."

Morning pretended to laugh. "No, not here. What about you?"

"What about me?"

"Are you alone?"

The man shook his head. The earlier smile was gone. "I'm afraid not."

The truck's passenger door opened. Two more men got out. One was about the same age as the first but heavier with a fleshy face covered in stubble. The third man was older, bald, and clean shaved. He carried an assault rifle, which he casually pointed at Morning. "What's this?"

"She thinks she's out of gas," the bearded man replied.

The older man stepped forward. "Out of luck is more like it. She has a few years on her, but she'll do."

"Wait," Morning said. "You can have the car. Please. Just let me go."

"Let you go?" The older man chuckled. "It never ceases to amaze me how many stupid people have managed to survive this long and yet here you are, by yourself, unarmed, with that tight little body just begging for some attention."

"You work for Vig."

"From time to time," the older man said. "Would you like to know what's going to happen next?"

"Not really."

"I'm going to tell you anyways. You're going to close the hood of that car, lean over it, and then let us all get acquainted with your backside. If you do a good enough job of showing us a good time, I might just let you live."

Morning decided then that she was done playing scared. "I don't think so."

The three men spread out across the road with the oldest standing in the middle. He clicked his tongue. "Don't make me shoot you first before the fun. That would be rude."

"You might want to look behind you."

"Eh?" The older man glanced back to see LoLo and Jacob standing on either side of the truck, pointing their weapons at him.

LoLo pulled up a corner of the tarp and then nodded. "It's all there."

"As agreed." The older man sounded impatient. "Where is he?"

"Hiding behind the cruiser," Jacob replied. "There's another one with him—a sheriff."

"That explains the car's decal," the older man said. He raised his voice. "Get out here."

Dillon stepped out first with his gun drawn. "You backstabbing piece of shit."

"It's just business, Sheriff," LoLo replied. "No hard feelings. Now, where's the bear?"

"There he is," Jacob answered as Bear emerged from the other side of the car.

The older man whistled. "As big as advertised." He pointed the assault rifle. "Don't get any ideas. I won't hesitate to shoot you dead like the mad dog you are."

"Vig wants him alive," LoLo said.

"She prefers alive, but dead will do if it can't be helped."

"I don't want her thinking I reneged on our deal to help deliver him to her alive."

The older man shot LoLo a look that made clear he believed he was the one in charge. "This is *my* operation. You load your bikes in the back of the truck and take it and the shipment back to whatever hole you crawled out of. I'll take the cruiser and the bear back to Vig."

"What about us?" Dillon asked.

"You were dead the moment I pulled up here," the older man replied. "As for the woman, I've already explained to her how she can live to see another miserable day in this hellish paradise."

Dillon clicked the hammer back on his revolver.

"Don't," the older man said. "If I start shooting, I won't stop until you're all dead and that'll be on *you*, Sheriff." He nodded at Bear. "Now turn around and back up slow so we can tie you down for the return trip to Vig. She's been waiting a long time to get her hands on you."

Bear didn't move.

The older man aimed the rifle at Bear's chest. "I won't ask again."

Dillon took a cautious step forward. "You said I was dead the moment you pulled up here."

"That's right."

"That would make me a man with nothing to lose."

"Are you willing to get everyone else killed? Fire the gun. You might get a round or two off, but then I shred you all."

"Not if he puts one right between your eyes first," Dillon sneered.

LoLo and Jacob aimed their pistols at Dillon. Then the other two men did the same. The older man smiled. "It's basic math, Sheriff. You're outgunned."

"The woman is also hiding a shotgun under the hood of the car," Jacob added.

"I know," the older man replied. "I noticed her glancing down at it."

Dillon cleared his throat. "You weren't listening."

For the first time since he arrived the older man appeared uncertain of the outcome. "To what?"

"I didn't say *I* would put one right between your eyes." Dillon paused. "I said *he* would."

Dillon, Morning, and Bear all ducked at the same time. LoLo and the other four men looked down at them, confused, not noticing the flash of metal coming from the rear of the car. Remington was already out of the trunk and aiming his rifle at the space right between the older man's eyes.

The night air crackled with that first shot.

The older man's head snapped back then rocked forward. His mouth fell open as he blinked several times. Wisps of smoke slithered out of the hole in his forehead while blood pumped from the gaping exit wound at the back of his head. The assault rifle clattered against the road. His mouth opened and closed; he blinked again, and then collapsed on top of the rifle.

Everything stopped after that—a moment that seemed to stretch out far longer than the actual few seconds between the older man's face smacking against the pavement and what happened next.

Morning grabbed the shotgun and then dove to the side. Dillon fired off two rounds into the tall, bearded man's chest while Remington shot at the shorter man who then cried out in pain as blood ran down his arm from a shoulder wound.

Then it was the bear's turn.

The sledgehammer flew across the road, causing both LoLo and Jacob to duck. By the time they looked up Bear was already on top of them. LoLo fired but missed wide. Bear kicked him backwards and then flung Jacob against the side of the truck with enough force it dented the door and shattered a window.

LoLo tried to crawl away on his hands and knees. "Wait," he gasped. "The shipment is yours. Take all of it." He pushed the pistol away. "I'm unarmed."

Bear picked up the hammer.

"Behind you," Dillon yelled.

Jacob had regained his feet and was turning toward Bear.

Morning aimed the shotgun and pulled the trigger.

One side of Jacob's face and neck were shredded by the pellets. He collapsed while holding his neck with one hand and still trying to aim his gun at Bear with the other. Bear swung the hammer over his head. He meant to crush Jacob's chest with it but missed and struck his shoulder instead. The sound of the collarbone breaking was nearly as loud the earlier gunshots.

Jacob tried to scream but could only gurgle and wheeze. He lay on his back, chest heaving, choking on his own blood.

"It's done," Dillon ordered. "Get on your feet."

"Please, I can help you. I know things. I can get things for you. I'm a good friend to have around here."

Dillon kept his gun aimed at LoLo. "Friend is not a word I would ever use to describe the likes of you. All you know is how to lie and steal, but this time it's going to cost you."

"You came to *me*, remember?" LoLo snarled. "I didn't seek you out. You wanted information and I gave it to you. We had a deal."

"Exactly and then you broke it. Your plan was to hand over Bear and take all of the shipment for yourself as payment. And now you want to try to play the victim? Unbelievable." Dillon sighed and then turned to Morning. "What we do with him?"

"Don't ask her," LoLo cried. Jacob had a coughing fit that sent blood bubbling out of his mouth and nose. "For God's sake put him out of his misery and then let me go. You're not killers."

"That's right," Morning said. "We're survivors. You're the killer." She raised the shotgun higher. "I have one more round."

Dillon reached over and pushed the barrel down. "Don't waste the ammo." His gaze again settled on LoLo. "Get walking."

LoLo closed his eyes. "Thank you." He opened them and then started moving to where the motorcycles were hidden.

"I said get walking not get riding."

"What?" LoLo turned around. "I'll die out here."

Dillon shrugged. "Maybe."

"You might as well just kill me now."

Dillon raised his revolver. "Okay."

"Wait!" LoLo waved his hands in front of him. "Okay. I'll walk."

"I thought you might."

"You better hope I never see you or your friends again, Sheriff."

"That right?"

"Yeah, that's right. I assure you it'll be a much different outcome."

Remington walked up to Dillon and stood next to him. "You talk too much."

"Where's the girl?"

"None of your business," Remington growled.

"Left her all alone, didn't you? What a shame it would be if someone were to pay her a visit while you were gone. It's such a cruel and dangerous world. I do hope she's safe by the time you get back to Savage."

LoLo had enjoyed having his way for far too long. His ability to sense true danger, to hear the roar of an approaching storm, had been greatly diminished over the years. That storm now towered directly behind him, a mountain of muscle and bone that had come to value Reagan's well-being above all things. LoLo realized this mere seconds after speaking of her, but that realization was already too late. This time, his arrogance and overconfidence would cost him everything. He turned, looked up, and stared into the unblinking eyes of his executioner.

The sledgehammer drove into the bottom of LoLo's chin, obliterating his jaw and sending several teeth into the soft tissue of his mouth and sinuses. Blood covered his neck and chest. He fell onto his side, his eyes open and vacant. Bear walked up to him, lifted his foot, and then slammed the heel of his boot into LoLo's skull, fracturing it in several places and crushing the brainstem.

"Drag the bodies into the ditch," Dillon said. "Give the coyotes and wolves a chance to pick their bones clean." He looked at Remington. "That was a good idea you hiding in the trunk like that. Caught them off guard and that made all the difference."

"Happy to help even if my knees and back are none too pleased." He shook his head. "Hope to never see so much death as this ever again."

"That was their choice," Morning replied, sounding as indifferent to the bloodshed as Bear appeared to be. "We would have been happy to just drive off with our half of the shipment as agreed, but LoLo's greed finally caught up to him." She looked at Dillon and Remington, two older men who more than proved they had plenty of serious fight left in them. "You both did good."

Dillon gave her a thin smile and his eyes hinted at the exhaustion he felt. "I appreciate the kind words, but outside of us surviving it, I'm afraid nothing about this was good."

"Fair enough," Morning said. "I'll take surviving and the chance to fight another day."

Bear was already grabbing bodies two at a time by their ankles and dragging them off the road. He was anxious to get back to Savage.

They all were.

.

19.
✦✧✦✧

"You're a natural in that saddle, Reagan."

It was an unusually warm day in Savage for the time of year. The skies were clear, the air dry, with just a whisper of a breeze that would occasionally caress the tops of the grass below Vaughn's Hill. Reagan tilted her head and smiled up at a flock of honking Canadian geese flying above her in perfect formation. "What's his name?"

"Justice," Morning replied as she walked alongside her horse while holding the reins.

"That's a good name."

"It suits him."

"Have you had him long?"

"Sixteen years. I was still considered a young woman when he was a wobbly legged foal."

Reagan looked down. "You're not old."

"Thanks. I'm hanging in there."

"How long can horses live?"

"Not nearly long enough if you ask me."

"I thought I was."

"What?"

"Asking you."

"Right." Morning chuckled. "I guess you were. I had a veterinarian tell me once that a horse that reaches thirty-six is the equivalent of a person who turns one hundred."

"How old does that make Justice?"

Morning quickly did the math in her head. "About my age."

"So, neither one of you is very old." Morning sat up straight in the saddle and waved. Bear stood by the entrance to the tent with his arms folded over his chest. He smiled and waved back.

"He sure was worried about you being here alone last night," Morning said.

"I don't know why. I know how to get vegetables from the greenhouse and how to boil water from the river, and even catch fish. I could take care of myself if I had to."

"He cares about you a lot."

Reagan stroked Justice's powerful neck. "And I care about him."

"It's nice having people who care, don't you think?"

"I do." Reagan's brows pushed together like she was thinking hard about something. "Do you care about him?"

"Bear?"

"Yeah."

"Sure, I care about him and Remington and the sheriff and you."

"I mean do you like him?"

"I like all of you."

Reagan rolled her eyes. "C'mon, you know what I mean. Do you think he's cute?"

Morning stopped walking. "Cute isn't a word I would normally use to describe a man."

"Handsome?"

"Yes, Bear is a very handsome man."

Reagan's eyes twinkled. "You *do* like him."

"I'm not really interested in that kind of relationship."

"You don't want to fall in love?"

"I was in love with my husband Waylon. I guess I'm one of those people who thinks one true love is more than enough in this life."

"Do you think Waylon would have wanted you to stay alone?"

"We never really talked about it because I suppose we both figured we had a lot more years left together. If I had to guess I'd say what he wanted most of all was for me to be happy."

"I bet Bear could make you happy."

"I'm too old for him and he's too young for me."

"That's silly."

"No, that's how I feel."

"Feelings can change."

Morning gave Reagan a playful poke on her thigh. "You're tenacious."

"I just want people to be happy."

"Happy is a mighty tough sell these days."

Reagan giggled when Justice swished his tail and shook his skin, causing the saddle seat to tremble. "He wants you to know we can still be happy if we just try."

"That's what he said, huh? I didn't know you spoke equine."

"Happiness is a universal language. All we have to do is open our hearts and ears to understand it."

Morning pushed her hat up to get a better look at Reagan. "There you go again."

"What?"

"You have a knack for saying certain things a certain way that reveals a natural wisdom that far exceeds what would normally be found in someone your age."

Reagan pursed her lips. "Is that a compliment?"

Morning reached up and lightly pinched her nose. "You better believe it."

"Hello Mr. Wilkes," Reagan said.

Remington had the last of the shipment they had stolen from LoLo strapped across Peanut's back as he rode toward the tent. "Young lady, you know it's okay to call me Remington."

"Hello Mr. Remington Wilkes."

"Hah! You're full of mischief this morning." Remington winked. "I like it."

"Happy with the take?" Morning asked.

Remington stopped. "It's not bad. You'll be happy to know you have a few boxes of shotgun shells now. One of them is high-velocity slugs. You could take an elephant down with those. Beyond that it's mostly twenty-two caliber ammo—buckets and buckets of it along with a couple of older bolt-action twenty-two rifles that appear to be in decent shape. Either that's what LoLo wanted or he was getting ripped off."

"He seemed happy when he snuck a look under the tarp last night."

"Guess that's what he wanted then."

"Is all that twenty-two ammo a problem?"

"Not at all. I've heard plenty of people put down the twenty-two over the years, saying it's not good for anything but target practice and rodents, but none ever offered to be shot by one. It'll kill a man dead like anything else. You just might have to put two or three rounds in them instead of just one. I like the twenty-two though. Easy and accurate firing is a good combo in my book. The pistols we took from LoLo and Jacob are twenty-two semi-automatics—great little shooters. Reagan could easily learn on one of those. The assault rifle only had ten rounds left and none of the ammo in the shipment matches so that was a bit of a disappointment."

"You're going to teach me to shoot?" Reagan asked.

"Sure," Remington replied. "I don't see why not."

"Cool." Reagan smiled. "Thank you, Mr. Remington Wilkes."

Dog bounded across the hill toward them. Remington grunted as he watched him running. "That dog has been my shadow all morning. Won't leave my side—like he's expecting trouble or something."

"He slept in the tent with me when you were gone," Reagan said. "He's a good boy."

Remington looked down at Dog who sat staring back up at him, his long tongue hanging out of the side of his mouth as he panted happily. "He *is* a good boy, isn't he?"

Dog's panting abruptly stopped. He quickly turned, trotted to the edge of the hill, and started barking.

Peanut whinnied while Justice shook his head and snorted.

"Something has them spooked." Remington turned in the saddle. "Wonder what it could be."

"You hear that?" Reagan asked.

Morning scanned the clear blue morning sky and then pointed. "Airplane."

The small plane was coming from the north and descending fast, its single engine repeatedly cutting out. Bear jogged toward the others. Remington slid his rifle out and then clicked his tongue, riding Peanut to where Dog stood barking. Morning, Reagan, and Bear followed.

"Friend or foe?" Morning asked.

Remington checked to make sure his rifle was loaded. "It appears we're about to find out soon enough. That thing looks like an old crop duster from way back."

The plane's engine gave one final gasp and then cut out for good. They watched from the top of the hill as it continued to fall from the sky.

"Going to be a hard landing for whoever it is," Remington said. "At least they're keeping the nose up though—they know what they're doing."

The plane's wheels struck dirt and grass, bounced up, and then dropped again. The wings pushed the grass low as it skimmed across the valley floor for nearly two hundred yards before suddenly lurching right and then coming to a stop.

"Impressive," Remington whispered. He pulled his hat down tight. "Stay here."

"Where are you going?" Morning called out as he galloped away.

"To see who the hell it is," Remington yelled. "Grab those twenty-two rifles and cover me just in case. One of them has a decent scope on it."

Bear ran back into the tent to get the rifles while Morning and Reagan continued to watch the plane. Dog took off as well, trying to catch up to Remington and Peanut.

Reagan pointed again. "He's coming out."

A man in dark coveralls had opened the cockpit side door and then dropped out onto the ground. Bear returned with both twenty-two rifles and handed Morning the one with the scope. She looked through it. "I don't see any weapons. He seems about my age. Darkish skin and short salt-and-pepper hair. No beard. Average height and build." She moved the rifle slightly until she could spot Remington cautiously approaching the plane with his gun aimed at the man. Dog had run ahead and was keeping himself between the plane and Peanut.

"Dark skin like Bear's?" Reagan asked.

Morning shook her head. "No, not that dark. More like Lucian."

"Indian?"

"Maybe."

The man raised his hands up high. Remington pointed at him while Dog barked loudly. Morning squinted into the scope. "They're talking. Seems almost friendly." Remington jumped down from the saddle and then walked toward the plane with his hand out. The two men shook. Morning grunted. "Real friendly."

"Isn't friendly good?"

"I hope so because now they're coming this way."

Remington got back on Peanut. The man followed as they walked slowly toward Vaughn's Hill. Dog, seemingly satisfied that the unexpected visitor didn't pose any immediate threat, ran off. Remington and the man had nearly reached the bottom of the hill when Dillon's cruiser pulled up to the house. He exited the car and immediately walked toward them while holding his revolver at his side.

Morning looked through the rifle scope again. "The sheriff doesn't appear to be nearly so friendly." Dillon stopped and pointed at the pilot. The pilot said something and then pointed at his plane. Remington nodded. Dillon looked back and then holstered his weapon. Remington motioned for him to follow them up the hill.

"We're going to need to catch more fish today," Reagan said.

"Why?" Bear asked.

"Because there'll be another guest for dinner. You and I can do some fishing later, okay?"

Bear nodded.

Remington, Dillon, and the mystery pilot climbed the hill.

Morning held tightly to the rifle, ready to use it.

Just in case.

20.

✦✧✦✧

"I've been beat to hell so many times even my memories have bruises on them."

Leo Astor was bone tired and he looked it—and it wasn't just the marble-sized cancerous lumps that covered so much of his face and neck. He didn't talk so much as sigh his words. What Morning had seen while looking down at him from atop the hill as salt-and-pepper hair was clearly more salt than pepper up close. He was thin, almost frail, but his dark eyes were intelligent and earnest and he had an easy manner to him that made one want to listen to what he had to say.

Born on a military base in Anchorage to a white army officer and a Canadian Inuit woman, Leo had spent nearly the last half of his sixty years as a bush pilot doctor providing medical supplies and services to the native villages along the Alaska-Canada border. It was work he enjoyed largely because it allowed him long stretches of time to be alone. He had largely given up on society some time ago and the horrors that followed the collapse only served to further confirm his long-standing pessimism toward humankind.

"Strip away the phony, the distractions, all the other bullshit we were spoon-fed by so-called modern society and we get down to the truth of the matter—people are bastards."

"Yourself included?" Morning asked.

Leo nodded. "I'm no better."

"You were a pilot up north." Remington looked at him from across the fire inside of the tent where they had just finished a supper of fish and vegetables. "What are you doing in these parts?"

"Surviving. I fly supplies to and from various locations, which allows me to keep stocking up on essentials for myself in the process."

"What locations?"

Leo locked eyes with Remington. "I'm not lying about any of this."

"Didn't say you were, but like you just said, people are bastards, right?"

"Don't go using my words against me."

"Answer the question," Morning said. "How'd you end up in the field below this hill?"

"Vaughn's Hill," Leo replied.

Remington's hand edged toward his revolver. "I never told you that name."

"Didn't have to—someone else did."

"Who?"

"A man up at the Fort Peck reservation named Lucian."

"You know Lucian Cross?"

Leo nodded. "I do. When I was running low on fuel, I remembered his description of this place—namely the field where I could land the plane. I wanted to avoid landing on a road because you never know who might be watching. They're called road pirates for a reason. Cross is Lucian's white man name by the way. Up there they call him Lucian Rainwater. He's helping to run things on the reservation. Actually, he's trying to help run things on other reservations as well and doing a damn good job of it. The man is a natural leader. He's turning that reservation into a place his people can be proud of."

"He told us he was a former professor," Morning said.

"Lots of us were different things before the collapse." Leo pointed at Bear. "Like him."

Bear sat without movement or expression, but everyone could sense he was prepared to pounce should Leo prove himself a threat to Reagan and the others.

"You were a hell of a football player," Leo continued, "but that was a lifetime ago, wasn't it? From famous athlete to the man who quickly rose to the top of Vig's most-wanted list. I salute you. That woman has proven to be nearly as deadly to us as the vaccine was."

"Speaking of which," Morning said, "those tumors on you."

Leo grimaced. "Yeah, the vaccine most likely caused it. The first mass showed up on the side of my neck about eight weeks after I took the jab. The military bases I worked with required that I be vaccinated in order to keep my government shipment contracts with them. It was the kind of easy money I couldn't afford to give up. Part of the deal, though, was that I fly out and administer the vaccines to several remote villages in Alaska, but they wanted nothing to do with the shots."

"Who?" Dillon asked.

"The tribes. They refused—basically told me they wouldn't be putting that poison into their bodies no matter what. I'm sure it didn't help when I started showing up with these things growing on me. Had that first lump tested right away and it came back malignant. Some new version of a soft tissue carcinoma. The oncologist declared it a one-in-ten-million variant. Made me feel *really* special. They wanted to try chemo, radiation, the whole nine yards. I refused treatment. I might be a bush pilot version of a hick country doctor, but that doesn't mean I don't know how to interpret a fancy clinic's medical prognosis chart. The tumors you see on the outside are nothing compared to the ones on the inside. The cancer is everywhere. Nothing to be done. Without treatment they gave me nine months at best. That was over three years ago and I'm guessing that same oncologist who gave me the news is long dead by now just like most everyone else who took the jab. The way I figure, it's the flying that's keeping me alive. I have a purpose, something to get up each day for so that's what I've been doing."

"Until you ran out of gas in my field," Remington said.

"Diesel actually. I had this aircraft mechanic in Ketchikan convert it to diesel about ten years ago. He used a fabricated version of the old Packard DR engine from the nineteen thirties. On a full tank I can fly non-stop for almost forty hours without having to refuel. That allows me to cover a hell of a lot of area in a relatively short amount of time. The problem is that diesel, like every other kind of fuel, is getting tougher and tougher to find."

Dillon cleared his throat. "I know of some."

Leo's brows lifted. "You do? Where?"

"Nearby."

"Enough to get me back in the sky?"

"Yeah."

"What's the catch?"

"No catch. Not really. Would be nice if you could drop in and share information with us from time to time—especially anything you know regarding Vig and her road pirates."

"Sure," Leo replied. "I could do that. I've met her you know."

"Vig?" Bear exclaimed, his face suddenly animated.

"The one and only. Her primary base of operations is in Rapid City, South Dakota. I flew in and out of there a few times with supplies and she paid me back with diesel."

"She took control of the armory there," Dillon said.

"That's right. How'd you know?"

"Lucian told us."

"And not just the armory," Leo continued. "She locked down nearly all of the area between Deadwood and Sturgis and on up to Castle Rock. That was almost two years ago. She's sure to have expanded even further since then."

"Some of her road pirates made it here to Savage." Morning's tone took on a hard edge. "They didn't make it back."

"Do you know anything about a chopper in the area?" Dillon asked.

"I did hear she was trying to find someone to fly one that she got her hands on. Have you seen it?"

"It flew right over this hill. We shot at it and were hoping it might have crashed trying to get back to wherever it came from."

Leo shook his head. "Haven't heard or seen anything that could confirm that. Vig having a chopper isn't good though. Rumor is she has even been trying to gain access to a nuclear silo. The woman is mad. I kid you not. Saw it in her eyes—some kind of deep-rooted psychosis going on in there. She wants to make this world and everyone in it pay. For what I have no idea, but believe me, she is the living, breathing embodiment of pure rage." He looked at Bear again. "And if she finds out you're here, God help you all. She won't stop until there isn't even a blade of grass left alive in this place. And it isn't just because of how many of her road pirates you killed over the years. No, what you've done, what you've become, is a symbol of hope. Everyone knows the legend of the bear now. You actually put aside your fear and fought back. You stood up to her and you survived. That gives others hope that they can do the same and for a thing like Vig, hope can't be tolerated. It must be destroyed."

"We're not going anywhere," Remington said. "This is my hill and I intend to defend it to the very end."

Morning nodded. "We all do."

"I pray it doesn't come to that," Leo replied.

"Given your medical background and such," Dillon said, "who do you mostly blame for what happened regarding the vaccines?"

Leo shut his eyes tight and groaned. "Sorry. The internal pain is getting worse by the day. It sometimes feels like I have acid running through my veins." His eyes opened. "I already exceeded my expiration date years ago, but I'm afraid whatever time I do have left isn't much." He used the back of his trembling hand to wipe away the sweat that suddenly covered his forehead. "As for placing blame for the vaccines I really can't say. There are those who claim it was part of some big population control conspiracy or a deal gone wrong with a foreign power. Others are convinced it was nothing more than deadly government incompetence. I imagine the truth can be found somewhere in between all of those things. That said, I don't think anyone thought at first that it could possibly go as bad as it actually did. People were scared of the virus. The media and government officials certainly fed that fear. Then they ordered us to take the vaccine with the promise that everything would go back to normal after we did. That never happened. People died and they keep dying from those damn shots to this day. Ultimately, we did this to ourselves, right? We allowed it to happen using our own fear as an excuse. And don't give me any of that Democrat versus Republican or conservative versus liberal crap. This goes way beyond any of that foolishness. We got scared so we did as we were told. We sat down, shut up, and allowed them to inject us with hardly a complaint or even a question as to why. I have to think that if we hadn't allowed ourselves to be so easily divided so that more of us were actually paying attention to what was *really* going on, none of this would have happened."

"How do you think this all plays out in the end?" Morning asked.

"All I know is I won't be around to find out." Leo smiled at Reagan. "Those of you who will be around have to do everything you can to give ones like her a chance at some kind of future. Do you know why kids her age have become so valuable?"

"Because there are a lot of twisted sickos running around out there," Morning answered.

"No, it's because kids her age are so rare. They are the human versions of a four-leaf clover—they hardly exist. After the vaccines the miscarriage rate skyrocketed and births plummeted. Millions of healthy children died. And now so many of the women who remain alive are discovering that the vaccines destroyed their reproductive system."

"What's that mean for communities that largely rejected the vaccines?" Remington asked. "Places like those remote villages you were flying supplies into?"

"It means they might be the ones who will ultimately inherit whatever is left of this world." Leo warmed his hands over the fire. "Imagine that. Lands lost long ago by tribes such as my mother's people might soon be theirs again." He winked at Remington. "This hill being the exception of course."

Remington scowled. "Of course."

"Sheriff," Leo said, "are we still on for that diesel fuel you mentioned?"

"Sure. I'll keep my word so long as you keep yours. And say hi to Lucian for us."

"I will. He spoke very highly of all of you."

Remington picked the last bit of fish off his plate. "To be honest we weren't quite sure what to make of him."

"That's to be expected. It's unfortunate how potentially deadly trusting people can be these days."

"After you fuel up where are you off to next?" Morning asked.

"I'll be flying southwest over to the Crow reservation to deliver a message for Lucian and then likely rest up there for a few days before heading back to Fort Peck."

"Mind if I ask what that message is about?" Dillon asked.

"Lucian is trying to better organize the tribes in the region so that they can put up more of a united front against the Vigs of the world."

"Is that right?" Remington watched the tendrils of smoke rising up toward the ceiling. "You think he can pull that off?"

"Too early to say, but so far it's looking promising."

Bear wrote on his tablet and then showed it to the others.

It sounds like he has the makings of a chief.

"Maybe," Leo replied. "I'd support him. He's a smart man."

The sides of the big tent rippled as a blast of wind buffeted the hillside. The sound made Reagan flinch. Morning put her arm around her.

"Weather is turning," Dillon said. "Likely won't clear until tomorrow. If it's okay with you I think it's best that we wait until morning to go get that diesel."

"As long as I'm not intruding," Leo replied.

Remington groaned as he got up. "You're welcome to stay the night here. There's plenty of room around the fire. Only problem is Reagan is a bit of a terror when it comes to the snoring."

Leo laughed. "I never would have guessed."

"I don't snore," Reagan declared.

"You're right," Remington replied. "You roar."

The sound of the wind combined with the laughter of those inside of the tent, but eventually that laughter died while the storm grew stronger. The horses shifted nervously just inside the entrance, their nostrils flaring as long fingers of lightning singed the Montana sky.

They were all in for a long night.

21.
✦✧✦✧

One week later.

"Make it an extension of your hands. The grip should be firm but not tight. See the target. Relax and then hold your breath right before you pull that trigger."

Reagan gasped a little when she fired the gun. She missed the tin can perched atop a rotting stump where Remington was teaching her how to shoot. Warmer weather had returned to Savage. Vaughn's Hill was bustling with the approaching spring as birds chirped under the golden glow of the early afternoon sun and the scent of new growth filled the air around them.

"You did fine," Remington said, his voice soft and reassuring. "Not bad at all for a first time. Ready to try again?"

"Yeah." Reagan held the twenty-two pistol up, determined to do better. She aimed, fired, and missed. "Dang it."

"That was closer. You were off by no more than a foot to the right. Go through your checklist and stay relaxed. Adjust your aim. That's it."

The third shot sent the can spinning off the stump. Reagan let out a triumphant shout.

Remington tapped her shoulder. "Don't forget the safety."

"Right," Reagan said. "Sorry." She carefully made sure the safety was on again.

"You're a quick study, young lady—hit your target from forty feet out on just the third try. That's impressive."

"Will we be able to practice more?"

"Absolutely. Just remember that you never point a weapon unless you're willing to use it." Remington took the pistol. "These aren't toys."

"I know. Thank you for showing me. I wish I had a gun when the bad men came. Things might have been different."

"Well, these days you're among friends, which makes for a lot better situation than what a lot of others are facing out there. As much as it hurts to remember the past make sure you take time to appreciate the here and now. Do you understand?"

Reagan nodded.

Remington's craggy smile pushed deep wrinkles out from the corners of his twinkling eyes. "Good. Now, I wonder how Bear and Morning are doing with the rabbit snares? I was hoping to make a stew for supper. How's that sound?"

"Delicious."

At the same time as Remington was announcing his dinner plans Morning and Bear were walking side by side through the fields that surrounded Vaughn's Hill checking the snares. The first three were empty. Neither seemed to mind, though, each of them enjoying the other's company amidst the tranquil solitude of the Montana countryside.

"Grass is growing again," Morning said with her arms spread out so that the palms of her hands brushed against the tops of the grass stocks. "This was always my favorite time of year. You could open the door, walk outside, and be surrounded by the sights and sounds of a new beginning." She looked up at Bear who had the sledgehammer slung over his shoulder. "You always take that thing with you wherever you go?"

Bear snapped off a piece of grass and then playfully flicked it under Morning's nose. She pushed his hand away. He smiled. She rolled her eyes.

"Behave yourself, you big goof." Morning pointed at a pair of sticks that stuck up from the earth. "There's the next snare." She frowned. "Nothing."

Bear held up a finger.

Morning nodded. "Yeah, the last snare is over there by that thicket."

They both turned at the sound of barking. Dog was bounding toward them. His head would pop up above the field grass, disappear below it, and then pop up again. Bear set the sledgehammer down, clapped his big hands together, and then knelt down as Dog circled him, his tail happily wagging away. When Bear ducked his head lower, Dog licked his ears.

"I think you have a buddy."

Bear scooped Dog up in his arms and then laughed as the animal nuzzled his face.

"Yup," Morning said, "you're a big goof all right." They reached the last snare and found it empty as well. "Damn. I was really looking forward to some rabbit for dinner." She crouched next to the snare. "Check it out. There's blood and fur on the grass. We had one but something came along and took it."

Bear put Dog down and then looked around the thicket.

"What are you doing?" Morning asked.

Bear snapped his fingers in front of a rabbit hole. Dog came up to it, sniffed the hole, poked and prodded around the thicket with his nose, and then took off through the field again. He ran around them in wide circles, stopping from time to time to smell the ground.

"Is he actually hunting rabbit for us?"

Bear pointed at movement a hundred yards in front of them.

Morning squinted as she tried to see what was going on.

Dog barked, jumped above the grass, and then disappeared.

"There!" Morning shouted. Dog's head popped up for a second before he was off and running again. "He's definitely after something." She started jogging to catch up. "C'mon. Let's go."

Bear picked up his sledgehammer and followed.

Dog's barking intensified. Then he yelped, growled, and yelped some more.

"Wait." Morning held up her hand. "That doesn't sound right."

Bear strode past her with the sledgehammer held in front of him. Dog howled in pain and then broke through a wall of grass near where Bear stood, blood oozing from a gash on one of his ears.

Something was chasing him.

Something big.

Dog whirled around next to Bear, his tail between his legs, his head low and his jaws snapping.

"Careful," Morning said. "It's coming this way."

The stocks of grass shook and then parted until eventually the cause of the disruption revealed itself. They smelled its earthy musk first before they saw it.

Morning cursed under her breath for not bringing the shotgun.

The dark-haired wolf strode through the grass and then stopped. Dog continued to snap his jaws, barking and yelping as he did so. The wolf was a big male, young, near starving, and very much wanting to make the much smaller Dog its next meal.

"That's what took our rabbit from the snare," Morning said.

The wolf looked at her when she spoke, its feral eyes quickly sizing her up. Those eyes showed no fear. Rather, they made clear it considered Dog an easy kill but, failing that, Morning would be a welcome replacement.

Bear reached down and started to put his hand over Dog's nose. Overcome by adrenaline and panic, Dog nipped at his fingers, breaking the skin. Bear ignored the bite, gently patting Dog's snout. "Shh," he whispered. Dog whimpered, sounding guilty for having bitten his new friend.

The wolf growled low and deep as it crept closer.

Bear rose to his full height, bared his teeth, and growled back.

Morning froze as she watched Bear and the wild beast glaring at each other. Drool dripped from the wolf's fangs as it started to circle toward Dog, but Bear moved to the side and blocked its path. He thumped the ground with the hammer.

"Back," he said.

The wolf retreated slightly, as confused as it was hungry. Morning flinched at the sound of its jaws snapping closed like a toothy rat trap.

"Back," Bear repeated as he took a step forward.

Dog stood next to Morning just behind Bear, growling as he watched the conflict unfold. She glanced down at him, wondering if something happened to Bear if he would stay to help defend her. Seeing the hairs on Dog's neck and shoulders bristling, hearing the fury in his growl, she knew the answer was yes.

The wolf charged.

Bear stood his ground.

The wolf stopped.

Bear swung the hammer in a wide arc in front of him, missing the tip of the wolf's long nose by inches. The wolf backed off when Bear swung the hammer again. He paused, waiting, hoping, the wolf would run away.

It didn't.

The beast jumped, its front paws striking Bear's chest as its jaws snapped shut in front of his face. Bear stumbled backwards but kept the hammer's handle between himself and the wolf.

Dog dove forward, biting into the wolf's haunches and refusing to let go even as the wild creature turned its head to bite him back. Bear slammed the hammer's handle up into the bottom of the wolf's neck and then crunched a knee into its exposed belly. Dog let go and scrambled back to Morning as the wolf again retreated.

Thunder approached. Morning looked behind her and saw Remington riding toward them at a full gallop. He leaned forward low in the saddle holding the reins in one hand and his rifle in the other as Peanut's long, powerful legs propelled them across the field.

The wolf took off through the grass. Remington put the reins in his mouth, raised the rifle with both hands, and gave pursuit. The ground trembled as they sped past Morning and Bear. When the wolf emerged in a clearing, Peanut pinned her ears back and found just a little more speed. Remington took aim and fired. The wolf tumbled end over end. Remington circled it and then fired again. He pulled back on the reins, sat up in the saddle, and yelled across the field asking if everyone was okay.

Bear nodded. Morning yelled back yes. Dog ran toward Remington and Peanut.

"He's bleeding," Remington said.

"Got bit," Morning replied, "but I don't think it's serious."

"Lone wolf." Remington turned in the saddle and looked out over the ranch property. "Haven't had to deal with one of those in quite some time. Big one too."

"Bear was practically nose to nose with it."

Remington looked Bear up and down. "No kidding? And not a scratch on you."

"I think the wolf realized he was trying to bite off more than he could chew."

"No doubt," Remington replied. "I would have been here earlier but had to saddle Peanut up first. Just glad no one was badly hurt. A wolf like that can do some serious damage. I suppose we should be grateful it wasn't a whole pack of them. That's a young male likely kicked out by the alpha. Wolves aren't meant to live alone. Makes them desperate and desperate leads to dangerous. I hate to kill anything, but once they cross that fear barrier and are willing to consider people as prey they have to be put down."

"Dog sure was brave," Morning said. "He gave as good as he got."

"I should have given you one of the pistols by now." Remington pulled the brim of his hat down. "I apologize."

Morning shrugged. "I should have asked or been smart enough to bring my shotgun with me."

"Lesson learned."

"Indeed."

Bear scratched behind Dog's uninjured ear, slung the sledgehammer over his shoulder, and then looked up at Vaughn's Hill where Reagan stood looking down at them. He waved to let her know they were all okay. She waved back.

"Had our first round of target practice," Remington said. "It went well. I know I keep saying it, but that Reagan is a hell of a good kid. She really knows how to listen to what you're telling—"

They all heard it. They all knew what it was. Bear, Morning, and Remington watched Reagan turn around slowly and then look up at what loomed behind her, a tiny speck of a girl staring into the mechanical abyss as dust clouds swirled around her.

The chopper had returned.

"Yah!" Remington shouted as he nudged Peanut's flanks and then took off galloping toward the hill. Dog followed close behind, barking along the way.

Bear started to run and then he stopped. "Don't wait for me," Morning said. "I'll catch up." He dropped the sledgehammer, turned, and ran at a speed that nearly matched that of Peanut, his huge arms and legs pumping in unison.

The chopper continued to hover over Reagan. She stood motionless for a moment before slowly raising her arms. In her hands was the pistol she had been practicing with earlier. She did exactly how Remington had taught her, gripping the weapon firmly but not tight, relaxing her muscles, breathing in, holding it, seeing the target, and then firing once, twice, and then a third time into the windshield.

Two of the three shots hit their mark. The chopper veered sharply, tipping sideways far enough that its blades nearly touched the ground. It righted itself, elevated away from the hill, veered again, and then dropped almost straight down, its motor roaring under the sudden strain. Down it went, falling faster and faster.

Remington yanked on the reins, bringing Peanut to a full stop near where the Wilkes barn once stood. Seconds later, Bear was beside them as they watched the chopper struggling to regain control of its descent. It lurched and tipped wildly from side to side as it fell.

"Not the house," Remington whispered.

The chopper didn't listen. It crashed into the little ranch house, its blades ripping apart the metal roof and wood framing. The tail spun around and then dug into the ground. The chopper's metal shell screeched like nails on a chalkboard as it was torn apart. Smoke billowed out from the engine compartment. Soon after, it was on fire.

Then came the explosion.

The force of the blast nearly threw Remington from the saddle. He shielded his face with his arm as the smoke and flames erupted.

Bear hardly moved.

Morning ran up to them. "Your home," she gasped.

"Yeah," Remington muttered.

"What happened?"

Bear looked up at the hill where Reagan stood watching the fire. He waved. She waved back.

"Reagan happened," Remington said. "It's like I told you. She took what she learned and blew that chopper out of the sky."

"With a little twenty-two pistol?"

Remington watched the flames devour what little remained of his home. "It appears so."

"I'm so sorry, Remington."

"A pile of nails and wood are all that is. It can be replaced. I'd much rather have the peace of mind that comes with knowing we don't have to worry about that damn chopper bothering us anymore."

"Vig is certain to come looking for it."

"Sure. And you know what? I don't really care."

"What are we going to do?"

"The same as Reagan just did," Remington answered. "We fight."

Dillon arrived in the cruiser a few minutes later, stunned by what he saw. After Morning filled him in on what had happened, he too offered his condolences to Remington for the lost home.

Remington shrugged it off, repeating what he told Morning. "Nails and wood."

"That fire is going to burn all night," Dillon said.

"Let it all burn," Remington replied. "To a crisp."

Anxious to make sure Reagan was okay, Bear started walking toward the hill with Dog trotting by his side.

The heat from the fire was making the others sweat. Dillon wiped his face. "Are we still on for supper?"

"No rabbit," Morning said.

"No problem," Remington replied. "I'll cook up some spuds."

Morning shook her head. "I'll do the cooking tonight. You relax. This is a lot to take in."

"I'm fine—really."

"I know." Morning smiled. "You're a tough old bastard."

"Who the hell are you calling old?"

"You."

"None of us are winning any youth awards these days," Dillon said.

Remington stroked Peanut's neck. "Speak for yourself, Sheriff. I just shot a wolf dead at a full gallop. Never done that before and I'd like to see a younger man try."

Morning stared into Remington's eyes. "That was pretty badass."

"Really?" Remington looked like he might blush. "You mean it?"

"Even Bear was at a loss for words watching that."

"Wait, he's *always* at a loss for words."

Morning smiled again. "Exactly." She laughed.

A murder of crows circled above the area where the wolf corpse lay. One by one they descended until they were out of sight, hidden by the tall grass with only their collective cawing signaling that they were there. The fire's smoke drifted over the field like churning skin, pushed by a soft breeze from the northeast.

Twilight's curtain fell over Savage, signaling the end of one day and the whispered promise of another to come.

22.
✦✧✦✧

"They're coming for you." Leo sipped coffee from his cup. He had landed in Remington's field earlier that morning hoping to secure more diesel fuel from Dillon. While waiting for Dillon to arrive he accepted Morning's offer of coffee and sat with them inside the tent summarizing what he had learned during his recent travels. His voice trembled a little when he spoke and the hands that held the cup shook. He was getting weaker. "I wish I had better news, but word is Vig is on her way here *personally* and she's pissed."

"Better we know now," Remington said.

Leo looked at Reagan. "You did good shooting down that helicopter."

"But the house." Reagan scowled. "I didn't want to hurt the house." She had been apologizing for the chopper crashing into Remington's home since it happened, and each time he told her not to worry about it.

"There were people who wanted to use the chopper to do very bad things," Leo said. "You stopped them from doing that."

"That's right," Remington added. "We're all very proud of our Reagan."

Reagan got up. "I'm going for a walk outside." When Bear started to join her, she told him to stay because she wanted to be alone.

"Walk my ass." Remington poured more coffee. "She's going to sit out there looking down at the damage. The poor thing can't let it go." He held up his cup. "Where'd you say you got this coffee from? It's delicious."

"An old diner off of Highway Two between the Blackfeet Reservation and the city of Shelby. I was told there were still some supplies there. I found three bags of that coffee and some of these." He took out a chocolate candy bar and handed it to Morning. "Please make sure Reagan gets some. It might help to cheer her up."

Morning took the candy bar and then followed Reagan outside, telling Bear that Reagan might be more comfortable hanging out with her right now and that he should give it a little time before joining them.

"You were all the way over in Shelby?" Remington said. "That's on the other side of Montana. You really do get around. How are those other places doing?"

"Compared to here?"

"Yeah."

"About the same except for the reservations."

"Lucian's idea of having the reservations form some kind of cooperative—that's still coming together?"

"The tribes certainly appear to be taking the lead in this post-collapse world. I spoke with a Shoshone healer down in Idaho last week who is convinced that modern society's fall is merely the long-awaited realization of American Indian prophecy—that the lands are being returned to their rightful stewards. As far as Fort Peck where Lucian is running things, they have actually started up a school program for the children there. I won't say things have gone completely back to normal, but they aren't all that far off."

"What's the farthest location you've been to recently?"

"After I left the Shoshone, I flew down to Logan, Utah."

"What's there?"

Leo shrugged. "Same as here—peace and quiet."

"No road pirates?"

"Not that I saw. Didn't talk to anyone. Landed in a field like yours and spent the night under the stars. The weather is quite a bit warmer there."

"That means more people," Remington said.

"Probably."

"More people means more problems."

"Maybe."

Remington swallowed the last of his coffee. "Not maybe—definitely. I'll stick to taking my chances here in Savage thank you very much."

While Remington was telling Leo that, Morning was sitting beside Reagan looking down at the still smoldering pile of destruction that had been the longtime Wilkes family home. "Hey," she said, nudging Reagan with her elbow. "Want a bite?" She held up the candy bar.

Reagan's eyes widened as she nodded.

Morning broke off a piece and gave it to her. "You have to get over what happened to Remington's house. It's not your fault."

"Everyone keeps telling me that."

"Then maybe you should listen to them." Morning took a bite of chocolate and started chewing. "Pretty good."

Reagan nibbled the corner of her piece at first but then plopped the rest of it into her mouth. "*Really* good."

"Chocolate makes everything better."

"I feel terrible about the house."

"We know. Remington told you not to worry about it though—just nails and wood, right?"

"He's being nice is all."

"I don't think Remington is someone who would say something he didn't mean."

"What about Leo telling us that the bad woman Vig is definitely on her way here and that she's angry about what happened to her helicopter? That's definitely my fault."

"No, it's the fault of the people who flew that chopper here in the first place. They knew they weren't welcome. We made that clear the last time, which means they were up to no good when they came back again. For all we know they were about to capture you and try to kill the rest of us."

"You really think so?"

"I think it's very possible, yes. Don't forget how badly Vig and her road pirates want to get their hands on Bear. If you look at it that way you could even say it's Bear's fault that Remington's house was destroyed. Not that I actually think that of course. I just want you to know that it's really not necessary to be placing any blame on yourself."

"Okay, I'll try not to."

Bear walked out of the tent. "We were just talking about you," Morning said.

"I'm fine now," Reagan added. "You don't have to worry about me."

Bear nodded, pointed at Reagan, and then said something Morning couldn't quite understand.

"He's asking if you want to go fishing with him," Reagan explained.

"Me?" Morning shrugged. "Sure." She looked at Reagan. "Do you want to come?"

Reagan glanced up at Bear, smiled at Morning, and shook her head. "You two go." She held up the candy bar. "I have chocolate to enjoy."

Bear motioned toward the back of the hill where the trail to the river below began. "Right behind you," Morning replied.

They said little as they made their way down the somewhat precarious path. When they reached the river, Bear baited the hook and then carefully let the line out into the slow-moving water until it sank to the bottom.

Morning sat on a rock, closed her eyes, and tilted her head back. "This is the warmest it's been in months and I'm loving it." She kept her eyes closed but sensed Bear was standing next to her. He cleared his throat. She opened one eye. "Yeah?" He wrote something down.

Thank you for helping Reagan to feel better about what happened.

"It really didn't take much. She's a tough kid."

She didn't want to talk to me about it.

"Because she was worried that she let you down. Your approval means so much to her."

You were a big help. Thank you again.

Morning sat up. "Never in a million years would I have guessed someone who looks like you would be the person you really are."

Bear frowned.

"Sorry, I don't think that came out how I meant it. What I mean is that there's so much more to you than this already very impressive physical exterior. If anything, it's your personality, your intelligence, your kindness and consideration that I find most attractive."

Bear's frown was quickly replaced by a sly grin as he wrote out his reply.

Attractive?

"Oh, shut up. I don't believe for a second that a man who looks like you, the chiseled lines, those eyes, that body, *my goodness that body*, isn't aware of how fine a picture they present to the rest of the world."

You're not so bad yourself.

Morning hadn't felt flustered in years, but she did then. "I'm old is what I am."

Bear shook his head.

"Thanks, but the lines on this face tell a different story."

That's a story I'd like to take some time to read.

Morning laughed. "That was pretty smooth." Her face turned serious. "I'm not looking for that kind of relationship, Bear. I'm sorry. You're wonderful, you really are, but this just isn't the time for me to even be considering such a thing."

I'll wait.

"You could be waiting a very long time."

That's okay. I have time. Unlike you, I'm still young.

Morning slapped the notepad against Bear's arm. "You jerk. That's it—I take back every nice thing I said about you. Now go check the line and see if you managed to catch anything." She watched him walk to the river, silently admitting that he was one of those rare men who looked as good coming as he did going. *Stop it,* her inner voice demanded. *You're slobbering over him like you're starving and he's this big, beautiful piece of steak.*

Bear bent down to retrieve the fishing line and then he carefully pulled it towards him, the muscles in his forearms, back and shoulders rippling as he did so. Morning told herself to look away, but she didn't. Instead, her eyes fed off of every detail and each subtle shift, from the slope of his nose and the square, dark-bearded jaw, the extraordinary width of his shoulders, to the powerfully sculpted backside that struck her as impossibly perfect. It was the first time since Waylon's death that Morning had allowed herself to feel such things for another man. She struggled with the guilt and shame that followed the sudden rush of arousal that coursed through her mind and body. *To hell with this,* she thought. She had been so careful for so long, but why now? The world that had been was no more. Her old life was long gone, and it wasn't coming back. Time was likely short, tomorrow certainly wasn't guaranteed, and for reasons that she couldn't fully understand, Bear found her attractive.

Bear straightened and turned, happily holding up a trout by its gills. Then he saw Morning striding towards him, her hat left on the rock behind her, hair flowing, eyes blazing, looking at him as if she was seeing him, all of him, for the first time.

He dropped the fish.

"Full disclosure," Morning said between heavy breaths. "I've never done anything like this before." She put a hand behind his neck and pulled him down toward her.

Bear hesitated.

She didn't.

Their lips touched. Morning pressed her body against his, marveling at its power. He lifted her up as if she weighed almost nothing. Their eyes locked onto each other's as she wrapped her legs around his lower back.

Morning kissed Bear's neck and then his ear. "Yes," she whispered. It was just one word, but it meant so much more to the both of them than the mere sum of its three-lettered parts. She was stunned by the speed and depth of her desire, having thought she was long past feeling such things. She closed her eyes when Bear laid her down in a patch of grass near the hill, her heart thumping madly inside of her chest. Under the sun's warmth he caressed her cheek, kissed her again, and then looked down at her, waiting for confirmation to proceed.

He was perfect.

"Yes," Morning repeated—and she meant it. To hell with being careful. To hell with caution. To hell with not satisfying those natural needs she had been forcing herself to ignore for far too long.

They would each give.

They would each take.

And while it lasted that was all that mattered.

23.

"Thank you again for the diesel. I'm not sure how many more flights I have in me but without your help it wouldn't be any by now."

"No problem," Dillon replied. "I feel good knowing it's being put to good use."

It was the third trip from the Wilkes ranch to the Savage service station with the four red five-gallon fuel jugs lined up in the cruiser's trunk. Leo looked and sounded tired. Refilling the plane by hand with diesel was proving to be almost too much for him.

"Is this one of your bad days?"

Leo closed his eyes and rested his head against the passenger window. "Pretty sure bad days are all I have left. Won't be long before I lack the strength to even climb into my plane's cockpit let alone fly it."

"And then what happens?"

"I die."

"Yeah."

Leo opened his eyes and glanced at Dillon. "Thanks."

"For what?"

"For not trying to blow sunshine up my ass. I have cancer and it's killing me. I appreciate you not trying to pretend otherwise."

"I had a family. Now I don't. I know a thing or two about how life and death work."

"I'm truly sorry for your loss, Sheriff."

"You know," Dillon said, "when the time comes where you can't do things like fly your plane, if you need somewhere to rest up, you're welcome to make Vaughn's Hill that place."

"Do the others feel the same?"

"I'm sure they do, but I'll ask just to be sure."

"That's very kind. It's a special hill, isn't it?"

Dillon nodded as he turned onto the main road that ran directly through the middle of Savage. "You feel it too, huh?"

"I do. At first, I thought it was a proud place, but then I realized it wasn't merely proud but also defiant. You know that Revolutionary War slogan that went on the flag with the rattlesnake?"

"The Gadsden Flag," Dillon replied.

"Is that what it's called?"

"I believe so."

"Don't tread on me—that's what that hill seems to be warning to those who would do that land harm."

Dillon grinned. "Old Hap Wilkes would have gotten a real kick out of hearing you say that."

"You were fond of him."

"I was—him, my father, pretty much that whole era of people from back then. This country had an entirely different sensibility—simpler but also tougher. They could spot BS from a mile away and they didn't suffer foolishness. Folks worked hard, had a sense of community and pride for their country. All of that seemed to be lost from one generation to the next."

"Your father was a sheriff as well?"

"A damn good one too. My old man cast a mighty long shadow. The respect he accumulated over his years wearing the badge was considerable. It took me a hell of a long time to convince folks around here that I was up to the job. Hap was a big help with that. When we fought together on that hill against the feds, people came from all around to stand with us. My father had been wasting away in a hospital bed following surgery. He had given up. It was tough seeing such a proud man laid so low as that. When he heard about what was going on at the Wilkes place, though, he forced himself out of that bed. I'll never forget it. I owe a debt of gratitude to the Wilkes family. It was Hap then and it's Remington now. If Vig really does come for us I can think of no better place to make a stand than at the top of Vaughn's Hill."

"I'm still hoping it doesn't actually come to that."

Dillon turned into the old Savage service station and parked the car next to the diesel pump.

"How'd you know about the generator here?" Leo asked.

"The county bought it as part of its emergency response plan. We figured we should have backup power so we could still fuel our emergency vehicles in the event of a blackout. I was involved in those discussions and the original recommendation."

"How much fuel does this place have left?"

"There are two big underground tanks here. Gas is nearly out because I've been filling my cruiser from it for the last few years. There might be forty or fifty gallons left at most. The diesel tank, though, is still nearly half full."

"How many gallons of diesel is that?"

"I figure about two thousand—maybe more."

"So, I take it you'll be switching out your cruiser for a diesel vehicle soon."

Dillon nodded. "That's the plan." He opened the car door. "Ready?"

Leo took a deep breath. "As I'll ever be."

"It's okay if you need to rest. I can fill the jugs myself."

"I'd like to help as much as possible."

Dillon got out, walked over to the side of the service station, and unlocked the padlock that secured the metal gate behind which the big diesel generator was housed. The generator had already been run earlier that day, so it started easily. "This thing could probably power most of the homes in Savage." He shouted so Leo could hear him above the din of the generator's exhaust.

Leo didn't reply.

"Everything okay?" Dillon asked as he stepped out from behind the generator and then looked across the parking lot.

Two armed men stood next to Leo. One was older and taller, with a full white beard and a bald head and neck covered in tattoos. His heavy-lidded eyes locked onto Dillon. "Stop right there, Sheriff."

"Do I know you?"

The man shook his head. "Don't think so." He pressed his pistol into Leo's side. "You do anything stupid and he dies. Understood?"

The other man appeared to be in his forties, with short dark hair, a fleshy face, wide shoulders, and thick-fingered hands, one of which was pointing a gun at Dillon. "You know how to run these pumps?"

"That's why we're here," Dillon replied as he turned slightly to hide his hand inching closer to his sidearm.

"You're going to fill our bikes for us," the man said. "And then we'll be coming back with a tanker truck for the rest."

"Is that right?" Dillon's hand rested on his revolver. He had never been an especially fast draw, but he was accurate and felt confident he could hold his own in a shootout. "Are you doing okay there, Leo?"

"Peachy," Leo deadpanned.

Dillon looked around. "Where are your bikes?"

"Close," the older man replied. "You'll want to do what we say, Sheriff."

"And why is that?"

"We're with Vig."

"Road pirates."

When the man smiled, it exposed several missing teeth and blackened gums. "That's right. I take it you know what that means."

"By the looks of that smile it means the dental plan she's offering isn't very good."

"Well, aren't you the little smartass."

"Word is she plans on heading out this way. Is that why you two are here—to scout it out for her?"

"Why we're here isn't your concern. Whether or not we let you both live is the only thing you should be worried about."

"Ask him," the younger man said.

The older one shot him an annoyed look.

"Go on," the younger man repeated. He shook his head. "Never mind. I'll do it myself." He looked at Dillon. "Have you heard of the bear?"

Dillon shrugged. "Sure, most everyone has heard about him."

"Do you believe he's real?"

"Don't care much either way."

"He's real."

"Okay."

"Have you seen him?"

"I see people from time to time. Can't say for certain if any of them were the bear."

"You'd know," the older man said. "He's huge."

Dillon kept his breathing steady as he prepared to draw his weapon. "That's what the rumors say."

"Those aren't rumors," the older man snarled. "The bear is real."

"Gentlemen, I don't mean to be rude, but can you cut to the chase and explain what any of that has to do with me?"

"We've heard about you," the younger man said. "The Savage sheriff who keeps patrolling the roads like he's still getting a paycheck."

"I'm actually the Richland County sheriff. Savage is an unincorporated community within the county."

"Like I give a damn." The older man jabbed his pistol into Leo's side hard enough it made Leo wince. "Where is he?"

"Who?"

"The bear."

"I have no idea. You actually think he's here in Savage?"

"You're a bad liar, Sheriff."

"Go easy on my friend there. He's sick."

The older man glanced over at Leo. "Sick? What kind of sick?"

"It might be contagious," Dillon answered.

The younger man leaned away from Leo while keeping his gun pointed at Dillon. "He does look like death warmed over. Check out all those lumps on his skin."

Leo coughed.

"He really is sick," the younger man cried, his eyes wide with fear.

Leo coughed again.

Dillon watched and waited.

The older man pushed Leo away.

"Duck," Dillon said.

Leo ducked.

Dillon calmly drew his weapon and fired at the younger man, striking him in the stomach. Then he aimed at the other one. They pulled their triggers at the same time. Dillon's hat flew from his head. He fell backwards, the breath knocked out of him as his back and shoulders hit the pavement. *Keep your eyes open*, he told himself as he waited for air to return to his lungs. *I'm okay. I'm okay.* He heard a voice. His ears were ringing. He tried to inhale but nothing happened. His head hurt. A warm wetness covered one side of his face. *You gotta breathe or you're gonna die.*

The voice was calling his name over and over again. Dillon focused on the sound, blinked several times, and looked up. Leo stared down at him.

"Dillon!"

Dillon's body suddenly felt like it weighed a thousand pounds. He gasped as his lungs finally opened for him. "Are you okay?" he croaked.

"I'm fine," Leo replied. "Don't move. You've been shot."

"Where?"

"In the head."

Dillon chuckled. "At least it didn't hit something I use too much." He felt his face and then looked at his hand. It was covered in blood. "That's not good." His head started to thump. "Help me up."

"Stay down."

Dillon grabbed Leo's arm. "Help me up—NOW."

"At least let me have a look at the wound."

"Fine but be quick about it. Are they both dead?"

"I think the first one you shot is still breathing, but that second fella, well, you got him right between the eyes. He dropped like the sack of shit that he was."

"My dad would have been proud."

Leo wiped away some of the blood on Dillon's head.

"How's it look?"

"A lot of blood," Leo answered, "but I think it just grazed you. You're a very lucky man, Sheriff."

"And a pretty decent shot."

Leo grunted. "That too."

"I'd really like to get up now."

Leo took Dillon's hand and helped to pull him onto his feet. He pointed at the pumps. "There are towels over there. Let me grab some for you so you can clean up a little."

Dillon bent over with his hands on his knees, feeling like he might throw up. After the nausea passed, he straightened just as Leo returned with the towels.

"Here you go."

"Thanks," Dillon said. He dabbed the towel on his head, wincing when he touched the singed line left by the bullet's path. "A quarter inch lower and there'd be brains mixed in with this blood." After wiping his face off he turned around. "Where's my hat?"

Leo held it up. "I picked it up for you." He handed it to Dillon.

"Will you look at that." Dillon held the hat up and then stuck the tip of his pinky through the bullet hole. "Like I said, a quarter inch lower and you'd be looking around for a place to bury me." He put the hat back on and tugged the brim of it lower over his eyes. "That's better."

"What do we do with the one that's still alive?"

Dillon walked over to the younger of the two men and nudged his side with the toe of his boot. "Can you hear me?"

The man groaned as he rolled over with his back against the cruiser. "Help me."

"There's no helping you," Dillon said. "You're already dead."

The man looked down at the lower half of his blood-soaked shirt. "Gut shot."

"That's right." Dillon crouched down in front of him. "You have hours of painful suffering ahead of you or I can end it quick. Tell me how long before Vig gets to Savage."

"I'm not telling you anything."

Dillon made a fist and pressed it against the man's belly until he cried out. "I asked you a question and I expect you to answer it."

"Okay."

Dillon withdrew his hand.

"A week, maybe two."

"How many will she be bringing with her?"

The man grinned with bloodstained teeth. "More than enough to wipe this place clean. She's going to kill every last one of you."

"How many? A dozen?"

"It'll be a lot more than that."

"But no chopper."

The man's eyes widened. "What do you know about the chopper?"

"I know it'll never fly again."

"So, it *did* go down here."

"Like a rock. If Vig comes to Savage she's going to die the same as you."

"She has an army."

"And we have a bear."

The man gasped as he coughed up blood. He wiped it away with the back of his hand. "Please, I'm so thirsty."

"How many innocent people have you killed?"

The man reached for Dillon. "Please."

Dillon knocked the hand away. "Look at you. You chose to live like a cowardly animal and now you're dying the same. Why couldn't you just leave us alone? That's all we wanted—to be left alone."

"I was just following orders. You don't say no to Vig."

"How many kids have you raped?"

The man looked away.

Dillon stood. "Yeah, I thought so." He raised the revolver and pulled the hammer back. "I'm going to do you a favor."

"By putting a bullet in my head?"

"That's right."

"Go to hell."

"You first." Dillon fired. The man's body slid sideways onto the pavement. Dillon holstered his gun, opened the trunk, and grabbed one of the fuel cans. "Back to work."

"You're still bleeding," Leo said while pointing at the blood trickling down the side of Dillon's face.

"I'll live." He started pumping diesel into the first five-gallon tank.

"What do we do with the bodies?"

"When I'm done here, I'll drag them out back."

"Shouldn't we bury them?"

"No time."

"But Sheriff—"

Dillon slammed the pump handle back into its holder. "Dammit, Leo, let's just focus on getting this fuel into your plane so you can fly off to wherever it is you need to go. You heard the man. Vig and her army of road pirates are on their way here. There's going to be a whole lot more holes to be dug before this is over." He put the tank into the trunk, grabbed another one, and started pumping again. A few drops of blood fell into the open tank, mixing with the diesel. Some more blood dripped onto Dillon's lips. He licked them, spit, and kept on pumping until the second tank was full and then he went on to fill the last two remaining tanks. After that he dragged the bodies behind the service station and covered them with a tarp. His head hurt, his mouth tasted like he'd been sucking on copper pennies, and he was starving. He wondered if Remington had some rabbit stew waiting for them back at Vaughn's Hill.

Leo gripped the cruiser's roof and grimaced as he lowered his head. "Give me a moment."

"Take all the time you need."

"Time," Leo said. "Unfortunately, that's something I don't have much of. I just hope to be useful during whatever little time I have left." When he looked up, his face was covered in sweat and the tumors had an odd purple-red hue to them. "The pain is manageable again. We can go."

"Are you hurting all the time now?"

"Pretty much."

"That sucks."

"Yeah." Leo sighed. "It does."

"Are you afraid?"

"Of death?"

Dillon nodded.

Leo put both hands to his face and rubbed his eyes. "Part of me is."

"And the other part?"

"I just want the pain to end." Leo looked up at the blue sky, enjoying the sun on his face. "The fact is that no matter the age one gets to we all die too young."

Dillon thought of his parents, his wife, his children, and extended family and friends who were no longer a part of his life. A wave of regret washed over him. He looked away not wanting Leo to see the tears that fell.

There had been so much death.

No matter the age one gets to we all die too young.

"Wise words," Dillon said.

"I'm not sure how wise they are," Leo replied, "but it's the truth."

Dillon ignored his throbbing head and the taste of copper that still lingered in his mouth. He opened the door and got behind the wheel, anxious to get back to Vaughn's Hill where the world still felt reasonably safe.

That was likely to change soon, but for now it was enough.

24.
✦✧✦✧

"Now you're just showing off."

A shirtless Bear strode up the hill with four rocks in a net strapped across his massive shoulders. He grinned at Morning who was barely managing to carry just one smaller rock in her arms. It was their fifth trip down to the river and back since breakfast that morning.

When they dumped the rocks onto the growing pile near the edge of the hill facing the valley and the rubble of the helicopter crash below, Remington picked up one of the stones and gave them an approving nod. "We're making good progress," he said. "Should have enough for our first fortification by this afternoon."

Morning grimaced as she rubbed her lower back. "That's hard work walking those up this hill."

Remington tipped his head toward Bear. "He seems to be holding up fine."

"I'm starting to think he's not actually capable of getting tired," Morning replied. "He's a human pack mule."

"You should see how he does carrying five next time."

Bear turned around, raised his arm, and flexed.

Morning rolled her eyes. "Yup—you're definitely showing off now, you big goof."

"How much did you bench during your playing days?" Remington asked.

Bear held up seven fingers.

"Seven hundred pounds?" Remington looked at Morning. "Am I understanding him right? A seven-hundred-pound bench press?"

"That's what he says."

Remington leaned in close to Morning. "You think we can believe him?" he whispered and then winked.

"Not sure," Morning whispered back. "He does look a little shifty and if there's one thing I know about men it's their need to exaggerate about certain things."

Bear grabbed the net and started back down to the river for more rocks.

"Wait for me." Morning jogged to catch up.

"I'll start putting up the first wall," Remington yelled out behind her.

Halfway down the path to the river Morning poked the back of Bear's arm. "Hey, you know we were just kidding, right? We don't doubt what you said."

Bear whirled around, looked past Morning to make sure no one was following and then clasped his hands around her back and pulled her toward him. The dark skin of his chest and stomach was slick with sweat.

"You're going to need a bath," Morning said.

Bear nearly knocked off her cowboy hat when he kissed her.

Morning pulled away. "There's work to be done."

Bear let her go, scowling, confused, perhaps even a little hurt.

"Follow me," Morning said right before continuing down to the river. When she got there, she sat on a fallen tree trunk that partially hung over the riverbank, took off her boots, and dipped her feet into the pristine waters of the Yellowstone. She sensed Bear standing behind her waiting for her to say more. "I don't regret what we did. I want you to know that." She looked back. "It was wonderful. It really was."

Bear sat next to the log, wrapped his arms around his knees, and looked up at Morning.

"I was married to one man my whole adult life and even though he's been gone for some time now there's a part of me that will *always* be married to him."

Bear took out the notepad from his back pocket.

You're feeling guilty?

Morning watched the water swirling past her feet. "Yeah, I guess I am. I don't blame you for that though. It's me. When I was married, when I took those vows, it was for life, you know? Not that Waylon wouldn't have wanted me to be happy. He wasn't possessive like that, but he was loyal to me, and I was loyal to him and as much as I have been trying to convince myself that what you and I did wasn't a betrayal I can't push that bit of guilt out of my head."

What we did was beautiful.

"Yes, it was, but it's also complicated—at least for me. The physical part was great and frankly, if I'm being totally honest, I needed the release. Just because I'm a widow doesn't mean I'm not still a woman and you helped to reconnect me to that part of myself and for that I'm very grateful."

But the guilt.

"Exactly. I keep wondering if the roles were reversed, if I was the one gone and Waylon was the one still here, if he would have allowed himself to be with another woman or if he would have ended that part of his life after my passing."

You would have wanted him to be happy.

"Of course."

Weren't you happy when we slept together?

Morning arched a brow. "We weren't actually sleeping."

I'm trying to be respectful.

"I don't think happy is the right word. Satisfied is what I'd call it. Physically, it was amazing. I mean *really* amazing. That doesn't last, though, does it? It didn't take long for the emotional baggage to start piling up. Look, I'm a simple, old-fashioned Montana farm girl. For years my days consisted of getting up early, feeding the chickens, collecting the eggs, cleaning the stalls, raising my son, and being a devoted wife to my husband and the life we created together. That's all I ever needed because that's all I ever wanted."

We're living in very different times now.

"Yes, we are, but that doesn't mean I can forget who I was because that's still a big part of who I am, and it always will be."

I respect your feelings, but I also hope that after this situation with Vig is over, if we survive it, we can sit down and discuss a possible future together—you, me, and Reagan.

"I'm not leaving Savage. This is my home."

It could be our home together. I like it here.

"Oh, I think we need to slow way down on that line of thinking, Bear. I'll make you a promise though. If we get past this mess with Vig then you and I will have that discussion, okay?"

Thank you.

Morning smiled. "You're welcome." She dried her feet and put her socks and boots back on. "These rocks won't walk themselves." She carried one while this time Bear slung five over his back.

When they reached the top of the hill Remington had already stacked a row of rocks that was five feet long by nearly three feet high. "You did manage five," he declared while watching Bear unload the stones next to the wall. "These fortifications won't be much, but at least they'll give us some cover if and when the bullets start to fly. Let me know if you need to take a break. There's no rush. We're making good time."

Bear shook his head and then started walking toward the river trail.

"Is he okay?" Remington asked.

"As good as can be expected under the circumstances," Morning answered.

Remington grabbed a rock and added it to the wall. "You two arguing about something?"

"We're fine."

"Sorry." Remington took off his hat and slapped it against his thigh to shake off the dust. "None of my business."

"No, it isn't."

"I'll just say one more thing about it."

Morning waited.

"Your Waylon was a good man and so is Bear."

"Is that it?"

"Don't miss out on happiness now because of obligations you might feel about someone or something from the past. Time is the one thing you can't ever get back and sooner or later we all run out of time for second chances."

"Thanks for the advice."

"Is that sarcasm?"

"A little, but I also know you mean well. I'm not one to talk much about private matters." Morning started to turn away. "I should get back to the river and make sure Bear is doing okay."

Remington tipped the brim of his hat. "If I overstepped that wasn't my intent."

Morning pointed at the partially finished first wall. "Keep piling on those rocks old man. We'll be back soon with more." Down by the river Bear was nearly ready to bring up more stones. Morning asked that he wait so they could talk some more.

He put a hand on her shoulder.

"I don't want this to turn into something negative between us."

Bear struggled to enunciate the words, but Morning had become much better at understanding them. "I'm okay," he replied. "Are you okay?"

"I care about you." Morning laid her cheek against his chest and hugged him tight. When she stepped back, Bear started writing.

You were right. There's too much on our plates right now. We can push the pause button and then revisit our feelings for each other later. Does that work for you?

"That sounds like a very practical way for us to—" Morning stopped midsentence and then pointed at something across the river. "Look at that," she whispered.

It was a lone wild stallion grazing between a couple of old cottonwood trees. The horse raised its head when Morning began to walk slowly toward the riverbank, its dark eyes watching her every bit as much as she was watching it. She stopped at the river's edge and marveled at the creature's natural presence and power. It was dark brown, with a short, muscular neck and large head marked by a spot of white just above the center of the eyes. The mane that fell over one side of its neck was nearly black—the same color as its tail.

When Bear moved to stand next to Morning, the stallion lifted its head higher and its ears tilted forward as if to say it couldn't believe a man could be so big. Its tail swished as it continued staring at the two of them.

"Isn't he beautiful?" Morning said. "It's been some time since the wild horses have run in this valley. How wonderful if they're returning to Savage for the spring like they used to back when Hap Wilkes was still alive." She turned to look up at Bear, but he was no longer there. Only his notepad and pen were left on the ground where he had been standing. "What are you doing?"

Bear was already waist high in the river as he made his way across, easily pushing through the gentle current. The horse didn't move, seemingly content to watch and wait. Bear reached the other side and slowly walked out, his hands at his side, water dripping from his body. He looked back at Morning and smiled. Then he took a few careful steps toward the horse.

"Let him see your hands," Morning suggested. "And be careful. That's nearly a thousand pounds of wild stallion in front of you."

Bear shuffled closer. The horse's nostrils flared as it grunted through its nose and its ears pinned back against its skull.

"Hold up," Morning said. "That sounded like a warning."

Bear waited.

The stallion grunted again.

There was no more than ten feet between them.

Bear raised his arms with his hands out and the palms facing up.

The stallion let out a raucous squeal and then reared up onto its hind legs, its head and front feet towering over Bear. For the first time in a very long time, he actually felt small, but he wasn't afraid. He stood calmly looking up at the wild beast whose equine ancestors had roamed the lands of Eastern Montana for centuries. The stallion's front feet struck the earth with a heavy thud. It snorted, shook its head, and then reared back again.

Bear remained as unyielding as the hill behind them, his body wet and glistening from the waters of the Yellowstone. Morning gasped as she watched the stallion step toward him until its nose was inches from his face. She had never known a wild horse to do such a thing.

A gust of wind sent ripples across the river. Seconds later came the faraway rumble of thunder even though the sky above was calm and cloudless.

That's not thunder, Morning thought as the ground trembled beneath her feet. With a final snort the stallion took off galloping toward the sound of the approaching herd. Bear lowered his arms. Morning saw his shoulders rise as he took in a deep breath while she waited for him to turn around. The roar of hooves grew stronger. The wind carried the noise of Dog's barking from atop Vaughn's Hill down to the riverbank just as the horses broke out between a cluster of shrubs a hundred yards north of the river. They numbered nearly three dozen—a handful of newborn foals among them, surrounded and protected by the rest of the herd. At the front, setting the fast pace, was the same stallion that moments earlier had nearly nuzzled Bear's head.

The herd slowed and then stopped, facing the river in a v-formation behind the stallion. Bear backed away into the water, conceding the area to the horses. The stallion snorted before walking up to the riverbank, lowering its head, and then drinking in a series of loud, slurping gulps. Soon the other horses were all doing the same.

Bear's hand nudged Morning's. She looked up, saw the tears in his eyes, and wrapped her hand around his. Watching those majestic creatures lined up across the river from them was a remarkable sight—one they both knew they would never forget.

The wild horses had once again returned to Savage.

25.
✦✧✦✧

By early evening four stacked stone walls had been completed. Three were spread out across the top of the hillside while the fourth stood just beyond the start of the path that led from Vaughn's Hill down to the chopper crash and remaining remnants of the ranch house in the valley below.

"These will provide excellent cover while defending the hill," Dillon said. He had arrived that afternoon to help with the last two walls.

"Did Leo say where he was flying to when he left this morning?" Remington asked.

"Fort Peck." Dillon squinted as he watched the sun's slow descent over the horizon far to the west. "I won't be surprised if that's the last we see of him. He's in a bad way. I had to help him up into the cockpit because he's too weak to do it himself."

"Damn shame," Remington said. "He seems like a decent fella. You never know—maybe he'll get a second wind."

Dillon turned to watch Bear walking with Morning across the hill toward the trail to the river. "They seem to be getting close."

Remington leaned against one of the stone walls. "They make for an interesting pair, don't they?"

"If you can find something real then by all means grab on to it."

"Not sure how real it is between them."

"No?"

Remington scratched at his beard. "Given the stress of our current situation I don't know if a person can trust what they're feeling. Adrenaline and fear can sometimes do odd things to one's perspective."

"Morning isn't a woman given over to false emotion because she's stressed. As for Bear, he strikes me as a man who knows exactly what he does and doesn't want."

"Hope you're right, Sheriff. I don't wish to see either one of them get hurt."

"They'll be fine. Besides, what's life without some hurt from time to time?"

"We all need to be fully focused on the task at hand, which is surviving whatever it is Vig has coming for us because failing that nothing else will matter."

"What won't matter?" Morning said as she walked up behind the two men.

Remington stuttered something about the walls.

Morning frowned. "That's not what I heard."

"I thought you were down at the river with Bear?" Dillon asked.

"He's bathing. I figured he should have some privacy. Is that who you two were talking about?"

Remington looked like the kid who had just got caught with his hand halfway inside the cookie jar. "Bear?"

"Was it just Bear or were you talking about Bear and me?"

"Both," Dillon answered.

"Are you worried about something?"

"Well. . ." Remington's voice faded.

"Does Bear know you're worried?"

Dillon shrugged. "I never said I was worried."

"You never said you weren't." Morning pointed at Remington. "So, you're the one worrying about my private life. I'm a grown woman, which makes it none of your business. We have plenty of other important things to be focusing on don't you think?"

Remington's eyes flashed his annoyance. "That's enough."

"Who was the one who hauled up most of these rocks?"

"Bear," Remington answered.

"Then please don't repay him by talking behind his back."

Dillon stared down at Morning from under the brim of his hat. "We weren't. The discussion had more to do with preparation than personal matters. Remington had concerns about everyone being focused on the task at hand and on that we should all agree."

"I'm plenty focused," Morning said. "And so is Bear."

"Good." Dillon glanced over at Remington. "Right?"

Remington nodded. "As rain. Besides, the wild horses are back for the first time in a long time. I'd call that a positive omen."

Dillon looked at Morning. "There you go—a minor misunderstanding. All is well with our little corner of the world."

"Any sign of Vig's road pirates during your patrols?"

"None," Dillon answered. "But lately I haven't driven much further than a few miles beyond the county border."

"And the plan is to have a rifle and ammo sitting ready at each one of these walls you put up?" Morning continued.

Dillon nodded. "Anyone in that valley has to shoot up at the hill while we'll have the advantage of shooting down at them so even though we're likely to have far fewer numbers, they'll be like ducks in a barrel down there. They can only come up the trail two at a time at most so we should be able to defend that easily enough as well. I'm not calling our defenses ideal by any means, but it'll be a hard slog for anyone who thinks they can just show up and take this hill from us."

"Unless Vig has another chopper or airplane at her disposal."

Remington grimaced. "God forbid."

"If Reagan can shoot one down all by herself," Dillon said, "there's no reason any of us can't do the same."

"Speaking of which"—Morning looked back toward the tent, —"I should go check on her." She walked to the tent and then paused at the opening. Reagan was talking to someone. Morning quietly stepped inside and then closed the tent flap behind her. Reagan sat on her knees next to the old leather chair by the firepit.

"Were you scared?" Reagan asked the chair. "*Really*? That's a lot of people. I bet it made you feel good to have so many people who cared about you huh?" She shook her head. "All I know is that her name is Vig. She's the boss of the bad men who want to hurt us." Reagan grinned as she nodded excitedly. "I did see them. They were so beautiful and there were some young ones too. Remington says they haven't been in this valley in like forever but now here they are. I can tell how much it means to him because his eyes got all shiny when he was talking about it. He said that you were friends with the wild horses too."

On and on Reagan went, her face overly animated as she continued her conversation with the empty chair. Morning crept closer, not wanting to startle her. She cleared her throat. Reagan kept talking. Morning cleared her throat again.

"Oh," Reagan said with a start. "I didn't know anyone else was here."

"Who were you talking to?"

"Mr. Wilkes."

"Remington?"

"No." Reagan looked at the chair. "He's gone now."

"Who?"

"Hap."

"You were talking to Hap Wilkes just now?"

Reagan nodded. "Uh-huh. He was sitting right there."

"Honey, Hap Wilkes died years ago. You've seen his grave on this hill."

"Dead doesn't mean gone. I told Remington that very thing when I first saw Hap here. That's how I knew Hap's nickname."

Morning sat next to Reagan. "The Irish Cowboy?"

"Yeah. And that's also when Hap mentioned your great-grandpa Cy. He says they're all watching over us and that they're so pleased that the wild horses have returned."

"Is there anyone else in here with us?"

"It's just you and me now."

"Where did Hap go?"

"I don't know."

"Will he be back?"

"Probably. This is his special place." Reagan sat up straight. "Where's Bear?"

"Washing up down at the river."

"Good." Reagan pinched her nose. "He was getting stinky."

Morning laughed. "You're right about that."

"He better hurry. It's almost dark."

"I'm sure he'll be here any minute now. What else did Hap talk to you about?"

"Lots of stuff."

"Such as?"

"You're trying to find out if I'm making it all up. Well, I'm not. Hap was sitting right there and we were talking."

"I believe you believe it."

"Isn't that just a nicer way of calling me a liar?"

"No, Reagan, far from it. I would never call you that."

"Remember when I saw that man smoking his pipe and standing on the porch of your house?"

"I do."

"But you couldn't see him."

"No."

"Did you believe me then?"

"I believe you saw something that I couldn't."

"Stop it," Reagan said.

"What?"

"I don't understand your answer. You say I believe something but that doesn't mean you believe it too. It just sounds like you're finding different ways of calling me a liar, but I'm *not* a liar."

Morning took Reagan's hands and lightly squeezed them. "I know you're not."

"Hap knows you're worried about your son, but he said Cy is doing fine."

"He mentioned Cy?" Morning realized her grip on Reagan's hands had suddenly tightened so she let them go.

"Cy is living on an island."

"That's right—the San Juan Islands."

"Hap says he has a room in a hotel in a place called Roche Harbor where he's surrounded by good people. They all help each other out by catching fish and crab and growing food the same as we do here."

Morning had mentioned the San Juans to others, but she knew she had never said anything about Roche Harbor specifically, so she was startled to hear that name come out of Reagan's mouth. "Have you ever heard of Roche Harbor before today?"

"No," Reagan answered. "Is it a nice place?"

"I've never been there."

"Well, Hap thinks it's a nice place and it seemed important to him that you knew your son was doing okay so that you could concentrate more on defending Vaughn's Hill so hopefully my telling you will help with that because I don't want Hap mad at me. Even though he's nice I can tell he can be scary too if he wants to be."

"Was he mad about the helicopter crashing into the house?"

Reagan's face brightened. "I thought he was going to be, but instead he said I showed the bad people what happens when you mess with Savage. I felt a lot better about everything after he told me that." She paused. "Do you think you'll visit the San Juan Islands some day?"

"I'd like to."

"You should."

"I'll try."

Reagan leaned back. "Awesome."

Bear came into the tent and walked over to them.

"You clean up nice," Morning said.

"I was talking to Hap Wilkes," Reagan added.

Bear's brows lifted.

Morning touched the chair. "He was sitting here."

"She's not sure yet if she can believe me," Reagan said. When Morning started to protest, she stood up and then touched Morning's shoulder. "It's okay. I know you *want* to believe me. I'm going to use the outhouse before it gets too dark. I don't like walking out there at night—way too scary."

Morning watched Reagan leaving. "Be careful and don't be too long. We'll be starting dinner soon." She looked up at Bear. "I don't know how, but she knew about Roche Harbor. It's the place my son Cy has been staying at in the San Juan Islands."

Bear took out the notepad and then lowered himself next to Morning.

Maybe Hap Wilkes really did tell her.

"I so want to believe that."

But...

"I think it could be a matter of me convincing myself that something is real when it really isn't because I want it to be true."

Blessed are those who have not seen and yet believe.

"Look at you breaking out scripture to make a point. I'll have to add biblical knowledge to your already impressive list of talents. So, you think it's possible Hap Wilkes was sitting in this chair talking to Reagan a moment ago?"

I'm saying it's not impossible.

"And you know what? So do I. There's a whole chain of events I hope to tell you about someday regarding when I first came to Savage after finding my great-grandfather Cy's journal. In a lot of ways, it's both a love story and a ghost story."

I look forward to hearing it.

"Maybe I can tell it to you when we visit the San Juan Islands."

That's in Washington State, right?

"It is."

That's a long haul from here.

Morning smiled. "That's okay—it's a long story."

Deal. Bear stuck out his hand.

Morning shook it. "Deal."

Reagan returned into the tent with Remington and Dillon following close behind. Remington groaned as he sat down in the old chair, closed his eyes, and then stretched his legs out in front of him. "I'm beat." He opened his eyes. "Thanks to everyone for all the help. Those little walls out there went up a lot faster than I thought they would and could be the difference between life and death should things go sideways for us."

"How are the horses doing?" Morning asked.

"They're standing together by the outhouse," Reagan answered. "They're getting along like the best of friends." She looked at Morning. "Did you tell them about Hap?"

Remington frowned. "Hap? What about him?"

"According to Reagan he was sitting in that chair talking to her about twenty minutes ago," Morning replied.

"No kidding." Remington looked like he might get up. "I'm not sitting on him, am I?"

Reagan giggled. "He's not there anymore."

"Well, that's too bad. I'd like to see him. Did he have anything to say to me?"

"Uh-huh." Reagan looked at Morning again. "I didn't understand what it meant so I figured you wouldn't want to hear about it."

"Go ahead and tell us," Morning said.

"Umm, Hap wanted Remington to know that when the day is darkest to look to heaven for salvation."

Remington mouthed the words silently and then shrugged. "I don't understand."

"See?" Reagan said. "I told you it doesn't make any sense."

Bear held up his notepad.

Perhaps it will make sense when the time is right and we're meant to understand its meaning.

Remington got up from the chair. "I don't know anything about looking to heaven, but I do know I'm starving after stacking all those stones today. Who else is ready for some supper?"

"Me!" Reagan shouted.

"Then let's go pick some of those tasty carrots that are in the greenhouse." Remington held Reagan's hand as they made their way back outside.

"Sheriff?" Morning asked.

"Yeah?"

"How long do you think we have until Vig and her army of road pirates show up?"

"I wish I knew. A few days perhaps?"

"Do you think we might luck out and she moves on to easier or more profitable targets?"

"That'd be nice."

"But not likely."

Dillon shook his head. "No. Between the chopper being shot down and Bear's presence here this place has likely become personal to Vig. She wants to send a message to anyone else who might be thinking of standing up to her—namely that doing so will get you killed."

"How do you like our chances of coming out the other end of this okay?"

"We won't know that until we see exactly what we're up against. If it's just a couple dozen camped out in the valley at the bottom of this hill, I'd say we might do fine. If it's much more than that we could be in for some serious trouble."

"Are you afraid?"

"Not really. I'm more ready than anything—ready for a fight. Win or lose I just want to get to it. The waiting, the unknown, it's become the worst part of all of this." Dillon lowered his voice. "Do you think she really saw Hap Wilkes in that chair?"

Bear quickly scribbled a response.

Yes! Don't you?

Morning waited for Dillon to share what he thought. After a long pause he finally did.

"I believe *something* is going on up here on this hill. What it is exactly I can't say."

Remington and Reagan soon returned with the carrots that were ready for boiling. A fire was started.

Darkness descended.

A meal was shared.

Right before savoring the last bite of carrot Morning snuck glances at the others and then silently prayed to a god she hoped was actually listening that it wouldn't prove to be their last meal together.

God didn't answer her.

Yet.

26.

✦✧✦✧

"She has to know you trust her."

"What does that even mean?" Reagan asked.

Morning slowed her horse Justice's pace so that Reagan and Peanut could catch up to them. "It means when you relax, so will she."

"But she doesn't want to go."

"Because she senses *you* don't want her to. Your fear is confusing her. Take a deep breath and move your hands forward an inch or two so the bridle bit isn't so tight in her mouth."

Reagan sighed. "I didn't think riding a horse would be so much work."

"You'll get the hang of it. Remington is a patient and understanding man and that makes for a patient and understanding horse. There you go. See how Peanut is responding so positively to that little touch of freedom you're giving her now?"

"How'd you get so smart about horses?"

"There's no substitute for lots of time in the saddle," Morning replied. "My husband Waylon taught me that."

"Was Waylon smart?"

Morning grinned. "Smart enough to marry me."

"Or maybe *you* were smart enough to marry *him*."

"You're probably right about that. You want to do some trotting?"

"You mean go faster?"

"I think you're ready." What Morning wasn't telling Reagan was that her impromptu riding lesson that morning was the result of Remington's suggestion they try to get her as comfortable on a horse as quickly as possible in case something happened and she was forced to escape on her own. Morning agreed but also worried there was far too little time to adequately prepare Reagan for such a thing. Still, even a little practice was better than nothing.

"What do I do to make her trot?"

"Give her sides a little nudge with your heels," Morning answered.

Reagan flashed a big grin when Peanut started trotting, making her backside bounce up and down in the saddle.

"Stay relaxed," Morning said. "Move with the horse and you won't bounce so much."

"Like this?"

"That's right. You're a quick study."

"Can we go faster?"

"That would be a gallop. Are you sure you want to try that so soon?"

"Does Peanut know how to do a slow gallop?"

"I'm sure she can handle that. The question is if you can send her the correct signals so that she understands what you want from her."

"What signal is that?"

"Same as before," Morning replied. "A gentle squeeze into her flanks and also let out the reins a touch more. You'll want to lean forward in the saddle a little as well and remember—move with her not against her." Peanut started a relaxed gallop through the tall field grass near the bottom of Vaughn's Hill. Morning carefully rode alongside them, making sure both horse and rider continued working well together. "How are you doing?"

"Great!" Reagan exclaimed as her ponytail bumped against the back of her shoulders. "I'm actually riding a horse."

"You sure are. How do you like it?"

"I love it."

"Peanut seems to be enjoying the ride as well. Do you want to head toward the river and see if she wants a drink?"

"Yeah."

They reached the river in a few minutes. Both horses immediately lowered their heads and began drinking. Reagan winced as she adjusted her position in the saddle.

"Sore butt?"

Reagan's cheeks flushed. "A little."

"You'll get used to it."

"Does yours hurt too?"

"Nah. This old backside of mine is impervious to pain." Morning dipped her head lower. "Hey, you really did good, Reagan."

"Thank you."

"I mean it. I've seen too many give up after the first few minutes on a horse, but you listened, remained relaxed, and really proved to yourself and to Peanut that you belong in that saddle."

"Maybe I'll have my own horse someday."

"I bet you will."

Peanut and Justice had finished drinking and were touching noses. Vaughn's Hill rose up from the valley several hundred yards to the east and the main road into Savage was nearly equal in distance to the west. On the other side of the gurgling river was a cluster of blue and white wildflowers and beyond that a row of scraggly trees.

"This sure is a pretty place," Reagan said.

Morning leaned back in the saddle and looked up at the deep blue and white skyscape above her. "Yes, it is."

Justice's head raised and his tail twitched. He let out a high-pitched whinny.

"Two men on horses," Reagan whispered.

Morning grabbed the shotgun that was strapped to the side of her saddle. "Don't come any closer," she warned. The men weren't men so much as serious-looking, long-haired teenage boys dressed in leather hides and moccasins and sitting atop horses without saddles. "You sure don't look like road pirates."

"Lucian sent us to warn you," the older of the two said. His brown skin was smooth, his dark eyes clear and sharp, and his body lean and strong. A pistol hung from one hip and a long knife from the other. "We're Crow. My name is Joe and this is my younger brother Robert."

"Warn us about what?"

"Vig is coming."

"We know."

"Her army is very close—perhaps no more than another day's march."

Morning sat up straight. *"An army?"*

Joe nodded. "We counted at least three hundred of them, well-armed and with several vehicles, though most are walking on foot. It is believed Vig herself is with them."

"Good. I'd love to get a chance to end this once and for all with a bullet to her head."

"Careful what you wish for," Robert said. He appeared to be only fifteen or sixteen years old, but he spoke with a confident authority well beyond his years. A rifle was slung over his shoulder and, like his older brother, a knife hung off his hip. "She comes to settle a score with the one called Bear and her fury is said to burn white hot."

"Let it burn," Morning replied, "until it burns her up with it. Now, do you mind telling me what's with the garb?"

"You want to know why we look the way we look?" Joe asked.

"Yeah, the animal skins, moccasins, and the lack of saddles."

"The world that was is no more and the old world and our old ways are now returning."

"And so too will our ancestral lands be ours again," Robert added.

"I recall Lucian saying something very similar. When your lands are returned to you, will that include my place and the Wilkes ranch?"

"Lucian has made it clear that your claims will be honored by our people," Joe replied. "As long as you live your homes will remain."

"So, all we have to do is survive Vig's attack and this new old world of yours won't be bothering us?"

"Yes."

"Okay. I guess that's about as fair of a deal as we're going to get. Are you two heading back to the Crow Reservation? That's quite a long ride from here if you are."

"No. We are returning to Fort Peck to let Lucian know we spoke with you and to get further instructions from him."

"Any chance more of you might make the trip down here to help us fight Vig?"

"This is not yet our fight."

"I see. You're hoping we weaken Vig first for you."

Robert scowled at his brother. "We should be fighting her *now*. Vig travels in the open, which makes her more vulnerable. There is no honor in waiting."

"Quiet," Joe replied. "Do not speak out against the wisdom of the elders."

"You mistake cowardice for wisdom."

"Apologies for my brother," Joe said. "He is of an age when desire for violence too easily overwhelms good sense."

"You're only a few years older than me." Robert straightened his shoulders. "Leo begged Lucian to help them defend their hill and yet we hide at Fort Peck like mewling old women leaving these people here to die."

"These people are not *our* people," Joe replied. "Now say no more."

"You mentioned Leo," Morning said. "Is he still at Fort Peck?"

Joe nodded. "Yes, but he's very ill. He may already have passed by the time we return."

"He spoke passionately on your behalf." Robert's voice lowered. "It is our shame that we choose not to listen."

Morning stared into Joe's eyes and saw the inner conflict swirling within them. There was a part of him that wanted to fight Vig as badly as his younger brother did. "So, there's no chance Lucian will send us help?"

"I am sorry," Joe answered. "The tribes are gathering, but that takes time and I fear that is time you do not have."

"Your horses," Morning continued. "Where did you get them?"

Robert leaned forward and ran his hand over his mare's neck. "Do you recognize their bloodline? They are the descendants of the very herd that once roamed this valley since the time of my forefathers—the wild horses of Savage."

"When Hap Wilkes was alive."

"I know that name," Joe said. "Lucian has mentioned it. This Hap Wilkes was a friend to our people."

"All the more reason the tribes should be fighting Vig *now*," Robert seethed.

Joe shook his head. "You are so desperate for war, little brother."

"No, I am desperate to do what is right. Vig and her scum are coming here now, but how long before they are coming for us?

And how much more powerful will she be then? We hide from this conflict, yet we are many and we are strong. We should be—"

Reagan flinched in the saddle as she watched the top of Robert's head erupt in a red mist, his blood splattering her face. The world around her stopped. There was no sound or smell. Peanut shifted beneath her, instinctively backing away from the danger. Then she heard her name—faint, distant, spoken by a familiar voice. Something gripped her arm. She looked down, saw it, felt it, and then she looked up.

Robert's body toppled from his horse.

"Reagan!" Morning shouted. "Can you hear me?"

Reagan nodded.

"Ride back to the hill as fast as you can. Peanut knows the way. She'll get you there." Morning's grip tightened. "Do you understand?"

"What about you?" Reagan murmured. The shock of Robert's death was already fading. She knew bloodshed as well as she knew survival. Bear had taught her that.

Another shot rang out, splintering the bark of a nearby tree.

"I'll stay here until you're away. Bear and the others have likely already heard the gunfire. They'll be ready to help when you get there. Now go." Morning slapped Peanut's backside. "Hurry!"

Peanut took off at a full gallop, pushing through the field grass like a small four-legged tank of flesh and bone. Morning watched and waited until they were safely a hundred yards from her and then she turned to face Joe.

"Road pirates." Joe gazed at the lifeless body of his brother. Tears streamed down his cheeks. He held up the pistol, his lower lip trembling. "He was right. We should be the ones fighting them now."

Morning noted movement in the distance. "There are at least three of them," she said. "Likely scouting for Vig and they all appear to have hunting rifles." She reached for Joe. "Don't be stupid."

Joe pushed Morning's hand away. "I must avenge my brother."

"This isn't the time. You're outnumbered and with those rifles they'll pick you off long before you could reach them. Come back to Vaughn's Hill with me."

"No." Joe was no longer crying. His jaw clenched. "You go. Be with your people and prepare for what is coming."

"And leave you alone to die here? I don't think so."

Another bullet cut the air no more than a few feet behind Joe's head. He ignored it. "I'm not dying today, and neither are you." He leaned down while still somehow remaining on his horse, picked up his brother's rifle, and then quickly checked to make sure it was loaded. "You didn't tell me your name."

"Morning—Morning McGreevy."

"That is a good name. Be safe, Morning McGreevy, and protect the little girl. I do not need to tell you what the road pirates would do to someone like her."

The gunfire was getting closer. Justice snorted, anxious to be away from the approaching threat. Morning tightened her grip on the reins. "Don't do this. Come back with me and fight with us."

Joe yanked his horse around so that his back was to Morning. "I'm giving you a chance to escape. Please don't waste it."

"I'm not asking you to do that."

"You don't have to. I'm a warrior, Morning McGreevy." Joe glanced down at his brother. "A warrior who now must collect a blood debt from those road pirate devils." He holstered his pistol and raised the rifle. "It is time."

Before Morning could say more Joe unleashed a rage-filled howl, dug his heels into his horse's flanks, and took off through the field with his long, wind-whipped dark hair spread out behind him. She watched him aim his rifle and fire once, twice, and then a third time. A road pirate rose up from the grass and fired back. Then the two other road pirates did the same. Joe's horse screamed, stumbled, and fell, toppling face and neck-first into the ground. Joe was catapulted end over end from the horse, disappearing somewhere in the tall grass. Morning knew the impact alone could have been enough to kill him.

All three road pirates remained. One turned and aimed his rifle in her direction. Morning's shotgun was nearly useless at such long range, putting her at a considerable disadvantage. A bullet struck a log in front of her. Justice rolled his eyes and scampered sideways. Morning stared across the valley, hoping to see if Joe might still be alive but there was no sign of him.

Another shot hissed inches above Morning's shoulder. Justice strained against her hold on the reins, dripping froth where the bridle bit dug into the soft corners of his mouth. It was his way of telling her it was long past time they get moving.

There was nothing more to be done. Morning knew this was a fight she couldn't win alone and her dying now would only put Reagan and the others in that much more danger. Cursing under her breath, she finally allowed Justice to take off through the field.

The battle for Vaughn's Hill had begun.

27.

✦✧✦✧

"It looks so quiet down there," Dillon said. "Hard to believe what's coming."

The Wilkes property spread out before the group gathered at the top of Vaughn's Hill. The sun's slow descent cast long shadows over the valley floor. A gentle breeze carried the call of coyotes on the hunt from somewhere half a mile or more to the south. The hint of stars had already started to fill the emerging night sky.

"It's coming," Remington replied, his bushy brows pushing in against each other. "I've double-checked all the rifles at each wall station. They are ready to go with a bucket of ammo sitting next to them—enough ammo to hold out up here for a day or three."

"And then what?" Morning asked. Her question sat unanswered like an old toy abandoned on a shelf by those who didn't wish to play with it anymore. She looked into the faces of the others. "Well?"

Remington shrugged. "There's no answer to that."

"Why not? Shouldn't we be preparing?"

"For what? If we run out of ammo, we run out of ammo. There's nothing to be done about it, which is why we need to be stingy with how often any of us actually pulls those triggers. Don't fire unless you have a real shot. There is to be no firing over anyone's heads to send a message. We need to make every round count."

Bear held up the notepad.

When they are down there, once it's dark, I'll pay them a visit.

"A few hundred or more of Vig's road pirates could be camped in that valley by tomorrow." Dillon shook his head. "You're a big, powerful fella but even you won't stand a chance against those kinds of numbers."

I've done it before.

"Against three hundred of them?"

Not that many, but numbers don't mean nearly as much as lack of heart. They don't want to be here. Once they fear me more than they fear Vig the odds start to change. If you put up a strong enough fight most of these road pirates would rather run away.

"This time might be different," Dillon replied. "I've never heard of Vig assembling this many of her people to attack a single target."

Which means there's a good chance they have no idea what they're doing. This isn't a well-trained army we're talking about—it's road pirates. For every one or two of them that actually knows how to fight there's another dozen who are nothing more than drunks, drug addicts, and bullies whose first instincts are to scatter like cockroaches at the first sign of real trouble.

"He might be right about that," Remington said. "Vig has used fear as her primary weapon to grow and control her territory. She's been allowed to do that because so few have actually stood up to her. This little army of hers that's marching our way might not know the first thing about putting up an actual fight."

"There's another option we should consider." All eyes were on Dillon who cleared his throat before continuing. "There's plenty of diesel left in the tank at the station. We fuel up some vehicles and get the hell out of here."

"Leave Savage?" Morning shook her head. "No. This is my home and I'm not giving it up to Vig."

"Where would we possibly run to?" Remington asked.

"We could drive west," Dillon answered. "Or further north until we reach Fort Peck."

"No," Morning repeated. "If people keep running away from Vig then eventually they're going to run out of places to run to. I'm staying and fighting."

"Me too," Remington said. "This hill is my line in the sand. This is my time to make a stand. I'm a Wilkes. We don't run from trouble—we deal with it."

"Okay." Dillon nodded. "I feel the same, but I didn't want to assume all of you did as well." He paused. "We stay together and we fight together."

Remington squinted at something and then grinned. "There he is."

Dog sniffed the ground as he zigzagged his way toward them. When he reached Reagan, he licked her hand before going over to Remington and sitting next to him.

"He wants to fight with us," Reagan said.

"Damn right." Remington scratched behind Dog's ears. "He'll be our early warning system. Anything approaches this hill and Dog will bark out an alarm." Dog's tail wagged at the praise.

"Are we going to die?"

Bear knelt down on one knee in front of Reagan. "No. Not you."

"How do you know that?"

"I promise."

Reagan placed her hands around Bear's face. "You can't promise that, but it's okay. I'm not afraid."

A swirling storm of mixed emotions played out across Bear's face. Though he didn't speak the words clearly, they were all able to understand him. "I will protect you."

"But who will protect *you*?"

"For as long as any of us can," Morning said, "we'll protect each other."

Remington continued to scratch behind Dog's ears. "Absolutely. If I'm going down, I'm going down fighting. And the thing of it is. . ."

Morning cocked her head. "Yeah?"

"Well, as bad as things are right now, I have to admit it hasn't been *all* bad since the collapse."

Dillon grunted. "I think I know exactly what you're getting at."

"I bet you do, Sheriff," Remington replied.

"No damn cell phones," Dillon continued. "No bills. No taxes. No Internet. No social media. No reality television. No phony agenda-pushing politicians."

"For those of us who survived," Morning said, "life suddenly became very real. I only wish our loved ones could all be here to share it with us."

A shooting star flashed across the sky, followed by another and then another. "God is putting on a little light show for us," Remington said. "For there are as many souls in heaven as there are stars in an infinite sky, seeking life where there is death, peace where there is war, warmth where there is cold, and company where there is loneliness."

"Is that from one of your books?" Morning asked.

Bear started writing and then held it up.

Manitoba.

"That's right," Remington replied. "And the author?"

Decklan Stone.

"Right again. I can only wish to have written something as good as that."

Morning read Bear's answer and then looked at Remington. "I know that name."

"As well you might. He sold a great many copies over the years."

"No, that's not it. My son mentioned it to me once."

"The son named Cy who lives in the San Juan Islands."

"Yes."

"Decklan Stone lived among those islands as well. The locals there knew him simply as the writer. His life story is actually every bit as fascinating as anything he put down in the pages of his books. I recall how they were going to make a movie about it at one time, but for some reason it never happened."

"There was a tour," Morning said. "Cy visited his private island home. The wife opened it to the public after she moved full time to Roche Harbor."

"Calista."

Morning frowned. "Who?"

"Calista," Remington answered. "She was Decklan Stone's wife. There was a magazine article on her after his passing. The interview was conducted at the Roche Harbor Hotel where she was living with her longtime friend who also owned the hotel."

"That's right," Morning said as her memory of the conversation with Cy came rushing back to her. "As far as I know she still owns it. Her name is Tilda Ashland. Cy calls her Lady Ashland because he says she has this air of nobility about her. Apparently, she's quite old but still rules over that hotel with an iron fist."

"Morning, are you okay?" Reagan asked.

"I'm fine." Morning dabbed a tear away. "Just missing my son." She looked up. "I'm not afraid of dying on this hill. I'm really not but. . ." More tears followed.

"But you want to see your son again," Dillon said.

Morning wiped her nose. "Very much." She coughed. "I'd like to visit him and those islands he loves so much."

Dillon reached over and patted her hand. "You will—one way or another."

"Say, Sheriff," Remington said, "how about a song to lift our spirits? Your guitar is in the tent."

Reagan's eyes lit up. "*Please* Sheriff Potts, will you play for us?"

Dillon's face tightened. "Oh, I don't know."

"After supper." Remington winked. "A bowl of my rabbit stew is worth a song or two don't you think?"

"I tell you what—make it two bowls and you have a deal."

"Deal!" Remington shouted. "Who's hungry?" He led the way into the tent where all of the stew was then quickly devoured. Even Dog was able to enjoy a scrap or two of rabbit meat.

They sat around the fire with full bellies and heavy hearts, each of them worrying in silence over Vig's imminent arrival. Dog stretched out by Remington's feet while Peanut and Justice nibbled at some grass Reagan had left for them on the ground near the tent entrance.

"I kept my end of the bargain, Sheriff," Remington said. "Now it's your turn."

Dillon picked up the guitar and plucked at the strings. "There's no doubt you cook a fine stew." He strummed a few chords.

"You already have a song in mind?" Morning asked.

"I do."

"What is it?"

"Something I think is appropriate for our situation, but here's the deal—when I play it the first time, I need you to pay real close attention so that when I play it for a second time, we can all sing together, okay?"

"Nobody wants to hear me croaking out any songs," Remington said.

"Speak for yourself," Morning replied. "I'd buy tickets to the Remington show."

"Fine." Remington shrugged. "It's your ears that are going to suffer. Don't say I didn't warn you."

Dillon tuned the strings and then looked up at the others. "I actually heard this song in person years ago at that little roadside dive bar some miles north of Savage. I was out there on a public disturbance call. By the time I had finished up the report, my shift was over. The music was playing, and it sounded good, so I stayed for a beer and a listen. Still had my uniform on and everything. Folks didn't seem to mind my being there. Maybe they were grateful I cleared out that night's riffraff. Or maybe like me they were so into the music that as long as it played nothing else really mattered. It was just a singer and a guitar.

"He was a young man with the last name Bingham. Dark hair and beard, earnest eyes, wearing one of those big white ten-gallon hats you didn't see much of anymore outside of West Texas roughneck territory. Good looking kid, wiry strong, he had plenty of approving eyes on him as he worked those guitar strings. His voice was this dry warble dripping with the kind of yearning that made him sound much older than he was—like he had already seen and done things that left him with some serious scar tissue on his soul. Anyways, this is the song that had me hooked that night and for weeks after. I'd never heard anything like it before or since. He was selling signed CDs by the door and I made sure to pick one up on my way out and I played this damn thing over and over again until I had it right. About drove my wife and kids crazy."

"I like how you tell a story." Reagan smiled sheepishly as she touched the neck of Dillon's guitar. "I can see it all in my mind."

"Then I hope you like my singing as much as my story telling."

"It's the same thing," Reagan replied. "A song is a story, right?"

Dillon nodded. "I'd say the best ones are, yes." He picked at the strings and tapped the heel of his cowboy boot. "The song is called 'Wolves'."

"Like the four-legged ones?" Reagan asked.

"Not exactly. It's about standing up for what's right and doing what needs to be done even if it's unpopular or dangerous. We all have to fight off the wolves that would take from us. Those wolves can come in the form of losing loved ones, sickness, death, betrayal, violence, insecurity—basically the darkness that comes from living and makes people lose hope or take the easy path instead of the righteous one."

The fire flickered within Remington's eyes as he gazed at Dillon from under the brim of his cowboy hat. "That sounds like a hell of a story."

"It's a hell of a song. Now remember, I'll sing it first and you pay attention and then we can all sing it together. That was the deal."

"Yes, it was," Remington said. "So, get to singing, Sheriff."

The guitar played softly at first, matching the near whisper of Dillon's singing. By the third verse, though, the guitar was much louder, matching the defiant confidence of the song's message and Dillon's playing. Morning snuck a look at Bear who sat beside her cross-legged and leaning forward, his mouth partly open, brow furrowed, listening intently to every word. And as she listened as well, she soon understood his fascination. The song reflected so much that had happened to him.

It was his story.

It was her story.

It was all of their story.

Morning's hand crept over the ground toward Bear's. She wrapped her pinky around his. He looked down, his mouth hinting at a smile, then closed his eyes, lifted his head, and sang out the chorus, his voice rising like the fire's smoke. Some of the words were only partly formed but on he sang. It was the first time

Morning had seen him without any embarrassment or hesitation over his inability to speak clearly.

Dillon nodded his approval. "No need to wait, folks. Don't leave Bear hanging. We'll keep singing this thing until the wheels fall off."

The song ended and then started again. Remington clapped. Reagan joined him. Morning hugged Bear tightly as he continued to howl and wail. Dog wagged his tail as he walked slowly around their circle. Still standing near the tent's entrance, Peanut and Justice's ears perked forward, seemingly amused by the commotion.

They all sang and danced, laughing a lot, crying a little, fully aware of what waited for them the next day, and yet when fear threatened to overtake their courage, the song's refrain was repeated and their shared courage returned.

There would be no running away.

They were more determined than ever to stand their ground and fight to the last to keep the wolves at bay.

28.
✦✧✦✧

Reagan sat up, yawned, and stretched her arms over her head. The others around her were still sleeping. She looked for Dog but didn't see him in his normal spot curled up at Remington's feet as he slept in the chair. Last night's fire was completely out and the ground was cold to the touch.

Bear's roaring snore always made Reagan want to laugh because it sounded so very much like his nickname. She wondered if he ever considered hibernating for the winter.

Dog began barking outside.

Reagan got up, careful not to wake anyone. She pulled back the tent flap, happy to take in the crisp and clean Montana morning air. "Dog?"

Now he was growling at something.

Reagan stepped outside in her bare feet and turned toward the sound. "Dog?" she repeated.

The growling became more intense.

"What is it?" Reagan whispered.

Dog stood near the hill's edge facing the valley and snarling with his hackles raised. The early morning gloom made it difficult to see what was bothering him so much. Reagan stood next to him and put her hand on his shoulder. He ignored her, fixated on something at the bottom of the hill.

Then Reagan saw them.

A long procession of people was moving toward the helicopter crash site. Mixed in with the people were a few trucks and a large RV. Reagan tried to count how many there were but lost track after reaching a hundred. Nearly all of them were carrying guns. She turned and ran into the tent.

"Hey," Reagan hissed.

Nobody stirred. This time she shouted.

"Hey!"

Bear was the first to rise. He was already holding the sledgehammer by the time he reached Reagan. Seconds, later Dillon, Morning, and Remington stood next to him.

"What is it?" Dillon asked.

"People outside," Reagan answered. "Lots of them."

They spread out shoulder to shoulder and looked down. Remington scowled, spit, and then cursed under his breath.

"How many are there?" Morning asked.

"Too damn many," Dillon answered. "See that big fancy RV?"

"Vig," Morning said.

Dillon nodded. "My thoughts exactly. It appears their dear leader prefers to travel in style."

Remington strained to see the RV more clearly. "If we had one of those rocket launchers, we could light that thing up from here and send that lunatic woman straight to hell."

"You think they've seen us yet?" Morning asked.

"Probably," Dillon replied, "but I doubt they care. They have us so outnumbered they likely don't think we're any kind of real threat."

Morning knelt down next to Reagan. "Honey, I think it's best you go inside for a bit, okay?"

"Why?"

"I'd rather not have the bad men getting too good of a look at you."

"Because they'll want to take me away."

"That's right."

"Bear won't let them."

"You can take Dog with you," Remington said. "He'll keep you company."

Bear tipped his head toward the tent, letting Reagan know he agreed with Morning that she should go inside.

Reagan nodded. "Okay."

"Get in there," Remington said to Dog who then immediately walked alongside Reagan into the tent.

Dillon pointed at the helicopter wreckage. "They don't look too pleased about that."

Remington picked up the rifle that was leaning against one of the recently constructed river rock walls. "What if we just start shooting now and be done with it?" he asked Dillon.

"First we should find out exactly what it is that Vig wants from us."

"I don't give a damn what she wants. Look at the manpower she brought with her. She came to fight, and I intend to give her one."

Dillon reached out and pushed the rifle barrel down so that it was pointing at the ground. "Not yet."

"Then when?" Morning asked.

Dillon's expression was grim as he continued watching the gathering mass of people below them. "I'm sure it'll be soon—God help us." He looked into the eyes of each of the others. "We can't defeat that many of them."

"Don't give up on us yet, Sheriff," Morning said.

Bear grunted and pointed.

"Looks like they found your car." Remington raised his rifle. "I'm happy to plink a few for you. Just say the word."

Ten or so men encircled Dillon's cruiser. One of them poured gasoline over it while the others cheered. A match was struck. In seconds the car was engulfed in flames, sending a billowing cloud of black smoke high into the sky.

"Why?" Dillon asked. "Why do that?"

"To send a message," Remington replied. "They're making it very clear to us that they know we're up here."

"And as partial payback for what was done to their chopper," Morning added.

Remington nodded. "Yeah, likely that too."

The men around the cruiser backed away as the fire burned hotter and the smoke churned thicker. Two large explosions rocked the valley, sending remnants of the cruiser into the air. Vig's army cheered.

"Animals," Dillon seethed.

Inside the tent Reagan sat by the firepit with Dog who was resting his head on her lap while she massaged his neck. Both of them flinched when they heard the explosion. *I'm not scared of the bad men,* she kept telling herself and yet that whisper of fear threatened to turn into a full-throated scream. Her mouth was dry, her hands trembled, and her chest felt oddly tight.

Reagan was more afraid now than she had been in a very long time.

Memories of her life before the collapse came flooding back. Her mother's warmth, her father's sense of humor, their happy little home tucked within their equally happy little neighborhood—all gone. The man who had promised Reagan's mother he would take care of her abused her in every way possible and then sold her to a group of road pirates for nothing more than a few cans of bean with bacon soup and a case of beer.

Now those same kinds of men were back, no more than a short walk down the hill, hoping to kill her friends and get their hands on her. That wasn't what scared Reagan the most though. It was that Bear would fight to the death to protect her and she knew the pain of losing him would be too much. And it wasn't just Bear. She had come to love the rest of them as well—Morning, Remington, and Dillon had all been so kind to her. They had become a family and she didn't want to see any of them hurt.

Reagan closed her eyes tight and begged God to send Vig and the bad men away. "We're happy here," she whispered. "We just want to be left alone."

Don't forget what I told you.

Dog's ears perked up and his head lifted as he looked at the nearby chair.

Reagan smiled at the familiar voice. "When the day is darkest, look to heaven for salvation."

That's right.

"I still don't understand what it means."

You will.

"Promise?"

I give you my word. I don't ever lie, Reagan, and I don't intend to start with you.

Reagan shifted on the floor so she could directly face the chair. "I see you."

I know.

"Sometimes you look old but then you change and look young."

Young and old and everything in between. Regardless of the face I wear, it's still me.

"The Irish Cowboy—Hap Wilkes."

Green eyes twinkled within Hap's handsome, younger version face. Then those same eyes turned hard and serious when the image of old Hap suddenly replaced the younger one. His fingers dug into the arms of the chair as he leaned forward until the tip of his nose nearly touched Reagan's. He smelled of sun-dried leather, a warm summer field, and whiskey. When he spoke, his voice was the wind-pushed rustle of dry leaves over cold pavement.

Be ready.

"For what?"

Dog whimpered.

What comes next won't be easy. Being the cause of so much sacrifice never is.

"What is coming?"

Dog growled.

The hardness in Hap's eyes dissipated like fog in the light of a warm sun, replaced by the weight of sadness that comes with uncertain wisdom. He looked away.

"Tell me," Reagan nearly shouted.

Dog barked.

Hap's outline faded, leaving only the chair, but a final spoken word by him lingered after he was gone—an urgent warning to listen and to prepare.

That word was death.

29.
✦✧✦✧

"You sure about this?"

Dillon gave Remington a quick glance, clenched his jaw, and nodded. "Let's find out exactly what they're here for."

"We *know* what they're here for."

"Maybe we do. Maybe we don't."

"I don't like it."

"Duly noted."

"Sheriff—"

Dillon cut him off. "It's one unarmed man coming up the trail. We can handle that."

"A man taking mental notes on our defenses up here so he can report back to Vig what they are."

"And also confirming Bear is actually with us," Morning added.

Remington nodded. "Exactly."

Dillon pulled the brim of his hat down. "The time for discussion is over. He's already on his way."

Bear was marching a short, heavyset fifty-something-year-old man across the hill toward the others. The man's thinning brown hair hung nearly to his shoulders. His fleshy cheeks quivered when Bear pushed him in the back to walk faster.

When they reached him, Dillon looked the man up and down. "What's your name?"

"You're the sheriff," the man said between heavy breaths. His jeans and sweater were soiled and he smelled like he hadn't bathed in months.

"Name," Dillon repeated.

"Webster."

"You speak for Vig?"

"Nobody speaks for Vig but Vig."

"She's the one who sent you up here to meet with us."

"That's right."

"Why you?"

Webster shrugged. "Why not?"

Morning stepped forward. "Stop looking around. Keep your eyes on us."

Webster's surprised expression was clearly exaggerated. *"Looking around?* I don't know what you mean."

"Yeah, you do." Morning raised her rifle slightly. "That's why Vig sent you."

"Not exactly," Webster replied.

"No?"

Webster's grin revealed several missing teeth. "No." He half-turned to look up at Bear. "My job was to confirm he was real. He's the first thing Vig wants."

"She can't have him," Morning said.

Webster chuckled. "Oh, we'll see about that." His eyes narrowed. "Do you know how much the bear has cost her? She can't possibly allow him to go on. The question for the rest of you is whether or not you choose to die with him."

Morning didn't hesitate. "Yes."

"And the others?" Webster nodded to Dillon. "Are you willing to die for the bear as well, Sheriff?"

"Like we have a choice."

"But you do, Sheriff—you do! Allow me to return to the valley with the bear in tow and I assure you Vig will be much more willing to consider your longer-term chances for survival."

"Bear stays with us," Morning said. "That's not open to discussion. You tell Vig that."

"We're more than three hundred strong down there."

Remington grunted. "You might be three hundred, but if the rest are as sad a sight as you are then strong isn't a word I would use to describe that number."

"What did you do before the collapse?" Dillon asked.

Webster appeared surprised by the question. *"Do?"*

"For a living."

"Oh." Webster straightened. "I was a teacher for twenty-seven years."

"Where?"

"An elementary school down in Riverton."

"Wyoming."

"That's right. They addressed me as Mr. Dinklage. I so enjoyed helping shape those little young ones into more compassionate and capable activist citizens of the world. I truly believed it to be my life's calling."

"And now you're Vig's message boy."

"I'm no boy. I've done what needed to be done."

"To survive."

Webster nodded. "The same as you."

Dillon arched a brow. "I doubt that."

"Do you actually think you're better than me, Sheriff?"

"You're with Vig so, yeah, I'm better than you."

"She's no more a monster than the bear."

Morning jammed the tip of her rifle into Webster's soft, fleshy chest. "Bear isn't a monster."

"And neither is Vig."

"Then tell her to get off of my property," Remington growled.

"I'm afraid it's too late for that. Vig won't leave without the bear." Webster looked over at the tent. "Is it true he traveled here with a young girl?"

"Bear stays with us," Morning said.

"Refusing Vig will get all of you killed."

Dillon shrugged. "So be it."

Webster frowned. "You would actually sacrifice your lives for him?"

"Yeah," Remington answered. "We would."

"Why?"

"Because he's our friend and that makes it the right thing to do."

"The right thing?" Webster's laughter was almost girlish. "Look around. The right thing doesn't exist anymore. There is only survival."

"Not here." Remington stared into Webster's eyes. "This place is different."

Webster looked at the tent again. "Can I see her?"

"Who?" Dillon asked.

Webster licked his lips. "The girl. She's in there, isn't she?"

"You don't know that."

"But I do, Sheriff." Webster's nostrils flared. "I'm told she's beautiful. Can't you smell it?"

"What?"

"Innocence."

Remington drew his revolver, pointed it at Webster's face, and cocked the hammer back. "Are you looking to die?"

"Don't be stupid, old man. You kill me and Vig will end your lives far sooner than later."

"Like I give a shit."

"Are you aware of how valuable a girl like that is? She could be quite the bargaining chip for you. Think of it. A package deal—the bear and the girl together. Vig would be oh so appreciative of that—as would I."

Remington's eyes flared. "Sheriff, you best shut him up now. I'm a tick's hair away from blowing his head off."

Morning raised her rifle again. "I'd like to get in on some of that."

"You idiots," Webster said. "You're not safe from Vig on this hill and killing me won't change that. If anything, you need me."

"Why do you think we need you?" Dillon asked.

"Vig values my opinion, so if my opinion is that once she has the bear in her possession, she would be better served to leave the rest of you alone then don't you think that is at least worthy of some consideration?"

Morning continued to point her rifle at Webster's chest. "What's in it for you?"

Webster licked his lips again. "Vig gets the bear."

"And?"

"I get the girl."

Bear, who had been standing still and silent behind Webster while listening to their conversation, grabbed hold of Webster's shoulders and spun him around so that they were facing each other. He then put his hands around the much shorter man's neck and started to squeeze.

Webster's eyes bulged and his face turned shades of quickly deepening purple.

"That's enough," Dillon said.

Bear's fingers dug deeper into the soft folds of Webster's neck.

"He's not worth it. Let him go crawling back to Vig with his tail between his legs."

Bear held up his hands and stepped back.

Webster fell to the ground, gasping and sputtering. Dillon knelt down next to him. "He could have killed you easy," he whispered. "Now get your sorry fat ass off of this hill."

"You're all dead." Webster groaned as he regained his feet. "You can't stop us all. From the front and from the back—we're coming."

"You better get going before I change my mind," Dillon said.

Webster grimaced while rubbing his neck. "Sure thing, Sheriff. I look forward to seeing you all dead very soon."

"Wait." Morning approached Webster. "You said you'd be coming from the front and the back."

"You think I didn't notice the trail over there?" Webster pointed toward the back side of the hill. "It leads down to the river, doesn't it?"

Morning and Dillon shared a glance. Morning nodded. Dillon nodded as well right before he turned and shot Webster in the head.

Remington shrugged as he holstered his revolver. "I guess you changed your mind about letting him go."

"It had to be done," Morning said.

"We couldn't have him telling Vig about the trail to the river," Dillon added. "There's not enough of us to defend two separate entry points. For now, the only way they know to get up here is on the valley side and we need to keep it that way for as long as possible."

"He's not getting buried up here though," Remington said. "No way."

Bear bent down, grabbed hold of the back of Webster's shirt and jeans, lifted the body up like a sack of grain and walked it over to the hill's edge and then threw it over. It tumbled down end over end until eventually reaching the valley below. Soon after a crowd of road pirates gathered around it.

Remington clapped Bear on the back. "Thanks for taking out the trash, big fella. One down and a few hundred more to go."

"Now Vig knows who we are," Dillon said. "We're not making any deals and we're not going down without a fight."

Gunfire erupted from the bottom of the hill. "Get back!" Remington shouted.

"Don't return fire." Dillon crept toward the drop-off and looked down. "Remember, we can't afford to waste ammo. Bear, I need you at the trailhead. If anyone tries to make their way up here, you start blasting. Otherwise, we watch and we wait."

"For what?" Remington asked.

Dillon looked up at the clear sky. There was no wind, no clouds, only sun. "Hell if I know."

"*Hell if I know* doesn't sound like much of a plan."

"Feel free to share when you have a better one."

"They might decide to sit down there and wait us out."

"They can try."

"You know that eventually the bullets will have to start flying."

Dillon nodded. "Sure." He sounded as tired as he looked.

"Okay, Sheriff," Remington said. "Until then we watch and wait."

Morning went back into the tent to check on Reagan while Remington and Bear walked together to the trailhead to stand guard.

Dillon stood alone staring down at the road pirates below him. He had yet to see anyone enter or leave the RV that they assumed had Vig inside of it and wondered if she was actually even there.

It would be dark in a few hours.

Perhaps the night would deliver some answers.

30.
✦✧✦✧

The gunfire continued on and off for hours. Dillon estimated a thousand or more rounds had been fired at the hill. A few managed to leave holes in the tent's roof. Dog whimpered on the floor by the fire while the horses shifted nervously near the entrance.

Remington came back into the tent from checking on Bear who remained at the top of the trail making sure no road pirates attempted to force their way up. "We're good so far," he said. "The trail is clear."

"Why are they wasting so much ammo?" Morning asked.

"Because they can," Dillon replied. "And they want us to know it."

"When do we fire back?"

"We don't. Then we would be the ones wasting ammo and, unlike them, we can't afford to do that. Besides, it's still too dark. We can hardly see where they are."

"So, we just sit up here and wait?"

"Yeah."

Remington sat in the chair and warmed his hands by the fire. "Don't be surprised if they keep spraying bullets up this way all night. They don't want to give us a chance to sleep."

Reagan sat cross-legged on the ground watching and listening to the others talk. She would flinch every time another round of shots rang out from the bottom of the hill. Dog lay next to her trembling. "Is Bear really okay?" she asked.

Morning sat next to her and hugged her shoulders. "He's fine."

"The animals are scared."

"And so am I," Morning said. "We all are."

"Even Bear?"

"I know he's afraid for you."

"I don't want him to get hurt trying to keep me safe."

"Keeping you safe is the most important thing to him right now and nothing is going to change that."

"But I don't want him to die for me." Reagan's voice lowered. "I'm not worth it."

Morning turned and gripped both of Reagan's shoulders. "I don't want to hear you talking like that again."

"But—"

"You're worth it. Your life has more meaning to Bear and the rest of us than you could possibly know, but I hope someday you will." Morning took a deep breath. "Do you believe Bear has already saved your life more than once?"

Reagan's eyes were wide as she nodded.

"Then don't repay him by saying something as stupid as you not being worth it, understood?"

"Okay."

Morning let go of Reagan's shoulders. "Good."

"I'm sorry." Tears streamed down Reagan's cheeks.

"Stop crying."

"Sorry."

"And stop apologizing."

"I don't know what I'm supposed to do."

Morning gave Reagan a reassuring smile. "There's nothing wrong with wanting to cry. Believe me, there are days when I feel like that's all I want to do. It's just that right now isn't the time. We need to be strong, focused, and ready to help each other out. If Bear sees you crying that will make him worry and that won't do him any good and we can't have that."

Reagan pursed her lips and nodded. "I understand."

"Of course you do. You're a smart girl and more importantly you're a survivor."

"I don't think we can survive this though. There are so many of them."

Morning briefly considered lying but then decided Reagan deserved the truth. "You're right about that. The odds are against us. Do you remember what Remington taught you about shooting a gun?"

"Yeah."

"And are you ready to use one if you need to?"

"Are you asking me if I can kill a person?"

More gunfire erupted from below. Reagan glanced up at Remington and then stared at Morning. "I'm never going to let the road pirates take me again—*never*."

Morning nodded. "That's right. You do what you have to do to prevent that from happening."

"We all will," Remington added as he tried to rub the tired from his eyes. "We keep fighting until we can't fight no more."

"And then what?" Reagan asked.

Remington sat up in the chair, his eyes suddenly bright and clear. "Those animals at the bottom of this hill don't know what it is to live truly free, but we do. That means something. I am honored to call you both my friend and the same goes for how I feel about the sheriff and Bear. What happens today or tomorrow or the day after doesn't really matter because we've already won. Our dignity is intact and our humanity preserved. Vaughn's Hill is a special place, the kind of place not meant for most because most aren't worthy of it, but we are. We're worthy enough to live here and if need be, we're worthy enough to die here too."

He leaned down and took Reagan's small hands into his rough calloused ones. "There are far worse things than dying. What you went through at the hands of those road pirate scum, you know that all too well don't you? So, you keep fighting with us like the beautiful and powerful little woman that you are and don't worry about what might come next. Just promise me one thing."

Reagan arched her brows and waited.

"Should you get the chance," Remington continued, "and you have some of those road pirates in your sights, you shoot as many of them dead as you can. Can you promise me that?"

For a moment Morning saw in Reagan a glimpse of the determined woman she might become and said a silent prayer that she be given the time to do so. Then she turned at the sound of the tent flap opening and saw Dillon walking in.

"What is it, Sheriff?" Remington asked.

"Sun is coming up," Dillon replied.

Remington pushed himself up out of the chair. "After many years of study, I discovered that it tends to do that just about every day."

Dillon chuckled as he gave Remington a wry smile. "Nice to see you haven't lost your touch for not-so-subtle sarcasm." He pushed the flap open. "You're going to want to see this."

They followed him outside and then to the edge of the hill. There was just enough light to make out a flag billowing in the breeze in the valley below.

Remington scowled. "What the hell is that? They can't possibly be giving up."

"Seems more like a ceasefire," Dillon answered.

"But why?"

Dillon shrugged. "Not a clue."

Morning looked toward the other side of the hill. "Is Bear still guarding the trailhead?"

"Yeah." Dillon pointed at the flag. "They've already put out all their campfires."

"Any sign of Vig?" Morning asked. The RV was parked in the center of the valley.

"Nope."

Remington tipped his head. "There's movement by the crash site."

A group of twenty or so armed road pirates walked through the grass from the crash site to the flag.

Dillon squinted and then grunted. "The tallest among them appears to be a woman."

Remington picked up a rifle and looked through the scope. "Might be Vig." He glanced at the others. "I'm tempted to shoot."

"That's a nearly five-hundred-yard shot. Add in wind and elevation adjustments and your chances of hitting the target are likely about one in ten. What *is* guaranteed is pissing them off and escalating this situation into something we might not be able to handle."

The group stopped at the flag and then looked up at the top of the hill.

"Seems they want us to do something. I guess if you don't want me shooting at them, Sheriff, then we just stick around and see what it is."

Dillon reached for the rifle. "May I?"

Remington handed it to him. "Be my guest."

"You're right," Dillon said as he looked through the scope. "That woman could be Vig. The others are clearly deferring to her." His face tightened. "And you're right about something else. It's damn tempting to try to put a round through her skull."

Morning shook her head. "Don't."

Dillon lowered the rifle. "Why not?"

"Because that's what they want us to do. We haven't fired back yet. They have no idea what kind of weapons we have, if we can reach them from here, or how well we might be able to defend ourselves. They don't have any of those answers yet, which tells me there's no way that woman you're watching is Vig. She wouldn't risk getting shot at."

"Morning is right," Remington said. "Whoever that woman is, she most likely isn't Vig."

Dillon looked through the scope again. "She's coming toward the trail."

"What the hell for?" Remington took the rifle back to get a better look. "Huh," he grunted. "She's alone."

"Should we stop her?" Morning asked.

"I'd rather learn what she has to say," Dillon replied. "But one of us better give Bear a heads-up or he's liable to blow her away before we get that chance."

Morning started walking. "I'll do it. You two stay with Reagan." She picked up the pace, wanting to be sure she reached Bear before the mystery woman did. "Bear," she called out.

He turned around holding a rifle. "Yeah?"

"We have a visitor—a woman. She's alone."

Bear frowned and shrugged.

"Your guess is as good as mine," Morning replied. "Dillon wants to find out why she's coming up here. Let her by and I'll take her to the tent." She slung her shotgun over her shoulder. "Don't worry. I'll have my eyes on her the whole time."

Bear's frown remained.

Both of them turned at the sound of footsteps coming up the trail. They raised their weapons, watched, and waited.

The woman was even taller than anticipated—more than six foot. Her thick blonde hair was unusually clean and lustrous, as was her skin that, despite some lines around the eyes and mouth, was nearly flawless. Her shoulders were broad, her hips narrow, and her legs long and muscular. She wore tight blue jeans, a denim jacket, and dark brown work boots with the jeans tucked into the tops of them.

"Stop right there," Morning said.

"I'm unarmed," the woman replied as she held up her hands. Her voice was deep but also pleasant, like a kind yet no-nonsense librarian.

"Turn around."

The woman turned to show she wasn't hiding a weapon behind her back.

"Come this way," Morning continued, "but do it slow and keep those hands where we can see them."

The woman stopped next to Bear, looked up, and hinted at a smile. "And there you are," she said softly. "The bear. You've been such a naughty boy."

Bear's face was unreadable as he stared beyond the woman, keeping his attention on the trail behind her.

"And you." The woman stepped past Bear to stand in front of Morning. "Are you the one in charge?"

Morning kept the shotgun aimed at the woman's chest. "Why are you here?"

"To discuss the terms of your surrender."

"We're not surrendering."

The woman's smile was equally cruel and confident. "You will. The only thing not yet known is if you do it alive or dead. Where are the others?"

Morning continued to ignore the woman's questions while asking her own. "Do you speak for Vig?"

"I do."

"Where is she?"

"Close."

"In the RV?"

"Where are the others?" the woman repeated.

"What's your name?"

"You first."

"Morning."

The woman nodded. "Nice to meet you, Morning."

"And you?"

"Call me Alice."

"Okay, Alice, what do *really* want?"

"I told you—to discuss the terms of your surrender. Speaking of which, I should probably signal to the others in the valley so that they don't start to think you did something to me."

"Or I blast you now and throw your body down to them. That should clear up any confusion they might have."

Alice rolled her eyes. "You're not going to do that."

"I wouldn't be so sure."

Alice wagged her long pointer finger. "It's not in your nature. You see, I know people. You might be capable of killing but clearly you are no killer." She glanced back at Bear. "Now *this* one on the other hand. . ."

"We're not surrendering."

"I heard you the first time."

Morning's eyes narrowed. "Are you Vig?"

"Do you actually think we would risk sending Vig herself up here?"

"Maybe."

"Not likely. Now, can we please stop wasting time? Take me to the others so that we can try to resolve all of this with as little actual bloodshed as possible."

"If you want to do that then just turn around and go back where you came from."

"That's not possible."

"Why not?"

"The bear must be made to pay for his crimes. At the very least we'll be taking him with us."

"No, you won't."

"He's a killer."

"Nobody has taken more innocent lives around here than Vig's road pirates."

Alice sighed. "That's an exaggeration." She started to move closer to Morning, but Bear immediately reached back and clamped his hand around her upper arm and held her in place. "You're hurting me," she gasped.

Bear let her go and went back to watching the trail.

Alice rubbed her arm. "I wondered if you could be as strong as they say and now I know. You're every bit as strong and then some. Such an incredible physical specimen and not bad on the eyes either. We could have had so much fun. What a pity. What a waste. You would have been the greatest among all of our road pirates." She abruptly turned toward Morning. "Time is wasting."

"Get moving." Morning used the barrel of her gun to motion toward the other side of the hill where the tent stood. "And don't even think of trying anything."

"See you soon," Alice said to Bear before walking past Morning with her hands up.

Morning pressed the shotgun into the small of Alice's back. "Straight ahead." She watched her closely and noted how Alice's chin jutted out and up as she strode confidently across the hill like she owned the place. It made her again wonder if it was actually Vig who walked in front of her. Part of her wanted so badly to pull the trigger.

It would be so damn easy.

No, Morning told herself. *Now isn't the time. Whoever she is I need to give the others a chance to hear what she has to say.*

They continued walking toward the tent.

Two women.

One gun.

And a very uncertain future.

31.

✦✧✦✧

"Start talking and make it quick. I don't want you up here on my hill one second more than is necessary."

Alice's smile was that of a shark—all teeth and appetite. "And you are?"

"Remington Wilkes. This is my land including the valley your road pirate scum are currently camping out on without my permission."

Alice looked Dillon up and down. "Sheriff Potts?"

"That's right."

"I've heard of you."

"Same."

"All good things I hope."

Dillon stared back stone-faced.

Alice's eyes widened as did her grin. "And who is this little young lady?"

Dog, who sat leaning against Reagan's leg, growled.

"I'm Reagan."

"It's very nice to meet you, Reagan."

Dog growled more. Reagan stroked his head to let him know she was okay.

Remington sat in the chair and motioned for Alice to sit on the ground across from him. "You speak for Vig?"

Alice nodded after she sat. "Yes."

"Is she holed up in that RV?"

"Maybe."

"Why isn't she the one talking to us?"

"Too risky."

"So, she sees you as expendable," Morning said as she continued to hold the shotgun.

Alice glared at her. "Would you mind not pointing that at me?"

"Sure, if you want to start telling us why you're *really* here."

"It's the same as what I told you outside. I'm here to negotiate the terms of your surrender so that we might both avoid unnecessary loss of life."

"Surrender?" Remington scowled. "We're not surrendering."

"That's what I told her," Morning said. "She doesn't listen."

"I listen fine," Alice replied, "but the fact remains we won't leave here until we have what we want."

Dillon hooked his thumbs into his gun belt. "And what exactly is it that you want?"

"To start, the bear must pay for his crimes."

"That's it?"

Alice gave Dillon a thin smile. "For now."

"You're not taking Bear," Reagan said.

"No? Not even if it meant saving everyone else?"

Reagan shook her head.

"Does this child speak for all of you?" Alice asked.

"We all feel the same," Dillon replied. "You have a better chance of growing wings out of your ass and flying off this hill than you do of taking Bear from us."

"An ironic example, Sheriff, given you were the ones who shot down our chopper."

"Like you, that chopper wasn't invited."

"You seem like nice enough people. I would hate to see this situation turn seriously violent because that would clearly end badly for you. Despite what you might think, violence is not our first choice."

"Spare us your fake concern," Morning said.

Alice folded her arms over her chest. "Let me tell you my story."

"Why?"

"To prove I'm not the monster you think I am. I'm a woman, the same as you, who is trying her best to get through each day in this hellhole world of ours."

"If you really want to prove you're not the monster we think you are then go back down there and tell your people to pack up and leave us be."

"I was a mother to two wonderful children—emphasis on *was*. My oldest, a son, was an officer in the Marines while my daughter was enlisted in the Navy. They were both so dedicated to serving their country and I couldn't have been prouder."

"Lady," Remington held his hands up, "all due respect but we each have our stories of woe. What we don't have is the patience to listen to you trying to convince us you're anything more than the same road pirate filth that have been terrorizing those of us who were left still standing after the collapse. Morning is right. You want to show us different? Then get off my land and leave us alone."

"Anyways," Alice continued, "I raised them both as a single mother. Their father, well, let's just say I wasted far too many years thinking he would change into something better. He didn't of course. Men rarely do and not long after my second was born he was heading out the door leaving me to take care of everything on my own. So, the fact both of my children turned out so well was something of a small miracle for which I was so grateful. Then everything changed."

"The vaccine," Morning said, knowing that by doing so she was giving Alice the opening to keep talking and ignore Remington's declaration that she should leave.

Alice nodded. "My daughter was pregnant by the time the military told her she either had to take the jab or face a dishonorable discharge. The Marines said the same thing to my son. When they asked me for advice, I told them to get the shot. Millions had already taken it and our government declared it to be safe so what was the problem, right?"

She paused, her brow furrowed, and her hands clasped tightly in front of her. "Ten days after getting the vaccine my daughter had a miscarriage and then suffered a major stroke. Her brain swelled and she was put into an induced coma. Four days after that and I was standing by her hospital bed saying goodbye right before they took her off of life support. In a matter of days I went from looking forward to being a grandmother to burying my daughter."

"That must have been tough." Morning meant it. She couldn't imagine having to suffer through losing her son Cy.

"Tough." Alice grimaced. "If only that had been the only such loss. My son was next. Six weeks after I buried my daughter, I was notified that he had some kind of seizure while driving near his military base. There was an accident. He was airlifted to a trauma center with severe internal injuries but died on the operating table. Both my kids were gone and it was my fault."

"Your fault?" Morning said. "Why?"

"They came to me for advice, remember? I was the one who told them to get the shot—*me*. A mother is supposed to protect her children, but I didn't do that. I failed them."

"We all did." Dillon turned his back to the others but spoke loud enough so that they could still hear him. "God forgive us, we all did."

Alice's voice trembled. "You know my pain as well don't you, Sheriff Potts?"

"Yeah," Dillon replied. He turned around, his face grim and his eyes hard. "I do."

Remington cleared his throat. "I am sorry for your loss, but none of what you're telling us changes anything. You're not taking Bear and you're not staying here."

Alice stared at Remington. "It really is remarkable how you actually think you're in a position to dictate terms."

"We're willing to die on this hill," Remington said. "Are you?"

"Does your death wish also include young Reagan?"

"Keep her name out of your mouth." Morning stepped toward Alice ready to fight. "I mean it."

Alice appeared to almost laugh. "Of course you do." She got up, towering over Morning. "Know this. I will leave here, go back to my people in the valley, and explain to them how you were unwilling to hand over the bear, which of course only leaves us with the option of taking him by force. The firepower that will rain down over your heads after that will be unrelenting. You'll be begging us to stop but we won't for you will have had your chance to facilitate a different outcome—a chance you failed to take. I'll try to spare the girl's life because she's a valuable commodity, but I can't guarantee it. If she dies her death will be on you." She reached out to touch Reagan's cheek. "Such a sad thing that they have chosen this for you."

Dog snapped at Alice's hand, drawing blood from one of her fingers and causing her to cry out. "He doesn't like you," Reagan said.

"Filthy animal!" Alice hissed. She drew back, holding her hand. Dog's low-throated growl let her know he was ready to bite her again. "Get that thing under control."

Remington gave Dog's neck a playful squeeze. "Good boy." He looked up at Alice. "Seems we're all talked out and that means it's time for you to go."

"Last chance," Alice said. "The bear comes with me so that the rest of you are allowed to live another day."

Morning poked Alice in the stomach with the tip of the shotgun barrel. "No chance."

"Very well." Alice started reaching into her jacket.

Dillon drew his revolver and pointed it at her head. "Easy."

Remington got out of the chair. "What are you reaching for?"

"May I?" Alice asked.

"Do like the sheriff says—*easy*."

"See?" Alice held up a palm-sized black device. "Just a walkie-talkie." She pulled the antenna out and pressed the button. "I'm coming down—alone." A male voice confirmed he understood. She returned the walkie talkie into her jacket.

"Vig," Morning said.

Alice looked at her. "What about her?"

"We'd like to meet her. These discussions might turn out better for both sides if we were talking directly with the one in charge."

"Oh?" Alice's eyes twinkled mischief when she smiled. "I'll be sure to let her know you think so."

"Here." Remington held up a white handkerchief. "For your hand. You can keep it."

Alice took it and wrapped it around her injured finger. "Thank you."

Dillon lowered his gun. "I'll walk you to the trail."

"That's not necessary, Sheriff."

"I insist."

Alice shrugged. "Very well."

Dog growled again.

"Reagan is right," Remington said. "He *really* doesn't like you."

Little was said during the walk from the tent to where Bear stood at the top of the trail. When they arrived, Alice turned and faced the others. "You do know you're protecting a killer, right? And by doing so you will all end up dead because of him."

"You call him killer," Morning replied. "We call him friend."

Alice looked down into the valley. "It really is a beautiful place, isn't it? I take no pleasure in the blood that is about to flow here, but you leave me no choice. Still, I do admire your courage. If only more of us had shown such courage before the collapse, then perhaps many more could have been spared the trauma that followed."

"Is this what your son and daughter would have wanted?" Morning said. "Tell me, mother to mother, this person that you've become—would they even recognize you if they were still here?"

"But they aren't here." Alice clenched her fists at her sides while the corners of her mouth twitched.

Morning glanced down at Alice's fists. "You're a very angry woman, aren't you? Is that why you're really doing this? To feed that anger and then to justify it?"

"I help to bring order to the chaos and give others a purpose." Alice shot Bear a venomous look. "And don't you dare try to judge me while giving shelter to the likes of *him*."

"Bear fought against your version of order because it includes the abuse of children."

"He killed many."

"And he's likely to kill a lot more before we're done here. He could kill you right now in fact, but I don't think he would because that's not his way. You see, unlike you, Bear doesn't fight unless provoked or to help those unable to help themselves. Then again, you could still march down off of this hill and tell your people to go so that we can both live in peace away from each other."

"Too late." One by one Alice looked into the eyes of the others. "You have all chosen to pay for the bear's sins, which means you have all chosen death. The only one I pity now is Reagan because she wasn't allowed to choose for herself. You made that choice for her which makes you the tyrant not me."

"You mean Vig," Morning said.

"Eh?"

"You mean Vig isn't the tyrant because she's the one you answer to, right?"

"We're done talking." Alice started to make her way down the trail. After a few long strides she turned around to find Morning's shotgun staring back at her. "You would kill an unarmed woman?"

"If she was an evil bitch intent on spreading death and destruction? You bet."

Bear pushed the barrel of the shotgun down and shook his head.

"Listen to your friend," Alice said while pointing at Bear. "The only thing killing me now would do is hasten your own destruction." She turned away again and was gone.

"That was Vig," Morning said.

"You might be right about that," Dillon replied, "but we don't know for sure. To kill an unarmed woman because she *might* be someone isn't something I want to be a part of. We're better than that. At least I hope we are. Now, how about we take a look at how they're reacting down there?"

They stood at the top of the hill and watched as the road pirates massed together and then fell back upon Alice's return. She walked through the middle of them like Moses parting the Red Sea, her head held high, looking straight ahead. When she reached the RV, she opened the door and then disappeared inside.

"I knew it," Morning said. "We had her and we let her go."

"Perhaps she's reporting to Vig," Remington suggested.

Dillon propped his hands against his hips as he continued to watch the swirling mass of people below. "No, Morning has it right. Alice and Vig are the same person. She actually had the balls to come up here unarmed by herself to check us out."

"That scares me more than anything," Morning said. "To be that confident of the outcome—she has no fear of us."

"She has hundreds fighting for her," Remington replied. "She *should* be confident."

Morning shook her head. "It's more than that. She knows something we don't."

"Any idea what that might be?" Dillon asked.

"No but I think it's something—"

The road pirates in the valley let out a raucous cheer while the earth started to tremble. A familiar sound echoed across the hillside. Dog was barking inside the tent while Peanut and Justice scampered nervously near the outhouse.

The sound grew louder.

Morning and the others turned around slowly and then looked up into the sky.

Another helicopter was coming.

32.

The chopper flew directly over Vaughn's Hill as it crossed the valley. It made a wide turn and then hovered over an area near the river. Something was tossed from the cockpit and then a few seconds later there was a small explosion on the ground. The chopper turned again and landed behind the RV as road pirates gathered around it clapping and cheering.

"That changes things," Remington growled.

"Grenade," Dillon added.

Reagan ran out of the tent with Dog beside her. "Another one?"

"Looks that way," Morning replied.

"Can't we shoot it down like I did the last time?"

"If we have to, we'll sure try."

"Look." Remington pointed at a lone figure walking from the RV to the hill. "Vig is sending us another messenger."

The group walked together back to the trailhead where Bear stood watch. Dillon told him a man was coming up the trail. With guns drawn, they waited.

"I'm not armed," a male voice called out to them. He was of average height and build and appeared to be in his late twenties. His light brown hair was shaved short, and a long scar ran from the corner of one eye down to the bottom of his jaw. He was dressed in a sweatshirt and faded jeans with tennis shoes. "My name is Blair—Blair from Boston." He stopped on the trail about ten feet from Bear. "Damn, you're huge."

Dillon stepped forward. "I'm Sheriff Dillon Potts."

Blair snapped his fingers as he smiled and nodded. He had a pleasant face, but the eyes were cold and cruel. "Right, the sheriff who kept patrolling this area long after the collapse." He looked at the others. "It's nice to meet all of you."

"What's Vig want now?" Remington asked.

"As much as you might not believe it, she wants to avoid the situation from really going sideways."

Remington spit. "Sideways? What's that supposed to mean?"

"She doesn't want to see you all killed by your own stubbornness."

"You mean she wants us to hand over Bear," Morning said.

Blair nodded happily. "Exactly."

"We already gave her our answer on that."

"Well, that was before the helicopter's arrival, right?"

"You think that changes things?" Dillon shook his head. "It doesn't."

"Sheriff, be reasonable. Between our firepower below and the chopper dropping explosives from above we'll blow the top right off of this hill. Make no mistake, you'll all die up here."

"So be it," Morning said. "Just as long as I get to take a few of you road pirate rats with me."

Blair kept smiling. "I tell you what. Take an hour to think it over. It's not even afternoon yet—we have some time. There's no need to rush this, am I right?" His eyes lingered on Reagan. "Boy, would I hate to see anything happen to *your* pretty little head." He abruptly turned and waved without looking back. "Please take the hour to reconsider. Otherwise, I'd wager Vig will see you all dead before the sun goes down. Be back soon. I really do hope we can come to some kind of agreement."

Remington stared at the helicopter sitting in his field. "If that boy gets any happier he'll literally be skipping down this hill. Do you think his threats are legit? I was wondering if maybe that one grenade they threw down could be the only one they have and that they're just hoping to scare us into giving up easy."

"One grenade or a thousand, it doesn't matter," Dillon replied. "As we've said several times already, giving them Bear isn't an option." He glanced down at Reagan. "Besides, don't think for a second that once they have Bear, they won't be back asking for more. Vig has no intention of letting us survive this."

"I agree," Morning said. "That road pirate named Blair might have been smiling but he has the eyes of a killer. We can't trust a word that comes out of his mouth. We stay here and fight—*all of us*."

Bear looked away.

Morning stood in front of him. "Hey, you're not thinking about playing hero, are you? Whether the road pirates get their hands on you or not it won't make a difference regarding what happens to the rest of us. We need you here."

"Listen to her," Dillon said. "Handing yourself over to Vig won't save us."

Bear wrote on his pad and then held it up.

Waiting around to die isn't much of a plan. I need to know that we'll keep Reagan safe.

"Of course we'll try to do that," Morning replied. "Do you have something specific in mind that you want us to do differently?"

One of us needs to be prepared to get her away from here. Use the other trail down to the river and then head north from there.

"You want to take Reagan and leave?"

Not me. You.

Morning shook her head. "No, I'm staying and fighting. Savage is my home."

Let me stay and fight for you. Please. The only thing I ask is that you help give Reagan a chance to make it off of this hill alive.

"Agreed," Remington said with a tone that indicated the matter was settled.

"Wait a minute." Morning scowled at Remington. "You don't speak for me."

"Give Bear that assurance. It makes sense. We need him to fight and he needs Reagan safe. You can help us to have both of those things."

"And leave you three here alone to fend for yourselves? I don't think so."

"Don't I have a say?" Reagan asked. "I want to stay and fight too. Let me help."

"Get down!" Dillon yelled as bullets hissed over their heads. They scrambled behind one of the stone walls with their weapons drawn.

"Coming up," Blair shouted from further down the trail. "Don't shoot."

"Tell your people the same!" Dillon bellowed.

Blair was out of breath when he reached the top of the hill. "Vig sure has me working hard today. Hopefully this will be my last trip up here." He took several deep breaths. "That's better. Apologies for the gunfire. My people just wanted to make it clear that I'm to be respected. I know I said you had an hour to think it over, but Vig is impatient to get this whole thing resolved quickly. She has places to be."

Remington was the first to step out from behind the stone wall. "If she wants to resolve this like you say then that's a very simple fix—just go and leave us alone."

"You keep repeating that, but you and I both know that's not going to happen." Blair pointed at Reagan. "And one more thing—she's part of the deal. We get the bear *and* the girl."

"That's coming directly from Vig?" Morning asked.

"Yes."

"That's never going to happen and she knows it."

"I'm not comfortable saying what Vig does and doesn't know."

"You're wasting your time."

Blair frowned. "I'm trying to save your lives. I'd hardly consider that a waste of time."

Morning's voice raised. "You don't get Bear and you don't Reagan."

"And you don't dictate terms to me."

Bear's sledgehammer sat leaning against the stone wall. He reached down and picked it up.

Blair's eyes widened. "Don't be stupid. Anything happens to me and you'll all be dead in minutes."

"Our answer hasn't changed," Dillon said. "It's time you go."

"I'm sorry to hear that." Blair put his fingers to his mouth, whistled loudly and then turned toward the trail. "Vig wants the girl unharmed. Kill the others."

A line of armed men were running toward the top of the hill.

Morning pulled Reagan close and then leaned down in front of her. "Get to the tent. Hurry." Reagan took off running, the soles of her shoes kicking up little clouds of dirt as she went.

Blair reached behind him and then held up a gun. Bear moved in front of Morning, shielding her with his body. Blair grinned as his finger pressed against the trigger.

A shot cracked the air around them.

Blair crumpled to the ground.

Dillon turned and fired again at the first of the road pirates to reach the top of the hill. The man toppled against a rock. Three more followed close behind. The one in front was already firing an assault rifle. Bear pushed Morning behind the stone wall and then threw his hammer at the closest road pirate to them, hitting him in the chest. The man dropped his rifle and fell to his knees, gasping for breath. Remington finished him with a shot to the head.

"Don't do it," Dillon yelled at the next road pirate to emerge from the trail. "Put down your weapon and leave."

The road pirate fired. Dillon dove to the side.

Remington fired back but missed.

Bear grabbed the end of the road pirate's gun and yanked it and the road pirate toward him. He punched the man's face and then threw him against a boulder, crushing the side of his head and breaking his neck.

The last two road pirates stood shoulder to shoulder on the narrow hillside trail, aimed their guns at Bear, and opened fire. Bear ducked behind the same boulder he had thrown the other road pirate against. Rock fragments erupted around him as bullets ricocheted off the stone.

Dillon fired and missed. Remington did the same.

Morning strode down the trail holding the shotgun in front of her. By the time the road pirates looked away from where Bear was crouching behind the boulder and noticed her coming it was too late. The shotgun blast echoed across the hillside and valley below. Lead pellets ripped into the men's faces and upper bodies. One died immediately. The other fell to the ground screaming in pain. Morning put the gun to his head, hesitated, and then pulled the trigger, ending his suffering.

"Is everyone okay?" Dillon shouted.

"Good here," Remington replied.

"Me too," Morning answered.

Dillon came down the trail and brushed past Morning. "Bear? Are you good?"

Bear had a hand over his stomach when he turned. He looked down and then held his hand up in front of him. It dripped red.

"Is that blood yours?" Remington asked as he scrambled toward Bear. "Let me see."

Bear lifted his shirt. A wound the diameter of a pinky oozed blood so dark it appeared almost black.

"Oh no," Dillon muttered as he leaned down to get a better look. "Is there an exit wound?"

Bear turned. Remington lifted the back of his shirt, looked at Dillon, and shook his head. "Gut shot and the bullet is still in there."

"He's going to be okay, right?" When neither Remington nor Dillon answered Morning looked up and locked eyes with Bear. "You're going to be okay."

Bear nodded, pulled his shirt down, and stood up straight.

"We can try to slow the bleeding down some," Remington said. "Cauterize the wound and bandage it up."

"What about the bullet?" Morning asked.

Dillon shook his head. "We're not equipped to be cutting him open to try to fish it out. We'd just end up making a mess and killing him quicker."

"Quicker?" Morning felt her heartbeat slamming against her chest. "He's not dying. He's going to be okay." She looked up at Bear again. "You're not dying. Understand? I won't let you."

The chopper was coming to life again down in the valley. Dillon went to the edge of the hill. "It's starting for real now," he said. "They're getting ready to attack the hill—all of them."

Bear walked to the stone wall at the top of the trail and picked up his rifle. The front of his shirt was already soaked in blood.

"I can keep watch here," Remington said. "You go get yourself bandaged up."

Bear shook his head slowly, his jaw set, his eyes serious. He wasn't moving. "I'm good." He pointed at Morning and then at the tent. "Reagan." The next three words were difficult for him to form, but he managed. "Keep. Her. Safe."

"C'mon." Dillon touched Morning's arm. "We should check on Reagan."

"He's not dying." Morning shoved Dillon's hand away. "I mean it." She walked up to Bear glaring at him. "Don't you dare."

Bear shrugged. "I'm trying."

Morning poked him in the chest. "Try harder." She looked down, saw the blood, and nearly started to cry but forced the tears back. "I'm so sorry. I didn't mean to poke you like that. You've been shot, I wasn't thinking, I didn't mean to—"

Bear pulled Morning closer, careful not to get his blood on her. He leaned down and brushed his lips against her ear. Most would have struggled to make out the words, but she didn't have to hear them because she also felt them so clearly. "It's okay," he whispered. "I love you." The memory of their time together near the banks of the Yellowstone rushed back, filling her mind and senses with the smell of his skin and the powerful movement of his muscular body as it pressed against hers while they lay together under a forever blue Montana sky. How someone so strong could also be so gentle and considerate of her physical and emotional needs, so willing to give far more than take, was something she would never forget. She stiffened at the shot of guilt that suddenly coursed through her. Waylon had been the only man she had ever said she loved, but now, in this moment, she was prepared to say those words again to another while also telling herself that she couldn't.

And then she did.

Morning placed her hands around Bear's face, pressed her fingers into his thick beard, lightly kissed his forehead, his cheek, and then his mouth. "I love you too." Just four words, but they said so much because they meant so much. They were words Morning hardly ever spoke because she considered them precious and not to be wasted like so many others did who overused them as often and with as little thought as saying hello or small talk about the weather.

No, when Morning McGreevy used the word love she meant it.

Bear watched the others as they walked to the tent. He was surprised by how little the gunshot wound hurt. He knew it was bad, likely deadly, but for now it hardly bothered him. All he wanted at this point was to help keep the others safe for as long as he could.

Halfway to the tent Morning turned around, looked back, and waved as the wind whipped her hair into her face. Bear smiled. The distance between them made him appear far smaller and more fragile than he actually was.

I love you.

A sudden realization struck Morning hard, causing her to gasp. Try as she might to keep them away the tears were relentless this time, falling down her cheeks and then dropping to the ground.

Bear didn't only tell her he loved her.

He was also saying goodbye.

33.

✦ ✧ ✦ ✧

"Bear?" Morning walked faster toward the trailhead. "Where are you?" She carried a bandage and iodine in one hand and her shotgun in the other. "Bear?" she called out louder, her voice nearly drowned out by the din of the helicopter powering up below.

He was gone.

There were shouts, gunfire, and screams. Morning ran to the hill's edge and looked down. Bear was running through a mass of road pirates, swinging the sledgehammer, pushing, kicking, punching, and destroying anyone who dared get in his way. When the throng threatened to overwhelm him, he forced it back, leaving a crying and whimpering trail of broken arms and ribs, fractured jaws, and smashed skulls. He carved through them like a knife through butter and as Morning watched the crushing chaos unfold, she couldn't help but smile. It was the first time she had witnessed his full power unleashed upon an enemy and it left her both stunned and amazed.

It was beautiful.

"What's he doing down there?" Remington stood on one side of Morning.

"What little time he had left he is giving to us," Dillon answered from Morning's other side. "He's trying to draw as many of them away from the hill as he can."

The road pirates surged again. Bear pushed them back and then kept running through the field. There was more gunfire, more shouts to stop him, and more broken bodies strewn across the ranch property.

"They can't shoot for shit," Remington said. "As big of a target as he is and they haven't yet come close to hitting him."

"He moves so damn fast." Dillon shook his head. "How a man with a bullet in him can manage to do that is beyond me." He looked down at the bandage and iodine in Morning's hand. His voice lowered. "I guess he won't be needing that."

"No," Morning answered. "I suppose he won't."

Bear continued to run and fight while the road pirates continued chasing him.

"Even he won't be able to keep that up for much longer," Remington said. "It's a matter of what takes him down first—them or the blood loss from his wound."

Morning flinched when she watched Bear stumble face-first into the tall grass. He got back up quickly, turned, and faced a wall of road pirates. Even from the top of the hill she could tell the front of his shirt was soaked in blood. He held the sledgehammer in front of him, daring them to come closer. The road pirates jeered, mocking him for his inability to speak clearly as they spread out around him, like a pack of mad dogs right before the kill. Most held knives but a few had guns and those guns were raised. Part of Morning wanted to look away, but she couldn't.

The first two shots missed.

A third didn't.

Bear rocked backwards but stayed on his feet. His head lowered. He let out a roar and then he charged.

The road pirates panicked, knocking into each other as they tried to get out of the way. The sledgehammer fell, was raised, and then fell again, each time leaving a broken body in its wake. Over, and over, and over, Bear struck them down.

Something took Morning's hand. She looked down to find Reagan standing there.

"You shouldn't be watching this," Remington said to her. "I'll take you back to the tent."

Morning pulled Reagan close. "She's fine."

"Why?" Remington stared into Morning's eyes. "They're killing him down there. Why would you have her see that?"

"Bear is sacrificing himself for all of us but most of all for her. She deserves to see it, to know it, and to hopefully understand it. He fights so that we might live."

"But she's just a child."

"No, she's not. She's the future and we can't afford to have that future be ignorant of what happens here today."

"I want to stay." Reagan's eyes were clear with only a hint of sadness, but her voice trembled. "I need to see it so I can remember it—so I can remember him and everything he did for me."

Remington's look softened. He nodded. "Okay. You can stay."

"Twenty-seven," Dillon said as he pointed at the gathering of road pirates below them. "That's how many I've counted so far that Bear has killed or injured for us."

"And that's twenty-seven we no longer have to deal with," Remington replied. "It might not be enough but it's something. He's doing all he can to give us a chance to come out of this alive."

Bear swung the hammer one more time, fell to a knee, and then stood, chest heaving, blood oozing from multiple wounds including a nasty gash across his forehead that dripped blood into both his eyes. His teeth flashed white behind the dark beard when he grimaced. A road pirate stepped forward, gun raised, and pointed it at Bear's face.

Reagan's grip tightened around Morning's fingers.

The trigger was pulled. Bear fell. The road pirates applauded.

Dillon cursed. Remington shut his eyes and hung his head. A tear tracked down Reagan's cheek.

Morning stood watching where Bear's body had collapsed into the grass. There was pain for his loss, but that pain was a distant second to the rage that gathered within her like a fast-approaching storm. She hated this cruel world, despised the human animals who now controlled it, and wanted so badly to make them all pay.

"Here they come," Dillon said.

The road pirates left Bear's body in the field and gathered around the RV while the chopper blades turned faster as it continued to power up. The RV door opened and Vig stepped out and then raised her arms while holding a pistol in each hand. When she fired them both into the air, the road pirates cheered some more.

A long line formed in front of the RV. Vig pointed at the hill. The line began marching toward the trail.

"I'll take Bear's spot at the trailhead," Dillon said while checking to make sure his rifle and sidearm were both fully loaded. "I'll hold them off from the front while you shoot down at them from up here. Just make sure to keep yourself protected behind the walls."

"What about when that chopper starts making its way over our heads?" Remington asked.

Dillon looked up from checking his weapons. "Fire away. Maybe we get lucky and shoot it down like the last one."

"And if we don't?"

"Then it's been a pleasure knowing you." Dillon tipped his hat. "I sincerely mean that."

"Wait." Morning wrapped her arms around Dillon, hugged him tight, and then leaned back. "Hold that trail for us, Sheriff."

"I'll try to for as long as I can."

Remington stuck out his hand, took hold of Dillon's, and held it tight. "This isn't goodbye."

"Then what is it?"

"Good luck."

"Yeah," Dillon said. "You too." He left Remington, Morning, and Reagan and returned to the trailhead.

"Do you want to go back into the tent?" Morning asked.

Reagan shook her head. "I want to stay with you."

"If things start to really go sideways up here," Remington said, "you might want to do like Bear suggested and take the other trail down to the river. I'll do my best to give you time to get safely away before they even know you're gone."

"No," Reagan nearly shouted. "I'm staying on this hill."

"I guess that answers that." Morning loaded her shotgun with two high velocity slugs.

Remington nodded. "We'll take some of those sons of bitches with us."

"Damn right we will."

On the other side of the hill Dillon started shooting. Remington raised his rifle, stepped out from behind the stone wall, aimed, and fired three shots into the line of road pirates in the valley. One of them fell to the ground screaming. Remington grinned. "One down." A bullet struck the dirt near his feet. "Stay back," he said as he shuffled behind the wall.

For the next several minutes, the shooting continued. More road pirates were left dead or injured. Remington grunted. "Like I said, they can't shoot for shit." He fired off two more rounds while Dillon could be heard at the trailhead shooting every few seconds. "They aren't used to people actually putting up a serious fight. We might just have chance."

The helicopter started to rise off the ground.

Remington reloaded while Morning raised her shotgun. The shooting at the trailhead intensified.

"They're making their push," Remington said. "Stay calm, aim true, and keep that thing away from this hill. We don't want it getting close enough to drop more grenades on us."

The chopper hovered over the valley, sending waves of blade-driven wind across the hillside. Morning watched the panicked horses gallop into the tent.

"Where's Dog?" Reagan asked.

"I'm sure he's fine," Morning answered. "He knows how to take care of himself."

Remington's eyes narrowed as he aimed the rifle at the chopper. "It's moving fast." He fired twice. The chopper sped toward them, climbed higher, and then circled around the hill. "You ready with those slugs?"

Morning followed the helicopter's path with her shotgun. "As I'll ever be."

The chopper continued to circle before suddenly speeding toward Dillon's location. An explosion rocked the hillside. Reagan screamed. A second explosion followed soon after before the chopper swiftly returned to its position over the valley.

"Is Dillon okay?" Remington shouted.

"No idea," Morning replied as she tried to see over to the trailhead. There's still too much dust swirling from the explosions."

Reagan pointed. "There."

Dillon was running with a bad limp toward them. His hat was gone, blood trickled from one of his ears, but besides that and the limp he seemed to be okay. "I'm sorry." He coughed into his hand. "I couldn't hold them off—not once the grenades started to fall around me."

A row of road pirates emerged from the trailhead and stood at the top of the hill some two hundred yards away. They were all armed with rifles. Morning counted nine of them.

Remington fired first.

The road pirates fired back.

"Get her to the river," Dillon told Morning, "while you still can."

Reagan pulled her hand away from Morning's. "I said I'm staying."

Remington continued to shoot at the road pirates while Dillon knelt in front of Reagan. "We promised Bear we would do everything we could to keep you safe. Go with Morning."

"No." Reagan shook her head. "I won't leave here."

Bullets struck the ground all around them. Morning glanced toward the trail that led to the river and then did a double take. "We have more company."

Dillon turned. "Damn."

Remington looked over his shoulder between firing shots. "What is it?"

Four more road pirates walked out onto the hill from the riverside trail side.

"We're surrounded," Morning said as she made sure to keep herself in front of Reagan.

"Looks that way." Remington kept shooting.

The chopper sped across the valley. The road pirates paused their approach, watching as the helicopter climbed altitude, making it much more difficult to be targeted from below. Morning shot one of her slugs at it but missed. The cockpit door slid open. Seconds later, another explosion threw a cloud of dust and debris into the sky as the road pirates opened fire. Remington was thrown off of his feet. Dillon returned fire, reloaded, and then fired some more. The helicopter made a wide circle, hovered over the valley, ready to make another run at the hill.

"Are you okay?" Dillon asked.

Remington nodded, but the color had drained from his face. He got back to his feet, looked down, and noticed the splatters of blood on his boot. "That can't be good," he said right before falling back against the stone wall. "Shoulder," he gasped.

Morning had him lean forward and quickly found the bullet hole on his upper back. "Exit wound. It went in and out. Looks clean."

"Clean, eh?" Remington groaned. "I suppose that's good news, but it sure hurts like hell."

"Can you still shoot?" Dillon asked as he reached down to help pull Remington up.

"I'll manage."

"The bad men," Reagan said.

Both groups of road pirates were advancing along with the chopper. Morning, Remington, and Dillon all looked at each other. Bullets were coming from two sides and grenades from above. The understanding between them was unspoken yet clear.

There would be no escape.

The chopper's thrumming filled Morning's ears as it edged closer to the hill. She aimed her shotgun, said a silent prayer, and pulled the trigger.

Another miss. The chopper kept coming.

Remington handed Morning his revolver. "Save it," he said. "Whatever happens don't let them take her."

"Do you mean. . ." Morning's voice trailed off.

Remington nodded, his lips pressed tightly together and his eyes full of the pain from his wounded shoulder. "Think of it as a kindness. If they get their hands on her, the things they'll do—"

Morning nodded back. "I know." Though she said the words she was far from certain she could actually do what Remington was asking of her. To kill a child in order to protect her only felt like the lesser of two evils and not an act of kindness as Remington would have her believe.

Dillon unleashed a barrage of bullets at one group of road pirates and then aimed his rifle at the other group. Remington started shooting as well. The chopper was nearly above them by then, partially blocking out the sun and covering much of the hill in shadow.

"Please don't let the bad men have me," Reagan said. "I would rather die than be with them again."

Morning wanted to scream. To hear a child say those words and to mean them added further fuel to the fire that was her seething rage at a world that had created such an environment. *We let it happen*, she thought. *We did this to ourselves. Through cowardice, laziness, greed, and weakness, we made monsters of us all.* She stared up at the bottom of the chopper, felt the air swirling around her and tasted the red Savage dirt in her mouth.

Dillon cried out when a bullet grazed his upper arm. He fired back while unleashing a long blue streak of curses at their attackers.

"We're getting low," Remington said while tapping the nearly empty bucket of ammo with the toe of his boot. He looked up at the chopper just as the cockpit door opened. Another grenade was about to fall.

Morning stroked Reagan's hair and then pressed the tip of the gun against the back of her head. "I'm so sorry," she sobbed.

"It's okay." Reagan took a deep breath. "I understand. It's for the best."

"What the hell. . ." Dillon saw something in the sky beyond the other side of the hill.

Remington and Morning looked up at the same time. Remington's craggy face broke out into a wide smile. "Well, I'll be damned. It's just like Hap said." He looked down at Reagan. "Do you remember what he told you?"

Reagan nodded. "He said that when the day is darkest to look to heaven for salvation."

That salvation came in the form of Leo and his little plane speeding across the sky. The helicopter's engine let out an angry-sounding high-pitched whine as it suddenly backed away from the hill. The plane was moving much too fast though. It didn't slow even a little as it neared the chopper. The road pirates stopped shooting, their heads tilted back, their mouths hanging open, as they watched the collision unfold. The chopper was hovering over the valley when it was hit full-on by the plane. The impact made the entire hillside vibrate. The plane seemed to disintegrate into the chopper's metal frame, the two aircraft merging into one twisted lump of shrieking, smoking metal that somehow remained elevated for a few long seconds before dropping from the sky and crashing down onto the RV below. The valley went quiet as smoke billowed up from the wreckage and then a much larger secondary explosion followed, sending the road pirates in the valley who survived the blast scattering in all directions.

Remington stepped out from behind the stone wall firing his gun. "I've had about enough of your shit!" he bellowed as sunlight returned to the hill. The road pirates hesitated, confused and uncertain about what to do next. When one of them fell dead followed quickly by another, they took off running.

Morning drew the gun away from Reagan's head, turned to the side, and threw up. She had come so close to pulling the trigger.

"Are you okay?" Reagan asked.

"I am now." Morning wiped her mouth with the back of her hand. "And so are you, thank God."

The road pirates were gone from Vaughn's Hill but remained in the valley. The RV had been obliterated by the impact and resulting explosion.

Remington lowered his rifle. "How many of them are left?"

"No more than a hundred," Dillon replied from where he stood looking down into the valley. "And there's no sign of Vig."

"Killed in the RV?"

"That would be my guess."

"What now?"

Dillon shrugged. "Depends on whether they intend to stay and fight or not. There's still a hundred of them and just a few of us." He turned around, looked up, and cocked his head. "You hear that?"

"Like a drumbeat," Morning replied.

"Those aren't drums," Remington said. "That's the sound of horses galloping—a lot of them."

They looked toward the river to the south as the faraway rumble grew closer. From inside the tent Peanut and Justice whinnied with excitement.

The first horse and rider came into view, plunging into the river at full speed and then out the other side. A long row of other riders followed. Many wore intricate headdresses of feathers, furs, bones, beads, and stone. They were armed with rifles and knives and rode without saddles.

It seemed the once wild horses weren't the only things that had returned to the ancient lands of Savage.

So too had the Indians.

34.
✦✧✦✧

"He was so weak. Couldn't walk. Could barely talk. How Leo actually managed to fly here from Fort Peck I'll never know." Lucian sipped from his coffee as he sat around the fire inside of Remington's hilltop tent. "Our scouts had spotted the road pirates moving toward Savage some days ago. We also heard the rumors of another helicopter. As soon as Leo found out, he was determined to help and no amount of us trying to convince him that he wasn't capable of doing so would change his mind." He smiled as he stared down into his cup. "And then he started in on how we needed to help you as well. The tribe refused at first. Many felt that letting your people slaughter one another was in our best interest. Leo thought otherwise, though, and was unrelenting in his demand that we not live as cowards. And so, we gathered our forces and then marched from Fort Peck to here with Leo promising he would be following us soon after. As you all now know, he kept that promise and gave his life with one final act of sacrificial purpose."

Remington held up his coffee cup. "To Leo."

The others joined in the toast. While very appreciative of Leo's sacrifice, talking about him was also a welcome distraction from the painful grief they all felt over the loss of Bear.

"So, are you officially the chief up at Fort Peck?" Dillon asked.

Lucian nodded. "I am—chosen by my people." The lines that tracked across his otherwise smooth face appeared somewhat more pronounced. He wore the burden of leadership well enough, but it was also clearly taking its toll.

"That's quite an honor."

"It is. We have expanded our community services programs. Our schools are running, we have a fully functioning health clinic, and given how well our physician attended to your injuries here today you now know firsthand just how skilled we truly are."

"And an army of warriors to protect it all."

"Yes." Lucian's eyes twinkled. "We have that as well. And my people's revitalization isn't unique to Fort Peck. It is taking place all across these lands. We are many but we are also one."

Morning looked up from her thoughts of Bear. She intended to go down into the valley soon to give him a proper burial. Reagan's head was on her lap. "What's your intentions?" she asked.

Lucian leaned forward. "What do you mean?"

"Your people," Morning continued. "Your army. Your newfound power. What do you intend to do with it?"

"You mean in regard to places like Savage?"

"Yeah."

"Ah," Lucian said. "I think I understand now." He removed his eagle-feathered headdress and set it next to him. "History tells us how capable the white man was in taking land. Now, generations later, it seems it is *my* people who might very well prove to finally be just as capable of taking it back." When Remington started to protest, Lucian held up a hand. "I give you my word that so long as any here now continue to live in Savage your homes will remain your own. We came here to help not to take."

Remington shifted in the old leather chair, glanced at the others, and nodded. "Fair enough."

Dillon nodded as well. "I'll trust you to keep your word on this, Lucian."

"That word is given upon the honor of my people, Sheriff. It will not bend let alone break."

"Speaking of people," Remington said. "I have a question I've long wanted to ask on that."

Lucian nodded. "Go ahead."

Remington cleared his throat. "Uh, well, there are all of these terms for what you are—Native American, Indigenous People, Indian, American Indian—is there a right one that you prefer? It seems the rules kept changing and I always tried to be respectful of people and their proper titles, but I'll be damned if I know what the most appropriate designation is."

"Just call me friend."

"That's it?"

"That's it," Lucian replied. "All of those other things you listed off, think how much better society would have been if we had lessened our obsession to label everything and everyone. At the end of the day, for better or worse, we're all God's children."

"Absolutely," Dillon said. "Wise words, Chief. And thank you to you and your people for coming here today although I don't entirely agree with your decision to let the remaining road pirates go."

"They gave up their weapons and without Vig pushing them to go out and create more chaos, I think most will wish to return to some semblance of normalcy in their lives. There would have been no honor in killing them all." Lucian stood. "It is now time for me to rejoin my people in the valley and then return with them to Fort Peck. Our scouts will continue to monitor the area, though, and if you don't mind, it would please me to occasionally return here to visit."

Remington winced from the pain of his injured shoulder when he pushed himself out of the chair. "You're welcome here any time, Lucian." The two men shook hands.

Dog, who had been sleeping at Remington's feet, suddenly sat up, eyes wide, and then bolted outside. Seconds later he could be heard barking excitedly right before running back into the tent. He circled the group twice and then sat next to Remington panting happily.

"What's gotten into you?" Remington asked as he bent down to scratch under Dog's chin.

Dillon drew his gun and looked at Lucian. "Expecting someone?"

"No," Lucian answered.

Morning stood and then gently pushed Reagan behind her. "I can hear someone coming this way," she whispered. The footsteps were slow and heavy.

"Could be the horses," Remington said. "They're still outside."

Dillon stepped toward the tent flap. "I don't think so."

"If it was trouble, I'm certain Dog would be growling like crazy by now."

Dillon cocked the hammer back on his revolver as he cautiously moved toward the tent flap. "Better safe than sorry."

"Perhaps it is someone from my tribe," Lucian suggested.

Remington stared at the flap while he shook his head. "Again, Dog would be acting different if it was a stranger."

Dillon stopped and glanced behind him. "You actually think it's someone we know? Anyone who could be is already inside this tent."

Dog let out a friendly bark as if to tell Dillon to stop with all the talk and get to who was by then standing just outside.

"I know you're out there," Dillon shouted. "I'm armed so whoever you are don't think to do something stupid and get yourself killed."

A silhouette was reflected against the tent wall, put there by the late afternoon sun that made it appear unusually large. Morning's mouth was suddenly dry as she strained to make out the details of the shadowy form that was so familiar to her. She told herself it wasn't possible, that her pain from losing him was overcoming her better judgement and making her see something that wasn't really there.

A hand slowly reached inside the tent flap and started to pull it back. Dillon aimed his gun, ready to fire. "What do you want?"

Death entered the tent, and it carried a hammer—tall, powerful, fierce, yet bathed in blood and nearly broken.

Dillon lowered his weapon, mouth agape, blinking in disbelief at what he saw. Remington, eyes wide, shook his head. Morning was unable to move, to speak, to do anything but stand there stunned.

It was Reagan who finally broke the silence. "Bear!" she shouted as she ran toward him without hesitation despite his fearsome appearance, her arms spread wide. He smiled down at her when she hugged his tree-trunk-sized leg, but then he nearly toppled over sideways. Dillon scrambled to prop him up and then the others did the same. They led him over to the chair and helped him to settle into it. He was pale, his hands trembled slightly, and his face had an odd waxy sheen to it. His many wounds had been attended to including the gash over his forehead that had been expertly stitched closed.

"How?" Remington asked. Bear held up a small packet and handed it to him. Remington looked down at it and then turned toward the others. "Antibiotics."

"It appears you've been cared for by my tribe's physician," Lucian said.

Bear nodded and then made a writing motion with his hand.

Reagan brought him a pad and pencil. "Here you go." Her smile was so wide it seemed it could become a permanent fixture.

I'm not sure how long I was out for. When I opened my eyes, a young man was cleaning my wounds. He said he was a doctor and that Lucian was his chief. Bear pointed to the side of his scalp where a red line ran from the front to the back. *The bullet cut a groove into my skull. Knocked me out cold. It took the doctor some time to stop the bleeding. He said that if the shot had tracked a quarter inch deeper my brains would have been spread over that field.*

"I told you those road pirates couldn't shoot for shit," Remington said.

"What about the bullet in your gut?" Dillon asked.

Bear took the packet of antibiotics back from Remington, held them up, and then continued to write. *It's still in there. The doctor said to take these for the next five days to give my body a chance to counter the infection that's coming. I might still die, but at least now I have a fighting chance.*

"You won't die." Reagan looked very determined as she put her little hand over Bear's oversized one. "You won't."

When Bear smiled, a little flash of his old strength was reflected in his eyes. "I know," he whispered. "Not yet."

Morning stepped forward and then leaned down in front of Bear, sensing a very important part of his story was about to be revealed. "How do you know that?"

He told me.

"You saw him too," Reagan said. "The Irish Cowboy."

Bear nodded and then continued writing.

After he cleaned and stitched my wounds the doctor left to get the antibiotics. I was lying in the grass looking up at the sky. It was so blue, so beautiful, and so quiet. There was this big raven flying in circles above me and every so often, as I watched it, I swear I could hear and smell the ocean. It felt like I had been watching it for hours when something came up and blocked my view and I realized someone was standing over me. It wasn't the doctor. He was a white man, a cowboy, young, good-looking, but with a pair of those no-nonsense eyes some people have that lets you know they're not to be messed with. "Not your time," *he said.* "You have more days yet to spend with two wonderful ladies." *He knelt down and clasped my shoulder.* "Tell my nephew and the sheriff that they did good. I'm proud of them—we all are."

"We?" Remington said.

There was more than just Hap with me in that moment. I couldn't see their faces, but I sensed them there standing behind him—the souls of Savage.

"The souls of Savage," Remington whispered as he brushed a tear away. "I do like the sound of that."

Lucian put his headdress back on. "The Sioux have a term for this. It is *Hunka Tanka*—the ancestor spirit." He nodded at Bear. "It is a great privilege when they choose to reveal themselves to someone. You are a mighty warrior. It pleases me to know that you remain among the living." He looked at the others. "I must be going now. It's a long ride back to Fort Peck." When he reached the tent flap, Lucian turned around and his dark eyes settled on Morning. "Let me know when you are ready to travel to see your son in the San Juan Islands. I would be honored to help you arrive there and then return here safely."

"Thank you," Morning replied. "I might just take you up on that."

"I hope you do." And with that Lucian was gone.

"Can we wave goodbye to them?" Reagan asked.

"I don't see why not," Remington answered. "Seems that's the least we could do after they came all this way."

Morning suggested Bear stay and rest in the chair, but he refused. It took both Dillon and Remington to help him out of it. They all shuffled out of the tent, bodies aching, bone-tired, to stand on the edge of the hill and watch Lucian and his tribe ride out of the valley until only the wind-blown field grass and wrecked remnants of the earlier battle appeared to be left.

They knew better though.

Reagan stood between Morning and Bear. She reached up and held their hands tightly, signaling a bond between them that would never be broken in this life or the next.

The old world had gasped its last breath and from its smoldering ashes a new world emerged.

Time would pass, things would inevitably change, but through it all the souls of Savage would remain.

Epilogue

Reagan was haunted by memory, but she wasn't lonely despite having lived so many years alone atop Vaughn's Hill. She sang softly while tending to the vegetables in the greenhouse that stood next to the big tent. That morning had been spent catching an especially large river trout while the late afternoon would be occupied with her checking the rabbit snares in the valley below.

She did think of the others often though.

Remington had been the first to pass. He was put to rest on the hill in the Wilkes family cemetery behind the tent three years after the fight with the road pirates. The pneumonia took him quick that winter. He spent the last week of his life sleeping and sweating in his chair by the fire, his breathing becoming increasingly shallow and ragged; but very near the end, his eyes opened, and he gave them that old smile of his. "He's still proud of me," he muttered. In his last hours Morning held his hand, stroked his hair, and whispered to him that it was okay for him to go and not long after that's what he did.

Dillon demanded he be allowed to dig the hole for his old friend. It took him a while because his own health had started to decline and his body had never fully recovered from the battle for Vaughn's Hill. After Remington was buried, he turned to the others and declared his own time was coming. He still spent his days patrolling the area, wearing his sheriff's badge, cowboy hat, and sidearm, just in case trouble arrived. Trouble never did though—Lucian's tribe made certain of that. They were around often but careful not to intrude on Savage, proving Lucian was very much a man of his word.

It was Bear who found Dillon after they grew worried having not seen him for several days. He was face down in the well-manicured front yard of his longtime home near the roses that had been the pride of his wife when she still lived. Bear said it appeared he had been reaching for those roses when a massive heart attack or stroke cut him down. They took his body out to the Savage cemetery where he was buried with his family.

Bear continued to battle his own physical challenges during that time. The bullet in his gut didn't kill him but brought constant pain that would sometimes worsen to the point where he contemplated ending his suffering once and for all. If not for the love he had for Morning and Reagan that likely would have been his choice. Instead, he endured for months and then years, appreciative of those rare days when the pain would temporarily subside and he could feel somewhat like his old self. His greatest fear was over what might happen to Reagan and Morning after he was gone. Morning always shrugged it off, telling him to stop worrying about tomorrow when they should be grateful for today.

He hung on for seven years after Dillon's death but a bad fall down the trail while bringing water up from the river left him bedridden with a spirit nearly broken as his body. It was just ten days after that fall that Bear died in his sleep.

Having heard of Bear's passing Lucian and his tribe arrived to pay their respects, filling the valley as they had once done all those years earlier during the fight with the road pirates. They helped to dig the grave that overlooked the river side of the hill. It was then that Lucian took Morning aside to remind her of his longstanding offer to help get her safely to the San Juan Islands to see her son. She had sacrificed making that journey out of concern over leaving Bear alone, but now he was gone, and Lucian convinced her that her own time to make such a trip was running short. Reagan was a grown woman by then and quite capable of taking care of herself, especially with the help of Lucian's people so close by should she need it.

Morning was away from Savage for nearly a year and when she returned, Reagan immediately sensed a change in her. For the first few days she spoke glowingly of the beauty of the islands and its people, and how grateful she was that her son was so safe and content in such a remarkable place. She rattled off the names of the many interesting people she had met such as Lucas Pine, Roland Soros, and Fin Kearns. There was another name as well, revered by the others. It was the name of a woman Morning feared she would never meet and she almost didn't until the day before she was to leave and begin her journey back to Montana. She was walking the path in the woods through the nearby Roche Harbor cemetery grounds when she came upon someone standing over a grave.

The woman turned and looked at her. She was of average height but impressively strong and sinewy looking, with a lean face and mid-length brown hair that was streaked with strands of silver. A crystal hung from her neck that winked at Morning when the sun hit it. She appeared to be both older yet somehow ageless, and her voice, though hard and confident, was equally friendly and feminine as well. She was dressed casually in jeans, a sweatshirt, and a pair of comfortable-looking sneakers.

"Hello," the woman said. "I'm Adele. You wanted to meet me."

"Yes," Morning replied. "How did you know that?"

When Adele smiled, the air around them seemed to warm. "On these islands I tend to know just about everything."

"My name is Morning, but I'm guessing you already knew that as well."

"You're Cy's mother."

"That's right."

"Did you enjoy your time here?"

Morning went to answer but then paused to really consider the question. She had enjoyed her time on the islands far more than she thought she would. "It's a beautiful place—almost magical." Adele's eyes burned into Morning's in a way that made her feel completely safe yet also vulnerable. She knew then that she was in the presence of someone who understood the workings of the universe in a way that she never could.

"It certainly is," Adele replied. She looked down at the grave, rested her hand on the headstone for a moment, and then started walking deeper into the woods. "You and yours are welcome to return here anytime." Those were the last words she spoke before disappearing behind a thick row of evergreen trees. When Morning looked down at the grave, she noted the name inscribed on it was Tilda Ashland, the woman her son Cy had told her before had owned the Roche Harbor Hotel. Beneath the name was carved the image of a raven.

Morning retold the story of that meeting with Adele often in the years that followed her return to Savage, while always emphasizing the phrase *you and yours are welcome to return here anytime.* And then, like all of the others, she too was eventually gone, buried among her family and next to Waylon at the McGreevy homestead down the road from the Wilkes ranch.

Reagan walked out of the greenhouse and looked out over the valley. The weather was unusually warm, even by typical Eastern Montana standards. A large raven flew in slow circles above her. She took in a deep breath and then let it out, looking around for an explanation as to why the air suddenly smelled so different, and then she remembered what Bear had said when he described lying in the grass while looking up at the sky.

There was this big raven flying in circles above me and every so often, as I watched it, I swear I could hear and smell the ocean.

Though Reagan had never been to the sea she was certain that was the change in the air she sensed—a unique mix of saltwater and pine that was now somehow surrounding her on a hill in Savage, Montana.

You and yours are welcome to return here any time.

The words were spoken in a voice inside of Reagan's mind that she had never heard before, yet she knew exactly who it was. How or why didn't matter. All that did was whether or not she chose to listen.

The raven circled once more and then flew into the west, following the path of the setting sun where somewhere beyond the hills and mountains were the San Juan Islands, Morning's son Cy, and an open invitation from a mysterious woman named Adele that had yet to be accepted.

Until now.

Readers who would like to further explore the world of the best-selling San Juan Islands Mysteries by D.W. Ulsterman, including the characters of Adele Plank and others, are encouraged to check out the series page at Amazon.com. The stories are available now via e-book and paperback.

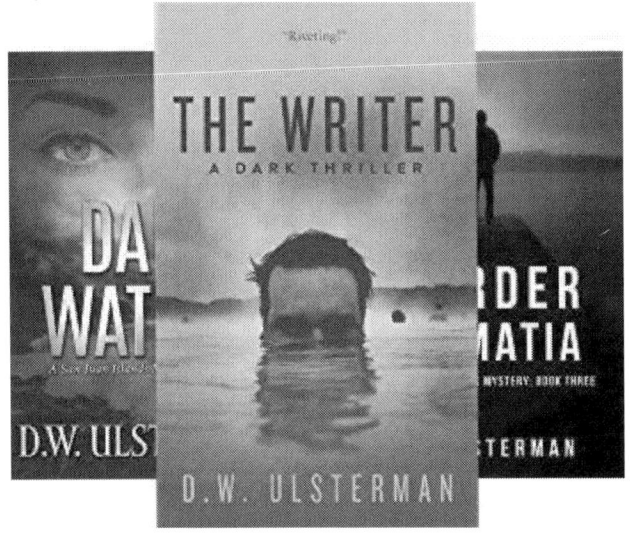

About the Author

D.W. Ulsterman resides in the Pacific Northwest with his wife of thirty years. His is the proud father of two grown children as well as being best friends with Dublin the Dobie.

During the summer months you will often find him navigating the beautiful waters of his beloved San Juan Islands and playing golf as a member of the San Juan Island Golf and Tennis Club.

In addition to the San Juan Islands Mysteries, he has also authored several other best-selling titles including The Irish Cowboy, Savage, and The Bowman Boys series.

All of his novels are available for purchase and/or download on his Amazon author page.

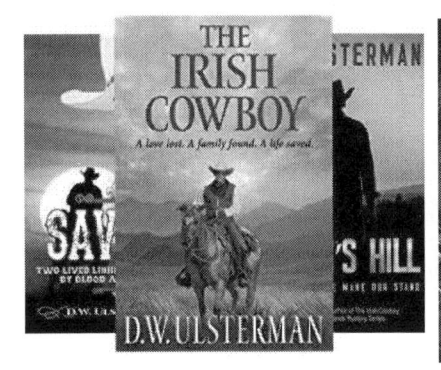

Made in the USA
Las Vegas, NV
05 November 2022